They could not see him, they could not feel his rage. His screaming curses were silent. Only sometimes . . . sometimes, he could sense an uneasiness about one or the other of the three. Just the vaguest sense that something was not quite right. It was not much, but it meant he *could* reach them. That kept Frazier going. One day he would have the power he needed, and on that day these three would suffer as they deserved.

Payback time was coming.

Also by Gary Brandner:

BILLY LIVES

Published by Fawcett Books:

THE HOWLING

THE HOWLING II

WALKERS

HELLBORN

CAT PEOPLE

QUINTANA ROO

THE BRAIN EATERS

THE HOWLING III

CARRION

CAMERON'S CLOSET

FLOATER

Gary Brandner

FAWCETT GOLD MEDAL • NEW YORK

A Fawcett Gold Medal Book
Published by Ballantine Books
 Published in the United States by Ballantine Books, a division of Random House, Inc., New York, and simultaneously in Canada by Random House of Canada Limited, Toronto.

Library of Congress Catalog Card Number: 87-91086

ISBN 0-449-13280-3

Printed in Canada

First Edition: April 1988

CHAPTER 1

Los Angeles, June 1987

LINDY

The intersection of Westwood Boulevard and Pico is not one of the glamour corners of Hollywood. It does not rank with Wilshire and Rodeo, Sunset and Vine, or even Beverly and Fairfax. Junior's Delicatessen, which shares the northwest corner with a newsstand and a dry cleaner, is not L'Orangerie, Spago's, or the Polo Lounge when it comes to high-visibility deal-making. However, it is at Junior's and other unpretentious eateries like Hugo's on Santa Monica and DuPars in the Valley that the nuts and bolts of movie deals are fitted together. Steven Spielberg or Francis Coppola or whoever is the head of Universal this week won't be seen there, but the independent producers, the eager young agents, the non-celebrity writers, directors, and others who butter the real bread of Hollywood meet over coffee and bagels in these modest surroundings to make career decisions.

Lindy Grant sat uncomfortably erect in a booth at Junior's with a copy of her screenplay, *Shadow Watcher*, lying flat on the table in front of her. Beside it were a cheese Danish with one bite taken out of it and a cooling cup of coffee. Across from her sat two men who were telling her all the things that were wrong with her script.

Lindy was trying hard to pay attention to what the men were saying, but her thoughts kept returning to a face. A terrible, angry face that belonged to her daughter but was not her daughter's face. And an inhuman voice that spoke strange, ominous words.

One of the men in the booth was Lou Davidoff. He was about thirty and wore his hair in a punkish semi-spike style. He had a pinched nose, crooked teeth, and a perpetually sour expression. Davidoff represented New Titan Films, an up-and-coming distributor, and was often mentioned in the trades as a comer.

The other man, tall, round-shouldered, with only a few strands of hair left to cover his high-domed head, was Lindy's producer, Josh Cleery. He was an independent, which in the movie business means he fit somewhere between having a secure studio contract and standing in the unemployment line. Only yesterday Josh was telling Lindy what a fine writer she was and how they had a sure winner with *Shadow Watcher.*

"I've got commitments for real money on this one, Lindy," he had told her. "They love your script, absolutely love it to pieces. All they want to see is a first line distributer tied into the package and we're on our way."

Now he was agreeing eagerly with Lou Davidoff that the script was a fair first draft, sure, but needed work. Lots of work.

First draft, hell, Lindy thought. She had already rewritten the thing completely three times, with half a dozen sets of revisions, even though her contract called for only two drafts and a polish. Now this kid with the punky hairdo—both the men were younger than she, Lindy reflected unhappily—was telling her that women-in-jeopardy stories were a tough sell without a commitment by a star, a major director, or a high-concept theme.

"Since we probably can't get Meryl Streep or one of the hot Italian directors on Josh's budget, maybe I could add a shower scene in a girl's dorm and we could sell it as a teenage sex comedy."

Davidoff's expression did not change. Josh forced an unconvincing laugh.

"She's kidding," he assured the distributor. "Seriously, Lindy, I think Lou makes some good points here. I mean, he's tight with the exhibitors, and he knows the kind of pictures they want. Why don't you go over some of those points again, Lou."

Sure, go over them twenty times, for all I care. Lindy already saw that the kid didn't know dip about story or character or suspense or real dialogue. But he knew the exhibitors. She arranged her features into a thoughtful expression and tried to listen to his dumb suggestions for changing her characters and juggling her plot points.

Lou Davidoff's monotonous voice faded into the background clatter of dishes and the chatter of other would-be deal makers. Lindy kept her chin propped on one fist and gazed attentively at his moving lips while her mind drifted back to her current worry number one.

What the hell, she wondered, was the matter with Nicole? Sure, there were the usual problems that went with a fourteen-year-old daughter—the clothes crises, the scuzzy boyfriends with earrings and Indian haircuts, the campaign for more liberal dating privileges, and a precocious breast development about which the girl was inordinately embarrassed. These were problems a parent of the eighties was expected to cope with, but lately a couple of things had happened that didn't fit any pattern.

It began a week ago at dinner with the face. Lindy had looked up from the script she was marking and saw a look of such malevolent hatred from her daughter that she spilled her wine. The girl's smooth, regular features were distorted into a grotesque mask that was somehow chillingly familiar to Lindy.

Then, in an instant, it was gone. Nicole was once again her usual chattery, goofy self. Lindy decided it was some trick of the lighting, some strange illusion. But the terrible distorted features had stayed in her mind.

Then, yesterday morning, as she was clearing away the breakfast dishes, she heard the voice. A harsh rasp that was barely recognizable as human.

"Lindy!"

Startled, Lindy had looked up to see no one in the room but Nicole. The girl had never called her anything but Mom. And she certainly never sounded anything like that. She was sitting cross-legged on the floor giving her full attention to adding another rip to her pre-ripped Guess Jeans.

"It's payback time," said the raspy voice coming from her daughter.

"What did you say?" Lindy stared.

For a moment Nicole did not look up. Lindy tensed, but when the girl lifted her head, her face was clear, the eyes wide and innocent.

"Huh?"

"What did you just say?"

"Me? Nothing."

"Didn't you . . . hear anything?"

"Like what?"

"Like somebody talking."

"Hey, are you okay?"

"I'm fine," Lindy snapped. "What was that voice?"

"I didn't hear anything, Mom. Maybe the neighbors are playing their TV loud again." She smiled tolerantly and returned to her work on the jeans.

Lindy studied the top of her daughter's head where the pale blond hair was parted along the pink scalp. The girl had her faults, but playing silly practical jokes was not among them. She was telling the truth.

And yet Lindy had heard it clearly. A rasping, angry call. Then the cryptic warning, if that's what it was. She had a flash of Linda Blair in *The Exorcist* talking in the demon voice, and quickly shook away the image. Still, the incident remained stuck in her mind like a shred of meat between her teeth.

She told Brendan Jordan about it last night as they sat close together on his double-width chaise watching *Aliens* on HBO.

"Are you sure it was Nicole you heard?" he asked.

"The voice came from her. There was nobody else in the house."

"I wouldn't worry about it," he said. "It's probably some new kick the teenagers are on."

"I don't think so. Nicole's not the type to fool around like that."

"Do you want me to have a talk with her?"

"Come on, Brendan. You doing the father part? Quit kidding."

He sat up and looked at her. "Just a minute. I *am* a father. My boy just graduated from Stanford, remember? Going on to medical school in the fall? Maybe I'm not Bill Cosby, and maybe his mother and I couldn't hack it as man and wife, but I don't think I did too badly with the kid."

She pulled his head toward her and kissed him. "I know, Brendan. I wasn't thinking when I said that. It's just that this isn't your problem. It's unfair of me to unload on you."

"Who says so? If you've got trouble, I want to hear about it. If I can't handle it, that's for me to decide."

"Okay. I'll keep you informed of any future developments. Just remember I gave you a way out."

"I'll remember." His eyes drifted back to the screen.

"Well, it's about time. We had to wait for the last scene of the picture to get Sigourney Weaver in her underwear."

"Are you saying you'd rather look at that woman's flesh than talk to me?"

He punched the remote control, darkening the screen, and pulled Lindy closer. "No contest. If Sigourney Weaver walked in here right this minute, with or without her underwear, and offered me a thousand dollars to fly her to Maui, I would tell her tough luck, Captain Jordan is otherwise engaged."

"What if she made it two thousand?"

"Not a chance."

"You're a liar, but I love it." They kissed then and never did see the end credits of *Aliens*.

The pleasant memory of Brendan faded as Lindy realized the two men in the booth at Junior's were looking at her. Davidoff sourly, as usual, and Josh with a hopeful, don't-screw-this-up expression.

"What do you think, Lindy?" Josh said.

This movie meant a lot to him. He had just two completed films to his credit—*Desert Frenzy*, a shoestring slasher that had made a few bucks in the video market, and *Street Mamas*, a piece of sleaze that was still on the shelf. *Shadow Watcher*, even with the modest budget he had planned, would be Cleery's ticket to respectability as a producer. A tie-up with New Titan would bring in dollars and could lead to bigger deals to come.

"I'll have to rethink it with the script in front of me," Lindy said, wondering what cockamamie ideas the dork had come up with while she was daydreaming.

"But we *can* do it, right, Lindy?" Josh said. "I mean, the changes aren't all that major."

How the hell would you know? Josh was a sweetheart of a guy when he wasn't scrambling to make a buck, but his feeling for a script was close to zero.

If only she could hit big with her novel, Lindy thought,

she could tell these Hollywood creeps to kiss off and never have to worry again about squeezing a screenplay into a convoluted mess that would please the most people with the least hassle. Trouble was, her novel had got no farther than Chapter Two, and so far no publisher had shown a flicker of interest.

"Let me think it through," she said. "Can you give me some notes?"

Davidoff consulted his Rolex. "I suppose I can go back this afternoon and dictate some of these thoughts to my secretary and shoot them back to you. I just don't want to delay this thing any more than we have to."

"My feeling exactly," Josh enthused. "Once we get your ideas we can show you pages—when, Lindy, a week?"

"Sure," Lindy said. *Why so long?* she thought. *Why not promise the toad we'll have a finished script for him tomorrow morning?*

It would mean no Brendan for the rest of the week, but both of them were used to that. His work as a charter pilot often took him away for days at a time on short notice, and working in the screen trade called for sudden, intense bursts of work for her with no time for fun.

And after all, making this deal was important to her, too. It would be her first solo credit, and if the flick made any money the majors would talk to her. And she did owe Josh. He'd gone out on a limb to sell her original screenplay to his backers. Lindy would do her damnedest to help him land a good distribution deal, even if she had to suck up to this creep Davidoff. Others in Hollywood had done a lot worse for a lot less.

Josh looked relieved. He beamed hopefully at Davidoff. "So, Lou, can we get together—when? Saturday?"

"You'll have to give me a call. If I'm not at Titan, try me at Warren Beatty's. You have his private number?"

"Right. Sure." Cleery kept a hand on the other man's shoulder as they walked out of the delicatessen.

Josh held Lindy back as they saw Lou Davidoff into his Mercedes in Junior's parking lot. When he was gone Josh said, "What do you think, Lindy? I mean, what do you really think?"

"I think he's an arrogant little prick who wouldn't know a good script from a seed catalog. Do you really know Warren Beatty's number?"

"No, but if I have to I'll kill somebody to get it by Saturday."

She reached out to smooth the worry lines from the producer's brow. "Hell of a business."

"Lindy, listen to me, Davidoff is an asshole, but he knows what makes money. He knows what the exhibitors want. Anyway, he's convinced Ben Zalic at New Titan Films that he knows, which is just as good."

"Don't worry, Josh, I'll have the rewrite for you."

The producer rubbed a hand across his lonely strands of hair. He peered down at Lindy. "I had a feeling there in the booth that you left us for a little while. Are you all right? I mean, are you really all right?"

"You know I don't do drugs," Lindy said. "If that's what you're talking about."

"Sure, I know that. It's just that I worry about you, you know."

"Sure Josh." *What you worry about is that I might snort myself into cuckoo-land like a couple of your other people and strand you with no movie and half a dozen investors who expect to see some of their money back.* "I've got to go. Nicole's home with a cold today."

"How soon can I see—"

"I'll call you when I get something on paper, Josh. Good-bye."

She left him standing there rubbing his scalp, and swung off toward her gray Tempo. She was conscious of the glances she got from men as she crossed the lot. She had always had looks, but now at thirty-seven, with her glossy black hair cut short, the contrast of the startling blue eyes, the firm body showing no signs of sag, she probably looked better than ever.

She got into the car and pulled the door shut. For a moment she sat there with the keys in her hand, chilled by a vague sense that something bad was going to happen.

CHAPTER 2

Seattle, June 1987

ROMAN

The girl bucked and twisted under him, her high, round breasts mashing his naked chest as his belly slapped wetly against hers. Roman Dixon worked at concentrating while the water bed undulated and a pornographic video played unwatched on the television set.

"Oh, Roman!" the girl gasped. "Oh, my God! Oh, fuck me!"

Why, he wondered, did so many of them get off on using the f-word while in the act? It didn't have the shock value anymore that it might have twenty years ago. In fact, Roman found it distinctly off-turning falling from the lips of some fresh-faced young girl.

Not as off-turning as this, though. With growing alarm he felt his erection soften and shrink inside the girl even as he pumped more vigorously. Finally he gave up and withdrew, rolling over to lie on his back beside her.

The girl lay still for a little while, then raised up on an

elbow and looked at him. For a moment he couldn't think of her name, then it came to him. Kathy Isles. Accounts receivable. They all seemed to be named Kathy or Christie. Or sometimes Debbie. Last week he had his first Heather. This Kathy had thick, dark hair that framed her pert little face in soft waves. She looked at him with worry in her clear young eyes.

If you say 'What's the matter?' I'll shit, he thought.

"Is anything wrong, honey?"

Roman did not shit. Instead, he lied. "Nothing's wrong."

"Is it me?"

"You're fine."

"Is there anything I can do?"

You can shut the fuck up and leave me alone, he thought. He said, "Don't worry about it. I'm just tired."

Kathy looked at him a moment longer, then lay back. On the television screen two naked women—one black, one white—did things to a naked young man who hung by his knees from a trapeze. The young man had a prodigious hard-on. The women were ardent in their attentions. All three looked to be having a better time than Roman Dixon was.

This was not the first time it had happened to him, of course. No man lived who did not now and then find himself incapable of performing the sex act. It was, however, the first time Roman had no ready excuse. Always before he had been too drunk or worried about business or distracted by some family problem. This afternoon, however, he was sober, his sporting goods stores were all in the black, and his home life was no more disagreeable than usual.

At thirty-eight it couldn't be his age. Hell, he was as randy as ever, and in good shape. Okay, so he was a little thicker around the middle than he'd like to be, and there was a softening of the jawline, but he had all his hair and the killer smile, and he still drew hungry looks from young women on the street, much to Stephanie's annoyance. No, it had to be something else.

Maybe his present incapacity was tied somehow to the funny thing that happened with his mother-in-law. No, not funny. Weird. The thought of Myrna Haaglund and the scene of the other night completed the shriveling of his organ.

If it was true that a woman's mother is an accurate picture of what the woman will become, he was in for a rotten future with Stephanie. Myrna Haaglund had been no prize twelve years ago when Roman was hustled into marrying her daughter. Fat and irritable then, at least she had most of her faculties. She wasn't all *that* old now, mid-seventies probably, but her mind was rotting. Half the time she couldn't remember where she was. Why Van didn't put the woman into a nursing home Roman did not know. The old man was as tough and ropy as ever, his mind just as keen. He sure didn't lack the money, and if Roman was any judge, Van Haaglund could still get it up, given the opportunity.

That thought brought Roman back to his predicament. He swung his legs out of the bed and got up, leaving Kathy bobbing there gently, like a pale dolphin on the tide.

"You don't want to try again?"

"Not today. I've got things to do. Things on my mind."

"Well, that's probably the trouble."

"Yeah, I guess."

Roman pulled on the bikini briefs Stephanie always told him he was too old to wear, and got into his shirt and pants.

"Are you going back to the store?" Kathy asked.

"What for? The place runs itself."

It was true. Each of the three D&H Sporting Goods Stores was managed efficiently by young men recruited from the University of Washington school of business. Roman kept an office in the original store in the U-District, but made an appearance there rarely. He scanned the monthly profit figures, made occasional recommendations on new lines of equipment, checked out the new hires, went to junior chamber meetings, but his presence at the store was largely symbolic. What it did for Roman was give him an excuse to get out of the house and away from Stephanie and the boys. Also, it let him personally hire certain key employees. Like Kathy Isles.

Kathy dressed rapidly, and they left the Olympus Adult Motel, discreetly located north of the city on old Highway 99. They stood for a moment under the portico out of the drizzling rain that was Seattle's trademark.

"You might as well take the rest of the day off too," he said.

"Thanks, boss." She kissed him lightly on the lips. "And don't worry about it. We'll make up for it next time."

"I'm not worried," he said.

At least not about what she thought he was. He watched Kathy cross the parking lot, pert and bouncy in her belted yellow raincoat. Then he walked through the drizzle to his Eldorado, thinking again of the bizarre experience last week with his mother-in-law.

Visits to the home of his wife's parents were always a drag for Roman. They had an expensive house in the rich suburb of Bothell, but he would rather go bowling.

His mother-in-law did little but sit and drool and babble about things that made no sense to anybody. Van only wanted to talk business, with the emphasis on how much tougher it had been for him than it was now for his son-in-law. Stephanie jabbered away foolishly as though everyone were having a fine time. The last visit, however, had been especially unsettling.

They made it through dinner—rib roast overdone the way Van liked it by the Haaglunds' surly black cook. No cocktails, no wine, and no after-dinner drinks. Van Haaglund was a teetotaler and a health freak. To smoke his cigarette Roman had to go out and stand in the rain on the brick patio. Mustn't contaminate the air. Balls. When he came back in he found himself alone with his mother-in-law, a situation he always tried to avoid.

Roman did his best to ignore her and checked his watch. If he could get Stephanie out of there in the next ten minutes he would get home in time for *Miami Vice*. While he waited for his wife to return he picked up a *Sports Illustrated* from the coffee table, hoping there might be a shot of some chick in a swimsuit. For a moment he successfully forgot about the drooling old woman, so he was startled when she spoke to him.

"Roman!"

At least the voice seemed to come from Myrna Haaglund. The tone was so harsh and the pronunciation so distinct that Roman almost dropped the magazine.

He looked at her in shocked surprise.

"It's payback time," she growled. In her watery, faded eyes there burned for an instant a hatred so palpable Roman could feel the heat of it. Then Myrna's head lolled to one side, the eyes dimmed to their customary stare, and the moment was gone.

When Stephanie and her father returned to the room Myrna was back to her dribbling, mumbling self. Roman said nothing about the strange outburst. It was over so suddenly that he could almost believe he had imagined it. Except that he *hadn't* imagined it. And for reasons he could not explain, the brief scene troubled him deeply.

Now he drove slowly through the light afternoon traffic across the Floating Bridge to the suburb of Bellevue, where his family waited. He was in no hurry to get back to Stephanie and her kids. Even after twelve years he was unable to think of her two boys as *theirs*. Maybe if he'd had some of his own, his life would be different now. But there was no use thinking about that. He'd made his bargain. A life of reasonable security for which he had to take on a homely woman and two homely kids. Sometimes—hell, often—he imagined how it might have been if he had not twisted his knee on that long ago football field.

He decided to stop at the Lion d'Or for a drink before going home. Maybe two drinks. They had a satellite dish, and there might be a ball game on from somewhere.

New York, June 1987

ALEC

Hard to believe, thought Alec McDowell, that there was a time when citizens could walk safely through Central Park in any season, night or day, without the imminent likelihood of losing their valuables, their virtue, their life, or all three. That time had vanished long before Alec McDowell arrived in the city in 1975, but he still sometimes thought about it with that odd nostalgia people feel for times they have never known.

It was not Alec's habit to stroll idly through the park, and he kept a wary eye on the other walkers on this June afternoon as he passed the heroic statue of General Sherman at the East Drive exit onto Fifth Avenue. He kept his stride brisk and let his arms swing purposefully as though packed into his narrow five-foot-six body there were a coiled machine ready to destroy an attacker with one or another of the martial arts. Not that he could hope to deceive a streetwise New York mugger for long, but at least he might be passed by for some decrepit old lady if he moved with alacrity.

There was a problem other than muggers bothering Alec this afternoon. He could not shake the unpleasant aftertaste of what seemed at the time to be a meaningless incident. It had happened the week before in his office at Laymon and Koontz, the consultant firm where Alec expected to have his own name added to the title soon.

He had been working late. The building had the silent, haunted feeling of offices at night, when ghostly echoes of the day still whisper through the halls and cubicles.

Alec's attention had been focused on the audio tape cassette playing in his portable machine. It was a conversation between an elected city official named Anton Scolari and the owner of a Newark construction company. The content of the conversation would have been enough to indict the official on charges of bribery and conflict of interest, had the tape not been obtained through the use of an illegal bug in the man's office. Alec McDowell, however, was unconcerned with the legal ramifications. What he was after was something to help elect his firm's client, Bo Walton, who would oppose Scolari in the upcoming election.

"Alec!"

He started at the unexpected sound of his own name spoken in the grating voice. At first it seemed to come from the tape recording, but logic quickly rejected that possibility.

Alec punched the cassette player into silence and looked around the roomy, deserted office. A young Puerto Rican woman in the blue uniform of the building maintenance crew was emptying ashtrays into a plastic-lined trash can.

"It's payback time."

Alec stared at her. "What did you say?"

The woman looked at him, and for a fraction of a heartbeat she wore a devil's smile, all teeth and hatred. Then her face lapsed into a soft Latin innocence.

"Sir?"

"Did you just speak to me?"

"No, sir. I di'n say nothing."

He held her eye for a long moment, then realized that what he had heard could not possibly have come from the throat of this woman. And what he thought he saw on her face was an illusion, a trick of the night shadows. What else could it be?

"Never mind," he told her. He punched the rewind button on the tape deck. "Can you come back and do this room later?"

"I got to do it like the list says or I get in trouble," the woman said.

"All right."

Alec swept the material he was working on into his desk and locked the drawer. What the hell, he'd got as much as he was going to out of the tape. It wasn't good enough.

Besides, the voice or hallucination or whatever it was had destroyed his concentration. It was nearly ten o'clock. He could go home to his Yorkville apartment, read some of the accumulated newsletters, then maybe get to sleep.

Sleep did not come easy that night. The grating voice would not leave his mind. There was something distantly, ominously familiar about it.

Now as he hurried along Fifth Avenue, where the danger of muggers was minimal, Alec still sensed a menacing presence somewhere nearby. Furtively he scanned the faces of the other pedestrians, but no one met his eye. He pulled up the collar of his jacket against a chill that only he could feel.

THE FLOATER

Darkness.

No light. No heat. No sound. No pain.

Only a terrible, crazy joy.

It had been a long, long time in the planning. There had been false starts and wrong turns. But now, at last, it had begun. The plot had been set in motion. There would be no stopping now.

It was payback time.

CHAPTER 3

Wolf River, September 1966

Wolf River, Wisconsin

"A nice place to live."

Population: 21,752

Location: 135 miles north of Milwaukee, 29 miles west of Green Bay

Principal industries: dairy farms, agriculture, Moderne Gloves, Allis Chalmers Farm Machinery

Hospitals: 1

Elementary schools: 4

High schools: 1

Colleges: 1

Hotels: 2; Motels: 4

Theaters: 2; one walk-in, one drive-in

Whorehouses: 2

Churches: 22

Taverns: 21

Cemeteries: 2

LINDY

"There's nothing like the smell of a new car," Todd Hartman said. He stroked the simulated leather dash panel of the burgundy Thunderbird as he headed up Elm Street.

"It's really nice, Todd," said Lindy. She didn't really care much about cars, but she knew what was expected of her. "I really appreciate your taking me down to Moreland's. This was the last day of the sale."

Merilee Lund spoke up from the back seat, thrusting her curly blond head in between them. "Yeah, me too, Todd. This really is a bitchin' car. How fast will it go, anyway?"

"As fast as you want," Todd said, talking back over his shoulder but still looking at Lindy. "You going down to Main Street this afternoon?" he asked her.

"I suppose so," Lindy said. "That's what everybody does on Saturday."

"It is a silly custom," Todd said, "but when in Rome . . . you have a ride?"

"Mm-hmm."

"Roman Dixon, I suppose."

"Sure. Who else?"

"I'm not riding with anybody," Merilee said. "I mean, I haven't promised anybody."

"You really like him, huh," Todd said. "Roman."

"Sure I like him. I wouldn't go with a boy if I didn't like him."

"You just don't seem like the usual type that hangs around jocks."

"I don't think I exactly hang around jocks," she said.

"You know what I mean. Anyway, if you ever get bored, or feel like a change . . ."

"I'll let you know," Lindy said.

"I'm not riding with anybody," Merilee said again.

"I guess you can ride with me if you want," Todd said without turning around.

"Oh, wow! Wait'll everybody sees us in this bitchin' car!"

Todd pulled the Thunderbird to a stop in front of the Grant house.

Lindy gathered up the sweater she'd bought at Moreland's and opened the door. "Thanks again, Todd," she said and stepped out.

"I guess you're going to the Halloween Ball with Roman too," he said.

"Yeah."

"Boy, it pays to be a football star."

"I don't know who I'm going with," Merilee said. She started to push the seat forward so she could move to the front, but Todd reached across, slammed the door, and drove off.

Lindy watched them drive away. She liked them both, but somehow this year their faults were glaringly apparent. Todd was the son of the town's richest banker, and couldn't let anybody forget it. He would probably be nice enough, but his family's money wouldn't let him. Merilee was nominally Lindy's best friend, but sometimes she could be painfully dumb.

She turned and went up the walk to her house.

Lindy would have liked to show Daddy the new sweater and let him admire her in it, but Wendell Grant was in his study, where she never disturbed him. Mrs. Krantz would appreciate her bargain, but she was busy out in the kitchen, her private domain. Lindy went on upstairs.

Lindy's room was in the front on the second floor of the big old house on upper Elm Street. Both windows were open to the warm Indian summer breeze. The pink-and-white curtains billowed softly, and the perfume of autumn filled the room. A stuffed panda, propped on the bed pillows, watched the girl come in with great sad eyes. It was the last of the little-girl things that Lindy kept in her room. The rest had been banished to the attic.

"Hi, Panda," she said. "Do you want to see my new sweater?"

She laid the box on the bed, opened it, and took out the layers of tissue paper. She held the maroon-and-white ski sweater up against her.

"See? It's too hot to wear it now, but it'll be nice this winter."

Abruptly, the sweater didn't seem all that wonderful anymore. She folded it up and put it back in the box. When she saw the sale ad in the *Chronicle* it had seemed like she had to have the sweater or perish. Daddy had given her the money, he always did, but now she wondered why it had seemed so important.

Feeling restless, she wandered over and sat down at her dressing table. She placed a hand to her cheek and inclined her head to the side. All around the mirror were Polaroid photos wedged in between the glass and the frame. Although none of the pictures was more than a year old, the edges of some had curled and the colors were already starting to fade. The events pictured seemed remote and nostalgic to sixteen-year-old Lindy, as though they had taken place in some Polaroid past.

There was a posed shot of the yell squad with Lindy, the yell queen, kneeling in front. Merilee was prominent in the first row, giving it the big openmouthed smile. The girls wore pleated red skirts, white letter sweaters decorated with red megaphones lettered WR, white socks, red-and-white saddle shoes. They held red-and-white crepe paper pompons, and the lot of them were smiling like the Pat Boone family.

The picture had been taken at last year's Thanksgiving Day game with Appleton, and at the time it had seemed exciting and fun. It should be even more kicky in this, her senior year, with a good chance for the team to win the state championship, plus the brand-new sweaters the school board had promised the yell squad. Why, Lindy wondered, couldn't she feel it?

She continued to study the photos, unemotionally, as though they belonged to somebody else. Here was a shot of her and Roman Dixon standing alongside his candy-apple 1957 Chevy. The car was dazzling, having just received its umpteenth coat of hand-rubbed lacquer. Roman, his thick blond hair BrylCreamed into a gleaming D.A., glowed with the pride of ownership. Lindy clung to his sweatered arm and smiled her All-American smile. She studied her white, even teeth. The braces Daddy insisted on when she was little had been a pain and a half, but the results were worth it.

And here was one from the Junior Prom—Lindy in pale green chiffon with orchid corsage, Roman stiff in white dinner jacket with scarlet cummerbund and matching carnation. They made a lovely couple. Just about perfect. Everybody said so.

The class picnic. Lindy and Roman at the lake, turning to grin up at the camera from the table where remains of chicken and potato salad crusted under the springtime sun.

The lovely couple again, this time after a football game, with Roman sweaty and triumphant in red-and-white uniform, helmet cradled under one arm like a knight after the tournament. Lindy, clutching her pompon, gazed fondly up at her champion.

And here they were costumed as Superman and Wonder Woman for the last year's Halloween Ball. How appropriate. Everybody said so.

There were other pictures of Lindy and friends, Lindy alone, and one of Lindy with her father. In many of the pictures the kids were seated in or standing next to somebody's car. There was one with Todd Hartman lounging against a shiny Cougar. Last year's car.

Lindy reflected that her father's high school album from thirty years before, with all the funny haircuts and the impossible clothes, also featured cars in many of the old black-and-white snapshots. Cars, Lindy decided, were treated like members of the family in America. She wondered if they did that in other cultures.

Bored with the Polaroid snaps, she got up and walked over to the chest of drawers. From the top she picked up a framed photograph of a dark-haired woman with fine cheekbones and smiling pale eyes.

"Hi, Mom," she said softly. "Here I am starting another school year. Last one. After this, no more Wolf River High. No more 'Fight, fight, fight for old Red and White.' I'll be glad to get out, I guess, but sometimes I wish you were around to tell me what happens next. Sometimes? Shoot, a lot of the time. I mean, Daddy's a prince, and he'll always take the time to talk to me, as long as I want. But there are things you just can't talk to your father about, you know? Aah, nuts."

She set the picture back in its place on the dresser. Lightly she touched the delicate Hummel shepherdess that stood next to it. The figurine had been a favorite of her mother's, brought down from the attic by her father as a special gift for Lindy's twelfth birthday. The little porcelain girl with her peasant dress and delicate crook always seemed to bring her mother closer.

Elizabeth Grant had died of lung cancer when Lindy was six years old. Her father talked about her only rarely, but Lindy could tell they had been very much in love. Old photographs showed them as a strikingly handsome pair. Had they once, back in the thirties or forties maybe, been known as the Perfect Couple?

Lindy Grant, one half of Wolf River's Perfect Couple of the sixties, was starting her senior year, and she was troubled by strange new feelings. It seemed to her that somehow during the summer she had outgrown her classmates. Not physically so much as, well, emotionally. They had all come back with the same flighty attitudes they had last year—concerned with their complexions, the hot new records, the football game, who was going with whom, and, of course, their cars.

It wasn't that Lindy had completely lost her interest in these pursuits, it was just that they didn't seem so all-consumingly important.

The influence of her gentle, educated grandmother, with whom Lindy had spent the summer in Boston, may have had something to do with her intellectual growth. She had taken her granddaughter to the ballet, the theater, and a Red Sox game in Fenway Park. Lindy began to understand that there was, after all, life beyond high school. Things were happening in the world that made shaking a pair of pompons seem just slightly ridiculous for anyone past puberty. A man had walked in space. Live television pictures were beamed from the moon. Rumors circulated that more American boys would be sent to that peculiar conflict in Vietnam. Nobody at Wolf River High seemed to care.

Lindy sighed. She felt old. By the time she graduated next June she would be seventeen. Childhood was behind her.

She returned to the mirror and leaned close to search for some new sign of maturity or wisdom in her face. The skin was clear and unlined, the pale blue eyes bright and arresting. The glossy black hair fell to the nape of her neck in soft waves. And the teeth, of course, were still perfect. Nothing there really to mark her new awareness of the world. She sighed again and put the heavy thoughts out of her mind. Plenty of time for that stuff.

She left the mirror and crossed the room to her record player. She selected a single by the Mamas and the Papas, dropped it on the spindle, and flopped down on the bed. She hugged the well-worn panda and listened to "California Dreamin."

What would it be like to live in California, she wondered, her newly acquired world-awareness slipping away. Could it be as dreamy as they said? It couldn't *all* be surfing and beach parties. But at least it would never be boring.

California was closer to where things were happening. Important things. The young people out there would surely be more aware of world events than they were here in the middle of Wisconsin. It wasn't as vital as New York or Boston, maybe, but the climate was a lot nicer.

Lindy let her fantasies take over as she thought about what a high school in Santa Monica must be like. Were all the girls blond, long-legged, and tanned to a beautiful creamy beige? Were the boys all dreamboat surfers and bongo players? She raised up on the bed and stuck out her tongue at the mirror. Of course not. That was just those silly beach party movies. Still, it would be kicks to live there.

A soft knock at her door.

"Come in, Daddy."

Wendell Grant at forty-seven was still a remarkably handsome man. He was straight and slim, and his hair was the same sexy shade of gray as Cary Grant's in *North by Northwest*. He smiled at his daughter, and Lindy felt the familiar little ache of pride.

"Busy?"

"I was just playing records."

"So, let's have a look at the sweater."

She held it up in front of her, kneeling on the bed.

"Terrific, honey, you'll knock 'em dead on the ski slopes."

"Daddy, you know there aren't any ski slopes around here."

"Oh, right. Well, you'll knock 'em dead anywhere you wear it."

Once again she felt a whole lot better about the sweater. It *would* look terrific.

"I stopped in to say good-bye," he said. "I've got to go up to Shawano, honey. There's a county committee meeting, and I might be late getting back."

She frowned. "You have to work on Saturday?"

"Judges don't have a union," he said. "Ida will fix you a nice dinner."

"I don't need any dinner. Roman's coming over. We'll get something downtown."

"Isn't he in training? I thought you guys had a football game next week. Clintonville, isn't it?"

"They don't put football players 'in training' anymore, Daddy. Besides, Roman's in great shape. So he says, and maybe he is. He worked all summer on some kind of construction job in Madison."

"Good for him. What's going on downtown tonight?"

"Nothing special. We'll just cruise around."

Wendell Grant shook his handsome head. "I'm darned if I can see what kick you kids get out of driving all the way up Main Street then turning around and driving all the way down Main Street."

"It's Saturday, Daddy. Everybody does it."

"Oh, well, if everybody does it, what the heck. Have a good time." He winked at her. "And don't get arrested. It would look bad for a judge's daughter."

He left her with a smile. He was right of course, she thought. Cruising was stupid and juvenile, an excuse for the boys to show off their cars and for the girls to wear the pretty new clothes they'd bought over the summer and fool around with the boys. It was all so very high school. But it *was* the first Saturday of the term, and *everybody* would be there.

Lindy didn't care about the flirting of fooling around. As the most popular girl in her class every year since ninth grade, she could have any boy she wanted. And she already had the prize catch of Wolf River High. Roman Dixon had been her acknowledged steady since she was old enough to date. The perfect couple—handsomest boy, star of the football team, and the prettiest girl, queen of everything. It was like a movie. It had been natural and inevitable. And it definitely had its advantages. Being known as Roman Dixon's girl saved her the trouble of fending off the creeps. Then there was knowing she was envied by every other girl in school, and that was a treat to be savored.

Roman might not be the brightest thing in pants, but he was easily the best-looking boy she'd ever seen, and he treated her well. Sometimes he got a little too eager with his hands. She let him get inside her blouse, but drew the line when he started going for the goodies down below. He was hot to go all the way, but he didn't hassle her about it.

Going all the way was something she had thought about a good deal during the summer. She had more or less decided that this year she would give in. It would be a nice farewell gift to Roman. She might even enjoy it, and it would save her the embarrassment of entering college next fall as a virgin.

She took the Mamas and the Papas record off the turntable, holding it carefully so as not to put fingerprints on the grooves, and slipped it back into the cardboard envelope. She slid the album into its place with the rest of her records and, with a last approving look at herself in the mirror, went downstairs.

Ida Krantz had been with the family eight years. After trying hard to be father and mother to Lindy after his wife's death, Wendell Grant was vastly relieved after two years to take the bony, capable woman into his household and let her assume charge of the domestic affairs.

For her part, Ida had come gratefully to work on Elm Street after her drunken bully of a husband fell asleep on the railroad tracks and failed to wake up at the approach of the 11:10 from Milwaukee. She had taken over as surrogate mother to the household, pulling together the pieces of the broken family.

Ida stood now at the foot of the stairs as Lindy came down. Her long bony face was tight with disapproval.

"Aren't you going to wear the rest of that skirt?"

"This is all of it, Ida."

"Does your father know you go out dressed like the town tramp?"

"Hey, this is nothing. The kids are wearing them up to here in the big cities. Miniskirts, they call them."

"I could think of a better name." Ida changed the subject. "Your father says you're not eating at home tonight."

"I'll get something downtown."

"A McDonald's burger, I suppose. With greasy French fries and one of those pasty milkshakes."

"The fries aren't greasy, the shakes are thick," Lindy said. "Besides, a government report came out last week that said McDonald's burgers are more nutritious ounce-for-ounce than wheat germ and alfalfa sprouts."

"I don't believe that for a minute," said Ida, her frown slipping a little.

"Well, it was worth a try." Lindy grew serious for a moment. "Ida, do you think Daddy has somebody over in Shawano?"

"Has somebody?"

"You know. A girlfriend."

"I'm sure I wouldn't know. Your father's private life is his own business."

"Come off it. You'd know if anybody did."

The thin woman sighed. "As far as I know your father is not dating anybody seriously at the moment. Not here or in Shawano or anywhere else."

"I didn't say anything about 'seriously.' "

"If you want to know about your father's love life, ask him."

"I have, but he's not ready to talk to me about it."

"Then I expect when he's ready he'll let you know."

"I wish he *would* find somebody. Get married again, even. Do you think he'll get married again, Ida?"

"I wouldn't be surprised." She started for the kitchen.

"I've got things to do. Say hello to Mr. Wonderful for me."

Lindy caught up with her and gave her a quick hug. "Roman likes you, too."

"There'll be cold cuts in the fridge if you're hungry when you come in."

Lindy fluffed her hair one more time and went out to the front porch to wait for the other half of the Perfect Couple.

CHAPTER 4

ROMAN

Roman Dixon stood out on the lawn in front of the white frame bungalow with green shutters where he lived with his parents. At six-feet-one, Roman was four inches taller than Howard, his father, who stood next to him. The family resemblance was there in the strong jaw, but Roman's hair was thick and blond where Howard's was black as coal dust. Roman had the lithe body of an athlete; Howard was still solid but had too much belly. The father's eyes were squinted and faintly bloodshot; the son's were a clear gray that gave him the look of being more intelligent than he really was.

Roman shifted nervously from foot to foot while he tried to hold on to the attentive expression he assumed when his father launched into a lecture. Roman was anxious to knock off the chatter, get into his candy-apple Chevy, and get downtown where things were happening. He wanted to pop in an 8-track cartridge, roll down the windows, and give everybody an earful of his new sound system. It had cost almost a thousand dollars, even putting it in himself, but it would be the best and loudest in town, and that made it easily worth the money. He was fairly itching to get started, but he knew the old man had to get in his say, so he held his impatience in check.

"You're not going to be doing any drinkin', are you Romey?"

"Hey, no way, Pop."

"Look, I know you put away a few beers last summer while you were working down in Madison."

"Just a couple of times," Roman said. "After work with the guys."

"Sure, I know that. And I'm nobody to be saying you should be a temperance freak or anything like that, but that was different. It's football season now. You're supposed to be in training, and the scouts are watching you. I mean, I know for a fact that both Illinois and Ohio State and at least one from the west coast are in town right now. Those guys watch both how you play on the field and what you do off it."

"Don't worry, Pop. I don't mess with anything during the season."

"I'm just thinking about you, Romey, you know that. You got a chance to do something with your life. Play some football, go to college, get an education. If I'd gone to college when I got out of the Navy I'd be something besides a friggin' factory hand now."

"Pop, you're a foreman. You got factory hands working for you."

"I still carry a lunch pail, son. I don't want to see you do that. Not ever."

"Don't worry, Pop." Roman stole a glance at his watch. Everybody would be cruising Main Street by now. Lindy Grant would be waiting for him. He remembered that he'd also promised to pick up Alec McDowell. Sometimes Alec could be a pain in the ass, the way he was always sucking up, but he was smart, and he came up with some fun ideas.

Roman would have liked to tell the old man to bag the lecture, but he knew better. Howard Dixon could still deliver a powerful punch if you got him pissed. Especially when he was drunk.

Happily, today the old man was sober, but when he got in one of his buddy-buddy moods he was almost as hard to take. Roman was relieved to see his mother come out of the house and walk toward them.

Fran Dixon was a plump woman with tired eyes who still carried traces of the pretty girl she had been. She said, "Howard are you going to keep the boy standing here all day? He wants to be off with his friends."

Roman grinned gratefully at her over his father's shoulder.

"Just havin' a little man talk," Howard said. He clapped his son on the shoulder. "Go ahead, Romey. Have a good time. Give the girls something to talk about."

"I guess I don't have to expect you home for dinner," his mother said.

"I'll get something downtown."

Howard frowned as though he wanted to say something more. He finally settled for, "Don't do anything I wouldn't do."

"That gives me plenty of room," Roman said in the ritual answer.

His father gave him a playful shove toward the car while his mother looked properly vexed.

Roman climbed gratefully into the Chevy, revved the sweet-running engine, and eased up on the gas, loving the baritone burble of the twin pipes. He took off, careful this time not to burn rubber, and waved back at his parents, who stood in the front yard watching him.

As soon as he was around the corner Roman popped in a Beach Boys cartridge and turned the volume up. He rolled down the window and let the mellow harmonies escape, even though the sounds were wasted in Grover's Meadows, the small tract where the Dixon family lived.

The Meadow, as it was now commonly called, had been named for himself by the developer who had built the tract homes there in the early 1950s. Fifteen years later some of the houses were beginning to show signs of age, but most, like the Dixons', were neatly kept up.

The Meadow was home to many of Wolf River's smaller merchants and the higher-salaried workers at Allis Chalmers and the glove factory. Although it was several cuts below Elm Street and the Hill, it was a respectable place to live, and Howard Dixon had worked hard to make a home there for his wife and son.

ALEC

At the very edge of the tract, in a house a little smaller and not quite as neat as the Dixons', lived Phelan McDowell, editor of the Wolf River *Chronicle*, his wife, Trudy, and their son, Alec.

The *Chronicle* did not publish on Saturday, but Alec's father was down at the office as usual, putting together the features for the Sunday edition. His mother clattered away in the living room at the old Underwood, finishing up the fashion column she did weekly for the women's page.

Trudy McDowell did much of the feature writing for the paper, mostly without a byline and without pay. Her regular work included the cooking column, social announcements, the Laff-A-Day feature, and the club news. Usually on a Saturday Alec would be helping out—proofreading, checking facts, and running copy down to the office on his bicycle, which he especially hated. However, since this was the first big Saturday of the school year, he had been given the day off.

Alec sat outside on the front stoop waiting for Roman Dixon. He was wearing the new red-and-white satin jacket he had bought with the money he was paid for his summer job at the *Chronicle*. He didn't much like working with his father, but the alternative would have been to hire out as a farm hand, which meant getting all dirty and physically tired.

The jacket was a size too large, but Alec had bought it that way on purpose. It was his hope that it would give the appearance of bulk to his narrow shoulders.

As he waited, Alec ran over in his mind a set of stock responses to Roman's descriptions of how great he was going to be this year on the football field. The hell of it was, the guy was good. He was the star of the team, and nobody knew it better than Roman. Still, he enjoyed having Alec around to agree with him.

Worse than listening to the jock heroics, Alex would have to hear about Roman's mostly imaginary sexual exploits. Roman Dixon was a dumb, conceited asshole, but he was popular. And he drove that fabulous candy-apple Chevy. When you didn't have a car of your own, and lacked the looks or the money or the athletic ability to be a part of the in-crowd, you did what you could to get close. What Alec McDowell did was kiss Roman Dixon's ass.

Alec's mother came out of the house carrying a sheaf of copy paper. Alec hoped she was not going to ask him to take it down to his father on the detested bicycle. How many high school seniors rode bicycles, anyway?

Trudy McDowell smiled fondly at her son. "Don't worry. Your father left the car for me so I can take the copy down myself."

She was a slim, intelligent woman who served as an anchor for his often erratic father. It was scary to Alec the way she sometimes seemed to read his mind.

"Is Roman picking you up?" she said.

"Yeah."

"That's nice."

She never commented one way or the other on Alec's choice of friends, or anything else having to do with his private life. It was one of the reasons Alec loved his mother so very much. She bent down and kissed him lightly on the ear.

"Have a good time, darling."

Her breast brushed against his arm as she straightened up, and Alec shivered. His mother was starting to turn gray, but she had retained a young, sexy body, which he found most disturbing.

Roman Dixon rumbled up with the windows rolled down, naturally, and the 8-track blasting at brain-damage level. Alec smiled, tried to close his ear passages, and got into the Chevy next to Roman.

With "Good Vibrations" booming from the four custom flush-mounted front and rear speakers, threatening to shatter the car's windshield, Roman tooled happily out of the Meadow and on down to Main Street. There everybody who counted at Wolf River High was either cruising the street or strolling the sidewalk. Roman seemed oblivious to the danger of imminent deafness. The admiring looks he got from the kids and the sour expressions from the adults made the pain worthwhile.

Main Street intersected with Elm at the bottom of the long gradual slope known locally as the Hill. The higher you went on the Hill, the higher was your position on the Wolf River social scale. At the very top stood the stone mansions of the Gotschke and Speith families, whose members had seldom been seen in Wolf River since the end of World War II. They preferred to live in places like Brown Deer or Evanston, but their names still brought respect in Wolf River.

Just below the fabled Gotschkes and Speiths lived people like Ralph Hartman, the banker, and his family. In descending order were found the houses of the town's top professionals, the landowners, and the leading merchants. Near the bottom were the police chief, management people from Allis Chalmers, and professors from the college.

As Roman and Alec rolled up to the corner of Elm and Main, a cluster of girls idled outside Weisfield's jewelry store, pretending to admire the window display of wristwatches. At the approach of the gleaming Chevy they giggled and waved.

Roman nudged Alec McDowell and said something.

Alec shook his head and cupped a hand to his ear.

Reluctantly Roman turned down the Beach Boys a few decibels. He pointed at the girls and said, "See anything you like?"

"Looks like the same old stuff to me," Alec said.

"Yeah, but you notice some of them are really filling out? Check the tits on Claire Hennesey."

"Yeah."

"How many of them you suppose got laid over the summer?"

Alec looked over the group and practiced his inexpert Elvis lip curl. "Them?"

"Sure. How many you think buried the old weenie?"

"None, if I know Wolf River girls."

"Don't kid yourself. They're female. The chicks want it as much as we do, and nowadays they're not afraid to ask for it."

"Nobody's asked me this week," Alec said.

"You got to let 'em know you're available. No shit. They all take the Pill now, so they don't have to worry about getting knocked up. There'll be plenty of pussy out there for a guy that knows how to get it."

Roman made the turn and headed up Elm between the rows of stately trees that gave the street its name. The houses near Main Street were well kept but modest. Up near the crest of the Hill where Lindy Grant lived, the houses were fifty years old and more—sturdy and sedate structures with gables and porches and leaded windows. The houses wore new paint, and the lush lawns were bordered by neat box hedges.

On this first Saturday of the school year social distinctions were not as important as they would soon become again. Kids from the old families on the Hill mingled freely and happily with classmates from the Meadow, and even the Poles from the South Side, Wolf River's oldest and poorest district. The cars were shined up, the sky was blue, the leaves just beginning to turn. The air was warm with a soft Indian summer breeze. Roman drove slowly, enjoying his sense of being young, healthy, and popular.

With the Beach Boys continuing to assault him from four speakers, Alec had some difficulty keeping the smile on his face. But he did. To him the California surfer sound was musical Pablum. If he was choosing the music, he'd have gone with Andre Kostelanetz, but that was a peculiarity he was not about to make public. The important thing was that if you were going to be Roman Dixon's friend and ride in Roman's car, you'd better listen to Roman's music. You either liked it or you kept your mouth shut.

As they headed up Elm Street, Alec leaned closer to the window so the other kids would be sure to see him. He knew a lot of them would kill to be riding up here in the school's sharpest car with the football hero. There were some payoffs to listening to the windbag.

Roman shifted down unnecessarily, rumbling the pipes. He stroked the floor stick lovingly, like it was his cock. He looked over, and Alec understood he was expected to comment.

"You sure got this baby running sweet," he said.

"I came home a week early to tune her up before school started."

"How come you didn't drive it down to Madison?" Much as he wanted to stay friends, Alec could not bring himself to refer to an automobile as "her."

"I was staying with my aunt and uncle, and they've only got room in their garage for one car, and I wasn't about to leave this baby out in the weather."

"I don't blame you," Alec said. "Not with a paint job like this."

"Besides, you don't need a car to score in that town.

The women have their own. They want to go somewhere, they take you."

"No shit."

"Yeah. They're really hungry for it. They'd hang around the construction site and watch us. You should have seen them lick their chops whenever we took off our shirts."

Alec widened his eyes. "Wow."

"Had to fight 'em off, practically."

"Wow."

"All they got for men in Madison is radicals and hippies from the university. Bunch of long-haired faggots. Women down there get a chance to see real men, they flip out."

I will not say "wow" one more time, Alec told himself.

"Wow," he said.

"So how'd the summer go for you?" Roman asked, making little effort to sound interested.

"Dull. I worked at the *Chronicle* with Dad, as usual."

"That what you gonna do? Work on a newspaper like your old man?"

"I guess, after college. I haven't thought too much about it."

"I know one thing I'm *not* going to do," said Roman, "and that's work in a factory. For one thing, factory work is a batch of shit, and for another, my old man would kill me."

"Your dad makes a good living."

"It's still working in a factory. He comes home with grease on his clothes, and his fingernails are always black."

"I see what you mean."

Roman brightened. "Hey, maybe you'll be a sportswriter and you can write about me."

"Wouldn't that be a kick."

Not fucking likely, Alec thought. Once he was out of this shit town he would be somebody and be on his own and wouldn't need to suck around with jocks. It was to his advantage now to be tight with the class hero—it got him invited to parties and it got him dates with girls who otherwise would have brushed him off. But pretending to agree with every simpleminded statement of the Star could be a giant pain. Someday he would love to tell Roman Dixon what a stupid prick he really was.

But not today.

CHAPTER 5

FRAZIER

In one of the big old wood frame houses on lower Elm Street, in the first block off Main, Frazier Nunley lived with his mother and father. His father had bought the place at the end of World War II with his GI loan. That was when he and his wife planned a large family, before Orva Nunley discovered that Frazier was the only child she could ever have.

The house was clearly too large for the three of them, but it would have been more expensive to move somewhere else than it was to keep it. During the summer they kept two of the upstairs bedrooms closed off. When the school year began, the extra rooms were rented out to students at Harvey College, the small liberal arts school at the edge of town.

This year the new dorm had gone up out on the campus, so the two upstairs rooms were not in use. The extra income was missed, for although Ellis Nunley was head of the English Department at Harvey, his salary was not large.

On this first Saturday of September, Frazier Nunley lay on the narrow bed in his upstairs room trying to keep his mind occupied by solving chess problems from a book his father had brought home. He enjoyed the intellectual challenge of the problems, but he never played the actual game. That was because there was simply no one in Wolf River good enough to play him.

One quick glance at the board layout was all Frazier needed for the hypothetical problems. He usually worked on several in his mind at the same time. When they were difficult enough, Frazier found some satisfaction in solving them quickly and systematically. Today, however, the mental exercise gave him no pleasure.

Through the window of his bedroom, even though it was tightly closed against drafts, he could hear the kids down on Main Street calling to each other, driving back and forth or strolling along the sidewalks. It was that way every Saturday of the school year, but especially the first. Frazier could lie here and listen to them talking and laughing and having a simpleminded good time.

Sure it was simpleminded, and pointless, but they were having fun. In the life of Frazier Nunley, straight-A student, chess master, acknowledged class genius, there was precious little fun. He would have given a lot to be a part of the foolish revelry on Main Street today.

At fourteen, Frazier was much younger than his senior classmates, to say nothing of being smarter. He had skipped three grades in elementary school but was still far ahead of the class in brain power. He could easily have passed the exams right now to get into Harvey. His father, in fact, was in favor of such a move. Frazier's mother, however, thought her son should not be too far removed from the ordinary experiences of the young, and wanted him to have a reasonably normal senior year in high school.

Normal my ass, thought Frazier. There was no way he would ever fit in. The other kids treated him with a certain respect for his mind, but he knew full well that privately they thought of him as the school nerd. Some, he knew, even thought he was queer, but in that they were dead wrong. Frazier Nunley's loins surged with as many heterosexual yearnings as any of his classmates. He daily lamented his lack of a chance to prove it.

Part of the problem was the way he looked. Forced to wear glasses since the first grade, his eyes were big and froggy behind the thick lenses. His body was lumpy and soft, bulging out like a girl at the hips. With his coarse, mud-colored hair and his pimply complexion, it was small wonder he had never had a real date.

Then there were his allergies. Hardly a pollen or an animal existed that did not set Frazier to sniffling and sneezing. The windows in his house had to be kept tightly closed. He took pills to alleviate the reaction when he did go out, but he still went through a big box of Kleenex in the course of a school day.

Frazier hated his body. He hated the way it looked, and he hated the way it was allergic to damn near everything. He could not blame heredity. His father was lean and wiry, a fraction under average height, but well proportioned and fiercely healthy. His mother was a tall, beautiful woman with the classic features of a Greek statue. No, for his physical flaws at least, Frazier had nobody to blame but himself—his fondness for candy bars and sweet soda, and his abhorrence of exercise. He was solely responsible for the way his body looked, but that didn't make it any easier to carry around.

Sometimes Frazier hated his mind, too. He would have liked to struggle along with the other kids over the problems that he sailed through using a fraction of his brain. At least in that he could be one of them. Sure, being a genius made school easier, but it also made him *different.* To be different in adolescence was to be shunned.

But much as Frazier enjoyed an occasional wallow in self-pity, he recognized it for what it was and snapped himself out of it when he figured he'd had enough. Now, with the laughter of his classmates still ringing outside, he wiped the chess problems out of his mind and filled it with a happier image, one he often summoned when he was depressed: Lindy Grant.

Lovely, laughing, popular, unattainable Lindy Grant. Last spring she had replaced Natalie Wood in Frazier's sex fantasies. Seeing Lindy in his mind was not quite as satisfying as covertly watching the real article in class, but it was better than nothing.

During the long summer, while Lindy was out of town, Frazier had filled the tedious hours with vivid, sensual mental pictures of her. Lindy, he had decided, was absolutely the most beautiful, most desirable creature he had ever seen. The first glimpse of her last week after the summer's drought had hit him like a punch to the stomach. She was in two of his classes. Unfortunately, her desk was located some distance from his in both classes, but at least she was in a position where he could get a good look at her.

Frazier lay on the bed and let the vision of Lindy Grant fill his mind. He slid a hand down inside his jockey shorts and felt his erection grow. He began a slow, purposeful stroking.

"Frazier, what are you doing?"

His mother was a loving, well-meaning woman, but she seemed to have some sixth sense that enabled her to intrude on Frazier's most private moments. He snatched his hand away as though she could see through the wooden door.

"Nothing," he said.

"I have a new record of the Bach-Busoni Chaconne. It's by Alicia de Larrocha. Would you like to listen with me?"

Orva Nunley was an accomplished musician herself, who once seriously considered a concert career. Wolf River, however, offered little opportunity for serious music. She loved her husband dearly, but Ellis was strictly a literary man with a tin ear. So she relied on her gifted son as someone to share her music with.

Frazier loved and understood his mother's music, and usually enjoyed their sessions together. But right at this minute, he would rather be left alone.

"I'll be down in a little while," he said.

"All right, dear," his mother said.

She never pressured him, never urged him to undertake anything he did not want to. Nor did his father. They were both a little in awe of the genius child they had produced.

Frazier lay back on the bed and drew in a series of deep breaths. He closed his eyes and imagined a blue dot directly in front of his forehead. The dot expanded into a window that irised open like a camera shutter. As he relaxed, the aperture grew larger. On the other side lay a soft blue sky with cottony clumps of white clouds. Frazier could hear tender, seductive sounds—the sighing of a gentle breeze, a girl's laughter. He focused his concentration on the spectral window, shutting out all external stimuli. Then, slowly, gently, he floated up and through the opening into the outside world.

This was Frazier Nunley's secret. No one—not his talented and loving mother, not his fond but preoccupied father, certainly not his classmates, knew what he could do. And Frazier was not about to tell anyone. They had reasons enough to laugh behind his back without thinking he was a certified wacko.

The marvelous power had come about almost by accident, and Frazier himself was much surprised at the discovery.

It had happened the first time three years ago, when Frazier was eleven. He was in bed, sick with the flu. Frazier always caught whatever form of flu was "going around." He lay on his back dreamily watching a spider spin a web at the junction of two walls and his bedroom ceiling. Such a beautiful construction for the single deadly purpose of entrapping an unwary fly. In Frazier's feverish mind the spider took on a mystical significance. The great Builder and Destroyer.

He followed its labors intently as each delicate strand of the web was spun out and attached at precisely the right spot to another strand. A work of art with a lethal intent. The construction was a miraculous and wonderful thing to watch, all the more so because Frazier knew it would not last out the day. No fly, even had one found its way into the Nunley house, would be ensnared there. His mother, for all her appreciation of the arts, would see the spiderweb only as something unclean, to be swept away. It would not long escape her eye, and that would be the end of both the web and its creator.

In his half-dozing, dreamlike state, Frazier urged the spider on. It became crucial that he see the web to its completion before the cataclysmic broom swept it away.

With every fiber of his concentration zeroed in on the tiny insect, Frazier became gradually aware of a change in his perspective, along with a pleasant floating sensation. The pain and fever of his illness drained away. Up and up he rose, silently, gently, like a helium-filled balloon, until he was right there with the industrious spider. He found he could examine at microscopic range the dainty filaments of the web, glistening with the sticky secretion that would ensnare the unwary fly.

His hearing, too, was unnaturally acute. As the spider moved delicately along the strands of the web, apparently unaware of his presence, it made soft, harplike twanging sounds. The sensation was exhilarating beyond anything in his limited experience.

The real shock came when his vision swiveled to survey the rest of the room from his new vantage point. There below on the bed lay Frazier Nunley. The detested pudgy body was awake, but unseeing and unfeeling. The pimply face was flushed and shining with perspiration. The eyes were closed. A beatific smile lay on the lips.

Frazier lost control then and felt his mind, his essence,

whatever it was that floated free, sucked down from the ceiling and back into the body. The brief flight had exhausted him, and he slept the clock around.

When he awoke, the fever had broken, and his sharp young mind was completely lucid. He examined his adventure coolly and rationally to determine whether it had actually happened or, what seemed more likely, it had been a product of delirium.

In his parents' library he sought out articles concerned with astral projection—the so-called out-of-body experiences. A child of logic, Frazier had always considered the reported experiences to be self-hypnosis, if not out-and-out fraud—material for the sensational tabloids, along with reports of hitchhiking on flying saucers.

Now he read everything he could find on the subject, looking at it with new eyes since his own experience. When he had exhausted the materials covering the subject in their home, he persuaded his father to take him to the college library. There he pored over the works of philosophers, psychologists, scientists, and mystics. The opinions were many and varied on what made up the essence of a human being, or mind, or soul, and how it was linked to the corporal reality of the body. He studied them all, weighing their merits and mistakes relative to what had happened to him.

Frazier distilled the knowledge gained from the disparate sources and began to practice as he might at some new physical task. At first his efforts met with failure, but he persisted. Then, gradually, he began to achieve partial success in setting free his spirit. At last his efforts were rewarded as he recaptured the precise state of mind that had allowed him to float free of his body and join the spider on the ceiling.

Methodically at first, then more quickly, he learned the techniques of breaking away from the bonds of his flesh. He noted the similarities and the contradictions between his new reality and the reported experiences of others.

As was frequently described in first-person accounts, he found he could look back and see his body exactly where he had left it. He could move through space, including solid barriers, without hindrance. Time had no meaning in his astral state.

In the floating condition, he could see and hear with outstanding clarity, but his other senses were left behind with the body. No taste, no touch, no smell. But that also meant no pain.

The major difference he found between his own experience and many of the reports was that there was no "silver cord" connecting his astral being to the flesh-and-blood self left behind. That, he assumed, was an invention of some imaginative writer with an Oedipal hangup, and had been picked up by suggestible "experts" who followed.

As he became more adept at disembodied journeying, Frazier ventured outside his house and along the block of Elm Street on which he lived. Theoretically, there was no limit to the distance he could travel, but in the early days of his experimenting Frazier never went out of sight of his house. He had a vague but powerful notion that he must not venture too far from his body. Although astral travel brought an overwhelming sense of freedom, there was always the underlying anxiety about the body left behind. A poor, shapeless, unlovely thing it might be, but it was home.

Now, on this Indian summer Saturday, the mind of Frazier Nunley floated up and away from the body on his bed, through the ceiling of his bedroom, up through the rock wool insulation and the attic filled with dusty memorabilia, through the shingled roof, and free into the September sky.

Down Elm Street he sailed to the intersection of Main, where, unseen and godlike, he could watch the revelry of his classmates. He settled down, down toward the slow-moving candy-apple Chevy owned by Roman Dixon. Roman, handsome, athletic, popular—all the things Frazier was not. More than once Frazier had thought how willingly he would give up his straight A's, his certain acceptance at any college of his choice, his string of academic awards, just to change places with Roman Dixon.

Roman drove with one tanned forearm resting carelessly on the windowsill. Beside Roman, his acolyte, Alec McDowell, talked with exaggerated liveliness, making sure he was part of the action. In his loneliness, Frazier would even have traded places with McDowell.

He moved in closer to listen.

"What time did you tell Lindy we'd be there?" Alec was saying.

"I told her to expect me when she sees me," Roman said.

"You tell her I was coming?"

"She won't care. We're not doing anything special."

As casually as that these two were preparing to enter the temple of the goddess. They would simply drive up to Lindy Grant's house, probably honk the horn, and she would come out and get in the car. Maybe she would sit between them. Her silky thighs would brush against theirs.

The picture was too painful for Frazier. With a groan no one could hear, he willed his mind up and away from the happy cruisers, over the sturdy elms, back up the street to his own house. In through the glass pane of his window he flew, and back into the doughy body that lay on the bed in its underwear.

There, alone, Frazier Nunley the young genius cried silently into his pillow.

CHAPTER 6

June 1987

LINDY

Old acquaintances vanished, dispatched to eternity by the stroke of the DELETE key, taking their pieces of the story with them. New people were born full-grown and imperfect. Slowly, painfully, the characters who survived shifted into new attitudes, their speech patterns changed along with the words they spoke, their motives dissolved and reformed in glowing green letters on the monitor screen.

Lindy Grant leaned back in the chair and looked at her work. "Shit," she said. "Sonofabitch."

She glowered at the screen for a moment longer, then punched the keys that would erase the scene she had spent the last two hours rewriting.

"How come you get to talk that way and I don't?" Nicole said.

Lindy swiveled in her chair to see her daughter standing in the doorway of the small storage room that served as her office.

"You didn't hear that," she said.

"Script not going so good?"

"The script is going lousy, and I'd have a few more choice words for it if you weren't around."

"Lighten up, Mom. Parents don't have to talk like Ward and June Cleaver anymore."

"I know that," Lindy said testily. "But somebody's got to maintain some kind of moral standards around here."

Nicole shrugged. An irritating habit she had picked up recently. "Okay. So who's the sonofabitch?"

"His name is Lou Davidoff. He knows as much about story values as Daffy Duck. Less. If I make my people do what he wants them to this script is going to make less sense than one of your Beastie Boys records."

"So why do it, then?"

"Because we want to eat. To eat well, we need a successful movie. For a movie to be successful it has to get into the theaters. Mr. Davidoff represents the people who can put it into a lot of theaters."

"But if it's a bad script nobody will go see it."

"You are beginning to perceive one of the basic principles of Hollywood."

"God, you live a glamorous life."

"So what are you doing home? Did they close the mall?"

"Nobody's around. Becky's spending a week with her father, Kim has to go to summer school, Tracey's got the flu or something. There's no sun for the beach, and I haven't got a thing to do."

"Want to try reading a book?"

"Get serious, Mom."

"You would think that the daughter of someone who depends on the written word to make a living would now and then take the time to crack a . . ."

She broke off, listening. From the street out in front of the house came the faint scrape of metal on metal. "You can go down and get the mail."

"It's not here yet. I looked when I came in."

"Trust me, it's here."

The girl cocked her head and squinted at her mother. "God, how do you *do* that?"

"A writer's ears are delicately attuned to the sounds of the mailman. His coming is the high point of the day—arrival of residuals and rejections. An acceptable excuse to take a break. Go see what he brought."

Nicole sighed and shrugged again and walked back out of the office.

Lindy's expression grew serious as she watched her daughter go. Since the troubling incident of the strange voice and the utterly foreign expression the other day, Nicole had been her normal self. Still, Lindy watched the girl closely. You could never be sure what the kids were into these days.

She turned back to her work, paging back through the marked-up script Lou Davidoff had messengered over. She held the bound copy gingerly away from her body as though something slimy might fall out.

"Eleanor needs to be stronger," he had written.

Jesus, everybody wanted women characters strong these days. Sigourney Weaver had birthed a race of Amazons. There was nothing wrong with Eleanor as written. She was smart, resourceful, reasonably courageous, and still feminine. But she was in fear of her life, dammit. Davidoff wanted some combination of Rambo and Miss Piggy. If that's what he thought would bring women into the theaters, he was wrong-o.

She punched the scene up on the monitor again and poised her fingers over the keyboard. Gratefully, she put everything on hold when she heard Nicole come back in the front door.

"Nothing from your agent," Nicole said, shuffling the envelopes as she came back in.

"Oh, thanks, mess up the one bright spot of my day.

You could have let me go through the pile slowly, keeping the possibility of good news alive a little longer.''

''God, you are in a mood.'' Nicole handed over the envelopes. ''Maybe I'll go see if Tracey's feeling any better.''

''Good idea. You can cheer her up now that you've taken care of me.''

With a last shrug Nicole sauntered out. Lindy smiled fondly after her. Considering the fact that Nicole's father had bailed out suddenly without bothering to marry her mother, the kid had turned out pretty well. She was glad now that she had not yielded to the urging of her friends to give the baby up for adoption.

''Somebody else could give her a good life,'' had run the arguments, ''and she'll only drag you down.'' Well, Lindy did not feel dragged down, and she was confident that Nicole had a pretty good life too.

She stood up to stretch her legs and carried the mail out to the living room, sorting it as she walked.

There was a credit card bill from Chevron, another from Bank of America for her MasterCard.

Cable TV bill. She reminded herself to cancel either HBO or Showtime. She would save twenty dollars a month, and they had the same movies anyway.

Announcement of a furniture sale at Levitz—for ''preferred customers.'' She had bought a coffee table there a year ago, which apparently qualified her.

The *Hollywood Reporter* and *Daily Variety*. Even before you picked up the telephone in Hollywood, you read the trades.

Calendar of events from the Writers Guild. Who had the time to attend those seminars, anyway?

This week's catalog from Publishers Central Bureau. That would cost her another twenty dollars or so. Lindy could never resist bargain books.

A handwritten letter. No return address. Postmark: Wolf River, WI.

Wolf River?

Lindy sat down suddenly on the sofa. She had not thought about Wolf River for a long time. Not consciously. Sometimes images from her childhood would sift through her dreams like oily smoke. Those were the nights when she woke up staring into the darkness, willing her heartbeat back to normal while she persuaded herself nothing was there.

She held the envelope from Wolf River by the edges, turning it over slowly. Thc paper was soft and smooth, like dead skin. The light in the room seemed to dim, though outside it was mid-afternoon and the sun was beginning to break through the cloud cover.

Since Ida Krantz had suffered her stroke there was no one in Wolf River Lindy had kept in touch with. Her father, as far as she knew, was still in Madison with his new wife. Friends from high school were scattered, forgotten, or dead.

Why me? she thought. Why now?

Why not open the letter and find out? asked the sardonic inner voice that sometimes called Lindy to attention.

"Yeah, why not," she said aloud, but without conviction.

She carried the mail back to her office, laid it out on the desk, and drew the Wolf River letter to her. She slit the envelope neatly with a silver letter opener and slid out the single sheet that was inside.

The message, like the name and address on the envelope, was written in careful script with a black felt-tip pen.

> Dear Lindy,
> Remember the Wolfpack? How could you forget! On Saturday, July 11, the Fabulous Class of '67 will hold its 20th reunion at the Wolf River Inn. Be There or Be Square.

Carefully, as though it might slither away, Lindy laid

the sheet of paper down on her desk beside the computer keyboard. She stared down at it, rereading the short, unsigned message.

What the hell was this, some macabre practical joke?

No. No joke. Could it be serious? Well, why not? Twenty years was traditional class reunion time. Buy why her class? And for God's sake, why her?

Lindy picked up the page with thumb and forefinger and dropped it into the trash basket beside her desk. The anonymous sender of the invitations had no way of knowing, but the Pope would marry Whoopi Goldberg before Lindy Grant would return to Wolf River, Wisconsin, for a high school reunion. Or any other reason.

She returned to the rewrite of her script, but could not get her mind back into the story. The cozy little room she used as an office felt cold. Shadows of Wolf River kept getting between Lindy and the glowing green letters on the screen.

ROMAN

Holy shit, what a headache.

Roman Dixon rolled over and shoved his face into the pillow, trying to smother the pain that lanced like a red-hot poker straight through his skull from temple to temple.

No good. It still hurt.

He rolled over on his back, and his stomach spasmed. Maybe if he could puke.

Roman lurched to his feet and shuffled across the bedroom and into the bathroom. He knelt in front of the beige toilet and retched. It seemed the lining of his stomach would rip loose and splatter out of his mouth, but all that came up was a dollop of biter yellow bile.

Roman flushed the toilet and staggered to his feet. He was definitely going to have to cut down on his drinking. Maybe go dry for a couple of months.

This time he meant it.

Really.

He made his way back to the king-size bed and fell across it, squeezing his eyes shut and praying for just one more hour of sleep that would ease his torment.

"Aren't you going in to the store today?"

Stephanie's voice sliced through his pain like a chain saw. He groaned.

"Shall I call and tell them you're not coming?"

"I don't have to call anybody. I'm the boss."

"It would be nice to let them know."

"They know it by now," he mumbled into the pillow.

Silence for several seconds, but he could feel her still standing there in the bedroom doorway, looking at him with those sad, sagging eyes of hers.

With agonizing effort he rolled over on his side to face his wife.

"Do you want some coffee?" she said.

"Jesus, no."

"An aspirin?"

"Not in this stomach."

She stood uncertainly for a moment. "The mail's here."

"So take care of it. You've got a checkbook."

"There's a personal letter addressed to you."

Something in his wife's tone pierced the pain and the nausea and made him shiver. "Who's it from?"

"There's no return address. Do you want me to bring it in here?"

"Never mind. I'll come out."

Stephanie looked at him for a beat longer, then turned and left the doorway. To Roman's aching eyes, her image seemed to remain standing there, slowly fading.

Never a beautiful woman, Stephanie Dixon had not aged well. At forty-three she was five years older than Roman but looked fifteen. Her body was flaccid, and her face sagged. Roman had encouraged her to exercise, and even suggested cosmetic surgery, but Stephanie resisted. She thought people looked the way they were supposed to, and tampering with it would be wrong.

He swung his feet out of bed and stood up, sweating and nude, on the thick bedroom carpet. He closed his eyes to let the wave of vertigo subside, then walked back into the bathroom. He stepped into the shower stall and turned the pointer to COLD, adjusting the head to needle spray.

The icy water raised goose bumps on his flesh and shriveled his pores, but after enduring five minutes of it he began to feel a little better. He turned on the hot water, soaped his body, rinsed, dried with a rough towel, and wiped a clear spot in the steamy mirror to look at himself.

Even with the slight pouchiness around the eyes, he was still a damn good-looking guy. Thick hair, good eyes, strong jaw. He tried a smile, but it didn't quite work.

Who would be writing him a letter? His first thought was that someone had seen him at the motel with Kathy Isles or one of the others. But what if they had? Stephanie knew about his fooling around. She didn't exactly like it, but as long as he kept it reasonably discreet, and played the part of husband and father when necessary, she tolerated it. Her father might not be so forgiving, but what could the old man do? The stores were in Roman's name now, part of his reward for marrying the plain daughter of the sporting goods magnate and taking her two kids.

His stomach tightened again at the thought of the boys. Brian and Eric. A couple of good manly-sounding names, but one was a sullen punk rocker type and the other a redheaded geek with thick glasses. Roman hated it when they had to go out together and people would assume they were his natural sons.

He pulled on a shirt and a pair of jeans and went out to the hall table where the mail lay. He picked up the hand-addressed envelope and scowled at the Wolf River postmark. It was not the old man's shaky handwriting, and nobody else back there would be writing to him. Nobody.

Stephanie was idling around in the living room where

she could watch him open the letter without seeming to watch. Roman took it back to the bedroom.

He sat on the bed and tore open the envelope.

> Dear Roman,
> Remember the Wolfpack? How could you forget! On Saturday, July 11, the Fabulous Class of '67 will hold its 20th reunion at the Wolf River Inn. Be There or Be Square.

He read and reread the short message. Reunion? Why in the name of God would he want to go back to that miserable town for a reunion? Any good memories of his days as a high school hero had died in that terrible senior year.

A couple of duty trips back to Wolf River to check on his old man was as much of the town as he could stand. After an hour or so of "How've you been?" they had nothing to say to each other. Roman would pass the old man some money and make some excuse to get the hell out of town.

Now they wanted him to go back for a high school reunion? Not fucking likely.

"Anything important?"

Stephanie was in the doorway again, watching him. Always watching, reproaching him with those sad, droopy eyes.

"No," he said. "I think I'll go into the store after all." He crumpled the letter, jammed it into a pocket of his jeans, and went to the closet for his waterproof windbreaker. He left the house without saying good-bye. The rain was cold on his bare head. Colder than usual.

ALEC

It was past eight o'clock when Alec McDowell walked up 55th Street past Eighth Avenue to his apartment building. The hooker on the corner of Eighth who used the pay phone there as an office leaned out as he passed.

"Hi, honey. You're getting home late. Need a massage?"

"Not tonight, Georgia, I'm too tired."

"I could wake you up."

"I'll bet you could, but I've got to work."

"Hell, ain't it," she said, and eased back inside her booth.

Not to Alec, it wasn't. Work was the one really meaningful thing in his life. He had no hobbies, no relatives closer than cousins, no friends to speak of, no sex life other than an occasional quick coupling with Georgia or someone like her.

The work he did might not rank in importance with curing cancer or clearing the slums, but it was all he had, and it kept him from crumbling into dust.

His mind tonight was filled with his current project—electing Bo Walton, an unqualified clod, to a position filled currently by Anton Scolari, a well-qualified crook. Alec had spent the afternoon and early evening talking to his client.

The talking was done at Walton's midtown club. Since the unsettling experience with the cleaning woman, Alec had avoided his own office at night. He came away from the meeting convinced that his client had the IQ of a radish. Luckily, elections were seldom decided on the basis of the candidates' intelligence. Alec had got hold of something much more useful—a juicy little scandal concerning Scolari. The public will forgive a certain amount of thievery in public office, but woe to the candidate who deviates from the sexual norm.

At the entrance to his building he glanced around automatically to make sure no one was following him, then he let himself into the foyer. There he keyed open the mailbox and gathered up the contents. Without bothering to look at the mail he headed for the elevator.

His studio apartment on the fourth floor was tidy, as he had left it. Alec always tensed as he opened the door, wondering if a burglar had rampaged through his rooms, stealing whatever he could carry and destroying the rest. Or worse, the burglar might still be there.

Nothing frightened Alec more than physical confrontation. He could hold his own in a battle of insults. Words were his business; talking was his forte. But the threat of violence to his person jellied his knees. He had engaged in just one fight in his life. As a high school sophomore he had made the mistake of teasing a classmate about his flagrant acne. The classmate punched Alec just once in the nose, and the fight was over. Soon after that Alec made it his business to become Roman Dixon's friend—a situation that made it unnecessary for him to fight again.

Since there was, on this occasion, no burglar or other threatening presence, Alec snapped on a light and eased his narrow buttocks into a chair. He sorted systematically through the mail, placing the bills in one neat pile, magazines in another, newsletters next to magazines, junk mail in the basket, letters . . . a letter?

Wolf River? What the hell? Nobody in that town would write to him, even if they remembered him, which was doubtful. His parents were dead and buried. Had been for a good many years. There was no one else.

Carefully he slit the envelope and read the message inside.

> Dear Alec,
> Remember the Wolfpack? How could you forget! On Saturday, July 11, the Fabulous Class of '67 will hold its 20th reunion at the Wolf River Inn. Be There or Be Square.

A sick joke? Who wanted to be reminded of that horrible year? Who would renew those disastrous friendships? Not he. Not Alec McDowell. More reason than most to stay away had Alec McDowell.

He tore the letter and its envelope into neat strips and let them flutter into the wastebasket. He brewed a pot of strong coffee and tried to concentrate on a campaign for his dull-witted client, but a dark part of his mind kept drifting back to Wolf River.

THE FLOATER

Mischief, thou art afoot.

The effort expended in preparing the letters of invitation was well repaid in the reactions of the three recipients. Let them squirm a little and wonder. Let them start to worry even as they destroyed the letters. Let them enjoy the last few days before the start of the pain.

If the Floater had had a voice, he would have laughed.

CHAPTER 7

Wolf River, October 1966

FRAZIER

One of the pleasures for the people who lived on lower Elm Street was the piano playing of Orva Nunley. Even the time she spent practicing, they said, was a delight. And when in the early evening Orva sat down to play for her small family, the neighbors opened their windows to share in the music.

On this October night Orva Nunley gave her full concentration to the sheet music before her as she played a Mozart sonata. It was a difficult piece, and she had worked some months at perfecting it. Orva was a tall, graceful woman, and her hands moved over the keys with a powerful authority.

Seated in the worn wingback chair that he refused to let his wife throw out, Ellis Nunley kept time to the sonata with the stem of his pipe as he read one of the little literary magazines he subscribed to. From time to time he would glance up at Orva and nod his approval.

Their son, Frazier, sat slumped on the couch, holding on to a polite listening attitude while his mother played. He was appreciative of her talent, and he did enjoy good music, but he had heard this piece many times, and just now his mind wanted to be elsewhere. He unwrapped an Almond Joy as quietly as he could and took a bite, letting his thoughts wander.

The school year was more than a month old, and school activities were well under way. Old friendships had been renewed, new ones formed. Couples got together, broke up, reunited. The football team was off to a good start, winning four of its first five games. Roman Dixon was being talked about for All-State. The Halloween Ball at the Hartmans' cabin on the lake was a week away, and everyone was busy planning costumes.

Well, not everyone. Not Frazier Nunley.

For Frazier Nunley it was the same old depressing story. As always, he was not a part of the action. His presence was acknowledged in a general way, but nobody ever thought to invite him anywhere. He was a snag in the stream of high school life, stuck helplessly in place while the fun flowed all around him.

It wasn't that he didn't want to join in, or that he didn't try. He made it a point to learn the way the kids were talking and to do his best to emulate it. He tried calling everybody "man," said "like" a lot, and used expressions like "far out" and "bitchin' " and "outasight."

He practiced walking around with an open, eager expression that would tell people he wanted to be friends. None of it worked for Frazier. It only made people back off further. Once he caught sight of himself in a mirror and was appalled at the sappy look he had been affecting. He quickly reverted to his normal vocabulary and the scholarly, distracted look that invited no one to come near him.

He tried going to the Friday night football games even though it wasn't much fun all by himself. He cheered wildly at all the right times, and did all the yells right along with the rest of the kids. But when the Wolves scored and everyone hugged and clapped each other on the back, Frazier remained alone, unhugged and unclapped.

After the game was worse. No one asked him along to the Dairy Queen or to Shakey's for pizza. He would go alone, buy himself a Coke, and hang around while the kids talked about what they were going to wear to the Halloween Ball. Nobody asked for Frazier's ideas on costumes, and nobody came close to inviting him.

The Halloween Ball was supposed to be a school-sponsored event, but in truth it was run by the Wolfpack, a tightly structured group of the most popular kids. It was made up of the jocks, the rich kids, the attractive ones, and a few connivers like Alec McDowell, who managed to be included in everything without possessing any special attributes. To belong to the Wolfpack was to be in. To be excluded made you a non-person. . . .

Frazier's mother finished the Mozart piece and sat back. She frowned at the sheet music in front of her.

"That was lovely, dear," said Ellis, using a finger to keep his place in the magazine.

"It's the best I've heard you play it," said Frazier.

"I don't know," Orva said. "The middle part isn't quite right. It needs work."

"You're a perfectionist, Mother," Frazier said. He swallowed a big chunk of the candy bar and stood up, hoping she wouldn't ask them to listen to it again.

"One does not play Mozart carelessly," she said. "But that's enough for now. Don't spoil your appetite, Frazier. Dinner will be ready in an hour."

"I won't," Frazier said, stuffing the rest of the Almond Joy into his mouth. He knew he should pay some attention to his diet for the sake of his complexion and his shapeless body, but the discipline a diet would require discouraged him. It didn't seem fair. Both his parents ate exactly what they wanted to, and his father hadn't an ounce of fat, while his mother's graceful form had remained unchanged since girlhood.

Frazier climbed the stairs to his room and sat gloomily at his desk. It was a room of books, chemical equipment, mounted biology specimens. Maps and charts covered the walls. Much of the floor was taken up by an eviscerated television set that he was repairing.

Frazier licked the chocolate off his fingers and then poked through the untidy drawers of the desk. He found a bag of salted Planter's peanuts and carried them to the bed. There he lay back and ate the nuts, popping them into his mouth and carefully chewing one at a time to make them last longer.

When the cellophane bag was empty, Frazier folded it neatly and tucked it into his shirt pocket. He lay staring at the ceiling, thinking about school and the Halloween Ball and how lonely he was.

And about Lindy Grant.

If only he could somehow make her notice him. Recognize the romantic soul that inhabited the lumpish body. What if she should be in the library sometime, frantically searching for a reference book for one of her classes. He could come along and she might ask him for help and then . . .

Jesus H. Christ, you're sounding like Charlie Brown and his little redheaded girl!

Angrily Frazier put the fantasy out of his mind. He breathed deeply and rhythmically, willing his mind to relax. Gradually, without his consciously summoning it, a pinpoint of soft blue light appeared directly over his forehead. As he began to focus, the dot of blue irised open, inviting him through, out of his fleshy prison. Frazier let his body go limp, and his spirit rose gently from the bed and out through the psychic window.

Floating free, he looked down on Elm Street through the branches of the tall old shade trees. Below in the dark houses lights glowed orange and inviting in the front windows. A wind sent the dry leaves skittering along the pavement. Frazier couldn't feel the wind; there was no feeling in this state, but he could sense it.

He let his mind glide up the hill, between the rooftops and the pinprick stars in the black velvet sky. He didn't think about where he was going, just let himself drift. When he eased back down among the sheltering trees and saw where he was, it came as no surprise.

It was Lindy Grant's house. Directly in front of him was a lighted window on the second floor. Her window. Frazier had been here many times. Sometimes in the flesh, down on the street, riding his bike past the house in feigned nonchalance. There was always the chance Lindy might come out just as he was riding by, see how easily he handled the machine, and . . . But she never did.

More recently, disembodied and free, he had gazed from up here into her room, savoring at close range the things Lindy touched and wore and lived with. The pleasure he felt in even such intangible contact was enough to make him ache.

He came to know Lindy's bedroom as well as he knew his own. There was her dressing table with its oversize mirror and the photos stuck in the frame. Her chest of drawers that held a Raggedy Ann doll, a carnival kewpie doll, the framed photograph of a woman, and a statuette of a shepherdess. There was her record player, there the posters tacked to her wall of the Beatles and the Monkees.

And over there, the shrine: her bed—all frilly in pink and white; and propped on the pillow, a stuffed panda. Lucky panda. Frazier could imagine the sweet smell of her body still clinging to the sheets as she left the warm bed in the morning.

Often before, he had devoured the bedroom with his imagination. He could have drawn a plan of its contents blindfolded. What happened next would change his life.

Lindy came into the bedroom.

LINDY

She closed the door and hugged the big box to her. She couldn't believe Daddy had actually gone all the way to Milwaukee just to buy this for her. Here she had been planning to wear some dumb homemade costume to the Halloween Ball and he had gone and found this simply marvelous outfit.

She laid the box down on the bedspread, set the top aside, and unwrapped the tissue paper. Inside was the beautiful, velvety, black cat costume with glittery sequined stripes. In a way it was Daddy's admission that she was growing up. No more clown or Dutch Girl or corny witch costumes for her.

Judge Grant had not thoroughly approved of Wonder Woman last year, but went along with it when Lindy promised to deemphasize the boobs. This year she would absolutely be the sexiest thing at the party.

Lindy could hardly wait to try it on. When Daddy gave it to her after dinner she had taken a quick look, squealed with delight, hugged him, and rushed up here to see how she would look wearing it.

She shucked the bulky knit sweater over her head and tossed it aside. The bra was next. Three hooks on the back and it was free. Lindy let the brassiere fall forward over her shoulders and stood for a moment enjoying the freedom of her unrestrained breasts. Some of the girls were starting to go braless, and Lindy thought it was a neat idea, but Daddy wasn't ready for that yet.

She admired herself in the mirror. Her breasts were high and beautifully rounded. Lindy would have liked them to be a bit larger, but that could still come. She lifted them gently in her two hands, playing over the nipples with her forefingers. The pleasant sensation tingled throughout her body, settling in her crotch.

She undid the plaid skirt and let it fall down over her smooth hips and long firm legs. She stepped out of the skirt and strolled back and forth in front of the dressing-table mirror.

Damn good body, she told herself. No wonder Roman Dixon and God knew how many other guys were drooling to get their hands on it. The blue nylon bikini panties barely covered her pubic mound in front, and revealed an expanse of downy curved buttocks behind.

Feeling sexy and good, and purposely delaying the excitement of trying on the cat costume, Lindy practiced a sensual walk, rolling her hips, jutting her breasts. She licked her lips and, with her eyes half-closed, blew an open-mouth Marilyn Monroe kiss toward her mirror. The result was less erotic than she had hoped for.

Well, she wasn't really the Marilyn Monroe type. Leave that to Merilee. Lindy saw herself as more a younger Elizabeth Taylor. She had the black hair/blue eyes combination, if not quite the cup size.

She slid her hands inside the elastic band of the panties and touched herself. She was moist and ready. Slowly, sensuously, she rolled the strip of blue nylon down over the silky triangle of black hair and slid the panties on down her legs and off. Tossing them on top of the discarded skirt, she stood again before the mirror, petting the soft pubic hair. A finger slipped between the lips of her vagina and touched the secret place.

A shiver went through her, and Lindy was tempted to bring herself to a climax, but she resisted. Reluctantly, she drew her hand away, watching herself in the mirror. Then she returned her attention to the cat costume.

It was a one-piece outfit of elasticized fabric that zipped up the back. There were black vinyl gloves with soft make-believe claws, and her own black boots would go perfectly. A silky domino mask fit over her eyes without hiding her face, and a hood was topped with velvety black cat ears. There was a stiffly curved detachable tail she would wear into the party for the effect, then remove when the dancing started.

When she had put on the entire costume, except the tail and mask, Lindy stepped in front of the mirror, making her movements sinuous and catlike. The effect was startling. She blushed, aroused by the way she looked. She was going to knock them dead, no doubt about it.

She picked up the tail, held it down behind her, and gave it an experimental swish. The end of the tail crooked up and knocked the Hummel shepherdess off the chest of drawers. Lindy made a grab for it but could not catch the figurine before it hit the floor and shattered.

The excitement of trying on the costume drained instantly away. Lindy peeled off the cat gloves and dropped to her knees. She fluttered her hands over the broken pieces, picking up the larger ones, trying to fit them together. It was hopeless. The shepherdess was destroyed. Gone. Just like that, a piece of her mother had been lost forever. As she knelt over the shattered figurine Lindy looked up at the photograph of the woman she had never gotten to know, and tears rolled down her cheeks.

FRAZIER

When the Hummel shepherdess smashed into fragments on the floor of Lindy's bedroom, the force that held Frazier's disembodied attention broke with it. The sight of the girl in the tight costume weeping as she knelt over the fragments flooded him with a guilty remorse at having watched her most private moments.

He withdrew swiftly from the window, up over the trees, and in a heartbeat was back slipping through the roof of his own house and into the inert form that lay on the bed where he had left it.

With the power to move restored to his body, Frazier sat up with a groan. Never in his life had he done anything so contemptible as to spy on a girl undressing. He felt evil. Unclean.

And yet he could not forget the exquisite excitement of looking upon the nude body of his goddess, watching her touch that most holy of places.

Shut up! he told his mind. Guilt washed away the erotic vision. He felt certain that the smashing of the figurine, which had obviously meant a lot to Lindy, was his fault. It was his evil, voyeuristic presence. He would have no peace until he had somehow made the loss up to her.

The next day Frazier left the school grounds during the lunch period. Feeling like a truant, he hurried down Main Street to Bonnie's Gift Shop. He hesitated outside the shop, looking at the display in the window. There were half a dozen ceramic statuettes among the decorative plates, the crystal decanters, the ornate candy dishes, and all the other useless things people give each other.

Although the statuettes were similar, none was exactly like the one he had seen dashed to pieces the night before in Lindy Grant's bedroom. With his spirits sinking, Frazier went into the shop.

A middle-aged saleslady came up from the rear of the store to greet him.

"Can I help you?"

Frazier pointed at the little figures in the window. "Do you have any more of these?"

"Hummel figurines? The ones you see are all I have at the moment. They're very popular. Were you looking for a particular one?"

"Yes. It's a girl in a long full dress and an apron kind of thing, standing, holding a crook."

"Ah, the little shepherdess."

"That sounds like it."

"I did have one, but it was chipped, and I sent it back to the supplier."

Frazier wilted, disappointed beyond all proportion.

"Some of these are quite nice," said the woman.

"Yes, I can see they are, but I really wanted the shepherdess."

The woman pressed a finger to her lips. "Let me just take a look in the back. I told my husband to take it to the post office with him this morning, but it's just possible he might have forgotten."

"I'd appreciate it," Frazier said.

While the woman walked back to the rear of the store, Frazier picked up one of the statuettes, a young minstrel holding a stringed instrument of some kind. He turned it over to see the tiny price tag glued on the base.

$69.95! He swallowed hard. This morning he had taken all his cash from the secret compartment at the back of his top dresser drawer. It totaled forty-seven dollars and change. He had no idea these delicate little chunks of ceramic cost so much.

The woman returned smiling from the storeroom. In her hand she carried a six-inch figurine that she wiped carefully with a soft cloth.

"We're in luck," she said. "For once my husband's absentmindedness paid off."

She gave the piece a final dab with the cloth and handed it to Frazier. He held it reverently, turning it over slowly like a sacred relic. It was almost a duplicate of the shepherdess in Lindy's room. Close enough to be a sister.

He swallowed hard. "Uh, how much is this one?"

"It was marked sixty-nine ninety-five."

Frazier sagged.

"But since there's a chip out of the base—see? right here—I'll let you have it for, oh, forty dollars. If you still want it."

Frazier nodded wordlessly and counted out the price from the bills that were folded neatly into his wallet. The woman wrapped the figurine and he carried it back to school, where he placed it reverently in his locker just as the bell signaled the end of lunch period.

CHAPTER 8

July 1987

LINDY

The printer beside her desk chattered busily while Lindy Grant leaned back in her chair feeling better than she had in a couple of weeks. Amazing, she thought, how bad news can suddenly turn into good. Just two days ago it had seemed that everything she had worked for was in the toilet.

She knew from the gingerly way Josh Cleery said her name over the telephone that his message was not going to be a pleasant one.

"Lindy?"

"What's wrong, Josh?"

"Wrong? Did I say anything was wrong?"

"You've got that funeral hush to your voice. Did somebody die? Or is it more serious?"

"Lindy, you were right about that Lou Davidoff. He knows dip about what makes a good script."

"He wants more changes?"

"Not exactly."

"He wants to call in another writer?"

"Well, no."

"Lou, for God's sake will you get to the point? What does he want?"

"He wants out."

"Out?"

"Out. Ben Zalic doesn't think the concept will go. New Titan is no longer interested in *Shadow Watcher.*"

"After I gutted the story and crippled the characters to make the changes Davidoff wanted?"

"Lindy, what can I say? It's not your fault. You did the best you could. Davidoff is a self-serving sonofabitch. There's a lot of them in this business."

Back to square one, Lindy had thought. Back even beyond that. Word traveled fast in Hollywood. It was a rare script that, once bounced, ever found a home. And if it got talked around that she was incompetent or, worse, uncooperative, she would play hell trying to sell another original.

She had spent forty-eight gloomy hours after that assessing her chances for a career change at thirty-seven. Then, while she was eating breakfast, came another call from Josh that rousted her from nightmares of unemployment.

"I hope you didn't burn the original script," he said, his tone unnaturally cheerful.

"I never burn anything. Don't tell me New Titan had a change of heart?"

"You have to have one to change it. Anyway, who needs those schmucks? I just talked to the top man at Cinema World. They got maybe not as many theaters as New Titan, but quality, Lindy, quality. They want *Shadow Watcher*, and they want it the way you wrote it."

Lindy burned her mouth on hot coffee. "Cinema World? They're buying the original script?"

"They love it, Lindy. I mean love it. We're dealing with

motion picture people here, not accountants. With a few minor changes they'll—"

"Minor changes?" Lindy's hopes sagged.

"Trust me, they love the script. Dialogue polish is all it amounts to. Can you meet with us today?"

She could and she did, not without strong misgivings about the "minor changes." Incredibly, they turned out to be truly minor, and the deal had gone ahead without a hitch. Josh was busy now renting studio space, lining up a director, a production manager, and other key people, giving Lindy a rare opportunity to work on her novel.

The printer's chatter ceased with a beep, and Lindy tore off the draft of a new Chapter 3. As she did so, she glanced at her watch and saw it was past eleven. Unlike Lindy, her daughter was by nature a late sleeper, but she had said she was going shopping early this morning for a new outfit to wear to the Duran Duran concert tonight at the Forum. It was a first date with some totally hunky guy from Beverly Hills High, and Nicole had let her mother know that this would be the single most devastating evening of her life.

Lindy left the compact room she used for an office and walked to her daughter's bedroom. She rapped on the door. No response from inside.

A twinge of apprehension caught like a bone in her throat. Although she had packed the incident of Nicole's wild look and the strange voice off to the attic of her mind, the ugly vision of a month ago would not go away.

She pushed open the bedroom door and walked in. Nicole lay on her side, facing away from the door, As usual she wore only the oversize top of a pair of men's pajamas. The sheet and blanket were crumpled around her feet, the pajamas pulled up over her pert little rump. Lindy crossed the room to the bedside and covered her. She touched the girl's shoulder. It was warm under her fingers. Too warm?

"Nickie? Nicole?"

The girl muttered something inaudible and rolled away from her mother's touch.

"Better get up if you want to get your shopping done."

Nicole gave a little moan of protest and buried her face more deeply in the pillows.

"Come on, kiddo, it's almost noon. Duran Duran tonight, remember? The hunk from Bev Hills?" Lindy took hold of her daughter's shoulder and rolled the girl gently over onto her back.

She straightened up with a gasp. Nicole's eyes were wide and staring. Her lips were slightly parted. Lindy had a terrible flash image of a death mask.

The girl blinked, rubbed her eyes, and looked at Lindy.

"Oh, hi, Mom. What time is it?"

Lindy could not immediately find her voice. She shook her head silently.

"Hey, what's the matter with you?"

"I . . . nothing. It's just that you looked so strange for a moment."

Nicole frowned. "I was having a dream. I don't remember exactly, but something icky." She rubbed the back of her head. "I must have slept with my head crooked."

"Do you want an aspirin?"

"You know I don't believe in pills." She looked past Lindy at the digital clock on the dresser. "God, look at the time. I've got lots to do. You shouldn't have let me sleep."

She was out of bed and across the hall into the bathroom before Lindy could collect her thoughts. . . .

Lindy caught her as she sailed toward the door on her way out of the house.

"Nickie, are you sure you're all right?"

"Yes, Mom," she said in the heavily patient way teenagers have of talking to slow-witted adults. "I'm just in a hurry, okay?"

"Okay." Lindy gave her a smile she did not quite feel. "Do you need any money?"

"I've got your Visa card, remember?"

"Oh, yeah. Try not to bankrupt me, will you."

"Mo-om!" Nicole gave her a shake of the head and danced on out.

Two hours later the front door banged open and Lindy jumped at the sound of Nicole's wailing cry. She ran to the door to find her daughter standing in the foyer, her hands covering her face, crying bitterly.

"Nickie, what is it?"

The girl's answer was to wail even louder.

"What happened?"

"I want to die!"

Lindy took hold of her daughter's wrists and pulled her hands down. She could not suppress a sharp intake of breath at what she saw. At the side of Nicole's nose, just over the nostril, was a red-and-purple boil the size of a grape. It was shiny and inflamed and looked ready to pop. Just about the ugliest thing Lindy had ever seen.

Nicole read her mother's expression and reached new volumes with her crying. "It just popped out there," she got out between sobs. "Don't look at me. I'm ugly, ugly, ugly!"

ROMAN

It was a rare sunny day in Seattle, with puffy white clouds that bustled across a bright sky, pushed by the breeze off Lake Washington. The atmosphere in the Lion d'Or was relaxed and promising. Roman Dixon swallowed his first good bourbon of the afternoon and wished he had someplace to go besides home.

The lilt of female voices attracted his gaze to the far end of the bar. There were two of them, in their twenties—a big healthy-looking redhead and a smaller trim-figured brunette with dark foxy eyes. Roman sucked in his stomach, knowing they were watching him. He could hear them whispering now, heads close together.

He looked them over in the mirror behind the bar and

felt the familiar stirring in his crotch. The girls were at an age when the skin was resilient and unwrinkled, the body firm, the breasts upthrust and insolent. Everything his wife Stephanie was not. Roman pushed away from his place at the bar and sauntered down to where they stood.

"Hi, girls. Are we having fun yet?"

They glanced at each other and at him. The bigger one, the redhead, looked up with frank interest. The dark one kind of peeked up at him through long lashes.

"We just got here," the redhead said.

Roman gave them his killer grin. "I'm sort of an unofficial greeter. Make sure everybody's happy, you know."

"I'll bet you're good at your job," the big one said, eyeing him up and down.

"I don't get too many complaints." Roman turned the grin on the shy one. "You local girls?"

"We're from Vancouver," the dark girl said.

"Canadians. Well, welcome to the U.S.A, eh?"

The girls smiled, but not broadly.

Roman switched his approach. "What are those things you're drinking there?"

"Banana daiquiris," said the redhead.

"No kidding. Well, let me buy you a couple, how about it?"

The girls looked at each other. The dark one said, "I don't know. We were just—"

"Good-neighbor policy," Roman said. "Hands across the border."

"Have you got any other plans for your hands?" the redhead asked.

Roman raised his palms innocently. "Hey, do I look like the kind of guy who would put the moves on two lovely Canadian visitors in a bar?"

"Yes," said the redhead, laughing. "As a matter of fact, you do."

Roman glowed. He hadn't lost it. Hell, if wanted to he could probably have both of them in a motel well before midnight. As a matter of fact, he wasn't in any hurry to get home. He raised a finger to signal the bartender.

That's when he felt it. A small thump at the base of his skull like a blow from a rubber hammer. Roman gave a small grunt, and for a moment the interior of the bar spun away from him. In a matter of seconds it was gone and the girls were looking at him.

"Hey, how many have you had, Ace?" asked the redhead.

"It's nothing," he ad-libbed. "Old war wound. Lucky I got it in the head. Nothing there to damage, ha ha. Hey, Jerry, a couple more of these banana things for these nice Canadian ladies."

Roman was talking fast to cover his concern about the momentary blackout. He had put down only one drink, and he never got dizzy like that. He had been a little off his feed since the dinner at the Haaglunds when his mother-in-law had acted so weird.

He pulled a stool over next to the redhead's and sat down, letting his thigh rest against hers. She made no move to pull away, and Roman grinned, back on familiar ground.

"So what are your plans for tonight?" he said.

"We thought we'd have a nice dinner somewhere, then . . ."

The redhead was still talking, but voice faded from Roman's consciousness. He had been hit suddenly with the most god-awful crotch itch of his life. Worse than the case of crabs he'd picked up in the Army. If he didn't get down there and scratch it right now, he was going to scream.

"Excuse me," he blurted, and staggered off toward the men's room, feeling like a thousand little parasites were chewing at his balls. The women stared after him, puzzled, but he didn't look back.

Barely giving the men's room door a chance to swing shut behind him, Roman yanked down his pants and the black satin briefs. He gasped at what he saw. His cock, his balls, and the surrounding flesh of his thighs was a flaming red, itching like nothing human. He grabbed himself, felt the unnatural heat of his skin, and almost cried out.

What the hell was this, some exotic new venereal disease? How could anything break out that suddenly? He had been fine this morning.

He shuffled to the sink, pants down around his ankles, and began splashing handfuls of water on his burning member. Tears welled in his eyes, and he wanted to scream.

ALEC

It was not often that both Dean Laymon and Richard Koontz appeared together at the offices that bore their names. Koontz, a dark, tightly coiled man with darting eyes, spent more time there than his partner, working fourteen-hour days in his corner office when he wasn't traveling among the movers and shakers of the international set. Laymon, big and open-faced, preferred to spend his time fishing in the Gulf of Mexico or hiking through the Adirondacks. The event that brought them both back at the same time was Alec McDowell's assessment of Bo Walton's chances of unseating Anton Scolari.

Koontz held a sheaf of papers and frowned down at it as he spoke. "Frankly, Alec, I don't see that this Newark business will do us any good. I mean, all right, so their guy raked back a few dollars on city contracts. Who doesn't? The voters don't give a damn about a little graft anymore. Hell, they're more likely to admire the guy for it than condemn him." He looked up, pinning Alec with his dark glare. "I'm disappointed. I expected more out of you on this one."

Laymon shifted his bulk in the leather chair. "It's not that we don't appreciate your efforts, Alec, but like Richard says, it really isn't enough. Scolari not only has the strong ethnic thing working for him, he's got a just-one-of-the-boys personality that comes across both in person and on television. He's a guy the voter wouldn't mind having a beer with. And let's face it, our man Walton comes across both in person and on the tube as a wimp."

Alec nodded sagely, as though he were thinking over what the partners had said. He had anticipated something like this, and he was ready. By holding his trump card until he had apparently failed, he would score the highest possible points with it.

He said, "That's exactly the way I saw it. Scolari is a crook, and we could prove it, but the fact is, who cares. Unless he personally shot somebody's mother in front of witnesses, people aren't interested. Maybe not even then. But I turned up something better."

The partners leaned forward. Alec savored the moment. As he was about to speak, something pressed his neck right at the base of his skull. A wave of dizziness came and went as he froze for an instant.

"Alec?" he heard Laymon say. "Are you all right?"

"Fine, fine. Just an allergy."

"You were saying you had something for us," Koontz prompted.

"Right. You remember what finished Gary Hart a couple of months ago?"

"You've got Scolari in a sex scandal?" Laymon asked.

Koontz was doubtful. "I don't know. Hart was running for President. You don't have to be all that clean to be elected on the municipal level. It might stop him from going any further, but that won't help us or Bo Walton now. Sleeping with a woman isn't good enough, Alec."

"How about sleeping with a boy?"

The partners leaned forward.

"Scolari's a faggot?" Koontz said.

"You've got proof?" Laymon asked.

"I've got the boy he was buggering," Alec told them. "He workth at dhe youemn . . ."

He realized the two men were staring at him a fraction of a second before he heard the distorted words from his own mouth.

"I gom to sime appadapit . . ."

"Alec, are you all right?" Laymon asked.

Koontz just stared.

Alec put a hand to his mouth. His tongue felt like a hunk of strange raw meat. It was swelling against his palate.

"Allagy," he mumbled. "Sowwy."

Laymon pushed out of his chair and came over to stand beside him. "Man, that came on suddenly. Is there something you can do for it?"

"Mmm-mmm," Alec shook his head.

Koontz said, "Look, you better get out of here and have that taken care of. We can continue this later."

Alec nodded, hand still clapped over his mouth, and fled from the office.

He stumbled out of the building and waved to a cab. He could barely keep his mouth shut now with the tongue forcing itself fatly between his teeth. The panic sweat was on him as he scribbled the address of his apartment on a card and shoved it at the driver.

CHAPTER 9

July 1987

LINDY

When Nicole's friends, including the hunk from Beverly Hills, arrived to take her to the Forum, Lindy met them at the door. She kept them waiting while she went into her daughter's bedroom.

"Your friends are here," she said softly.

Nicole pulled the covers up over her head. "I don't want to see anybody. I don't want to talk to anybody."

"All right, honey, I'll take care of it."

Lindy went back and invented a sudden case of the flu. When the others had left she debated whether to chew her daughter out or try to comfort her.

On the one hand she was impatient with Nicole for making such a big deal out of what was, really, a small adolescent problem. However, she still remembered from her own girlhood how devastating a pimple on prom night could be, and decided to leave it alone.

She poured a cup of coffee, took it to her cozy little office, and went back to work.

At least she tried to go back to work. The intermittent wails from Nicole's room as the girl explored anew her swollen nose destroyed concentration.

When at last her daughter was quiet it was after nine o'clock. Moving softly, Lindy went back to the girl's bedroom and eased open the door. Nicole lay on her side, breathing regularly, the pillow bunched beneath her head. Lindy tiptoed around the bed and knelt to examine her nose.

Miraculously, the boil had subsided to almost nothing. Only a pink patch of skin remained where the swollen boil had been. Lindy decided against waking her daughter for the good news. It might just start a new lament that she had missed the rock concert for nothing. She slipped back out of the bedroom and softly closed the door.

Lindy returned to her desk and began tapping out the scene she had left off earlier. It took a couple of seconds for her to realize that no corresponding green letters were appearing on the screen.

"Oh, damn," she said. She checked the power switch, the monitor control, the cable connections. Everything was as it should be.

"Sonofabitch."

Writing with a computer could be a blessing in speed and ease of making corrections—a quantum leap from working with a typewriter. However, when something went wrong with it you were in trouble. Any work you hadn't printed out was locked away from your reach as surely as though it were buried in the ocean floor. And whereas you could drop a busted typewriter off at the shop and take home a loaner, getting a computer repaired was a frustrating operation.

In the four years Lindy had used the computer with word-processing softwear, she had had only one breakdown. She had learned then about the independence of computer repairmen. It had been just before the four-day Thanksgiving holiday, and with a deadline approaching she could not afford to sit idle the better part of a week. In the end it had cost her a hundred-dollar ''priority fee'' on top of the hefty repair bill to get her machine back in twenty-four hours.

This would be a hell of a time for another breakdown—just as she was getting into the meat of her novel. She tapped experimentally at the keys again. The computer replied with a series of beeps and ominous grinding noises.

''Goddamn sonofabitch!''

HELLO, LINDY, the monitor screen spelled out.

She stared. What the hell was this? Some kind of a joke? But whose? Only Nicole was in the house with her, and Nicole avoided the computer like she would a Pat Boone album.

The marching green letters continued:

WOLF RIVER INN

SATURDAY, JULY 11

BE THERE OR THE GIRL REALLY GETS HURT

Lindy's thoughts rattled around wildly. What the hell was going on here? She thought about the unexplained blooming boil on her daughter's nose, and she thought about the weird look and the inhuman voice Nicole had spoken in a couple of weeks ago.

She reread the message on the screen. She could go ahead and deny the reality of it. Try to convince herself it was some bizarre form of computer glitch. Wait and see if anything more really did happen to Nicole.

Who was she kidding? Ghosts of the past ran spectral hands over her flesh. She knew for a certainty that the warning was real.

Lindy reached under her desk for the telephone book and flipped through the Yellow Pages for a twenty-four-hour airline ticket service.

ROMAN

As soon as he had called Dr. Gaines and insisted on an appointment first thing in the morning, the inflammation and the itching of Roman's crotch had started to subside. It was a damn good thing, because another hour or so without relief and he would have gone crazy.

Now as he stood at the receptionist's desk he had only a faint tingle around his balls. He was half tempted to call the whole thing off.

"Doctor is expecting you," the receptionist said. "You may go right in."

What the hell, he decided, it couldn't do any harm to get it looked at. He went into the examination room and dropped his pants.

"Nothing I can see wrong with you," said Gaines, studying Roman's naked genitals as he sat on the examination table with pants and briefs down. "No crabs, no rash to speak of. You say it came on suddenly?"

"Like a shot," Roman said. "One minute I was fine, the next I'm itching like I sat on an anthill."

The doctor determined there had been no change in Roman's diet or clothing, negating the possibility of an allergy.

"I'll take a blood sample just to be sure you haven't got one of the new exotic venereal diseases."

"I've never had VD in my life."

"That doesn't make you immune, you know. Did you tell your wife about this episode?"

"Stephanie? No way."

"It might be a good idea to refrain from sex until we get the results of the blood tests."

"That'll be easy enough."

"I mean *all* sex, not just with your wife."

"How long till you get the results?"

"Three–four days. Think you can hold out?"

"It'll be tough, but I'll manage."

The doctor rubbed the back of his head and sat down heavily in a white enameled chair. His thoughts seemed to drift off for a moment, then he focused on Roman again.

"You can put your pants back on now."

While Roman rebuckled his belt, Dr. Gaines scribbled on a prescription pad. He tore off the top sheet and handed it over.

"What's this?" Roman asked without looking at the prescription.

"Just a mild antibiotic. Can't do you any harm. Take it according to instructions and call me in three days for the blood test results."

Roman walked out of the doctor's office feeling pretty good. He was back to normal, the itch was gone, and nothing serious had ever been wrong with him. It was foolish to worry. He was in great shape. What did he need with antibiotics?

He glanced at the prescription blank before pitching it into a trash can, then came to a dead stop. He felt cold, and the breath seemed to have been knocked out of him.

Instead of Dr. Gaines's medical scrawl, the message on the paper was printed in heavy block letters. It read:

ROMAN—

WOLF RIVER INN

SATURDAY, JULY 11

BE THERE OR I'LL MAKE IT REALLY HURT.

As weird as the whole thing was, the part that started Roman Dixon shivering was the way REALLY was underlined. His groin seemed to start aching even as he read it.

Wolf River. Shit, what he would give never to hear the name of that town again. Memories filtered back of that fateful senior year. Memories he had kept sealed away for a long time.

He never had any doubt that the threat was real. Someone . . . something knew about him and was out to get him. With a grimace he remembered the words that seemed to come from his senile mother-in-law: *"It's payback time."* He had no choice. He would have to go back there and try to make a deal.

Stephanie would have to be given some kind of a story, and it would mean rearranging the work schedules at the stores, but on Saturday, July 11, like it or not, he was going to be in Wolf River.

ALEC

The wild panic that had seized Alec MacDowell when he feared he was about to strangle on his own tongue began to subside during the cab ride, along with the size of his tongue. By the time they reached Eighth Avenue he could feel some space inside his mouth and decided he wanted to be out on the street to breathe free air.

"Me out here," he mumbled.

The cabby gave him a peculiar look and pulled over at the old entrance to the Edison Hotel. Alec overtipped him and hurried away to lose himself among the sidewalk traffic.

Alec's shirt clung to his body, and he could smell his own panic sweat. Nothing remotely like this had ever happened to him. Possible causes marched through his mind: Something he ate for lunch? Not likely, he had the same Swiss-on-white sandwich washed down with cream soda that he ate three times a week. Job nerves? Bullshit, he thrived on stress. Some exotic disease? He'd had a thorough physical just last month, and was found to be in excellent health. No, there was something . . . unnatural about the episode. Something Alec did not want to think about.

So intent was he on his problems that he didn't see the gypsy woman until he bumped into her. An orange-haired hag in a grimy flowered dress who might have been any age from twenty to sixty, she materialized in front of him, her red-rimmed eyes shining, gap-toothed mouth wide and smiling.

Alec mumbled an apology and started around her, but the woman clutched at the sleeve of his jacket and held him.

"Let go," he snapped.

"I have a message for you, Alec."

The panic sweat froze against his body. The grating voice was icily reminiscent of the old cleaning woman in his office a couple of weeks back. *It's payback time.*

"Come inside," the gypsy said.

With all resistance drained, Alec let the woman pull him into her storefront cubbyhole decorated outside with a badly painted palm and zodiacal symbols. He sat down dumbly across a rickety card table from her, his nostrils pinched against the mingled smells of incense, garlic, and urine.

The woman's hands clawed on the faded tablecloth. Her eyes burned into him.

She said, "Saturday, July 11. Wolf River Inn. Be there or you will never speak again."

"What did you say?" Alec leaned across the table and grasped the gypsy woman by the wrists. Her bones felt frail as a bird's through the dried skin.

"How do you know my name?"

But the gypsy's eyes unfocused for a moment, and she was not hearing him. Then she came back to herself and smiled in a hideous parody of seduction.

"What would you like, sir? A palm reading? The Tarot, perhaps? Your horoscope? Or maybe you would like one of my . . . special services?"

Alec stared at her. The expression, the voice, the whole attitude was completely different from the crone who had confronted him.

"Sir?" she said, looking at him strangely.

Alec realized his expression must have startled her. He

pulled a bill from his money clip, dropped it on the table, and hurried out of the foul-smelling room to Eighth Avenue.

He still didn't know what was happening to him, but he was sure as death that if he ignored the bizarre invitation to return to Wolf River he would, indeed, never speak again.

THE FLOATER

It had taken a great deal of effort, but the message was at last driven home to the three people. Threaten each of them with the loss of something they treasured dearly, and they will do your bidding.

Touching each of them on his home ground had been satisfying, but the final scene had to be played out back where it all began.

Today was July 6. In five days they would all be back in Wolf River for the first time in twenty years. It would be a reunion none of them would ever forget.

CHAPTER 10

Johnny Carson's monologue was from a two-year-old repeat, and the topical references were sorely dated. Neither Lindy Grant nor Brendan Jordan paid any attention. While the *Tonight* show, at low volume, murmured away on Brendan's bedroom television set, the two people in the bed were interested only in each other.

Lindy turned in his arms to look back up at the dark window behind them. "Are the curtains all the way closed?"

"I think so. Who cares?"

"I don't know . . . it felt cold on the back of my neck. I just had a creepy feeling somebody was looking at us."

"He'd have to fly by in a helicopter to do it," Brendan said. "I live on the side of a hill, remember?"

Lindy shivered. "I guess I'm just nervous about the reunion."

"You're determined to go to that?"

"I have to," she said, then quickly added, "I've already got my ticket for tomorrow. I don't expect to be there long, no more than the weekend. Maybe I'll be back Sunday."

Brendan stroked her bare flank. "You know, in two years I've never heard you talk about your high school class, or your hometown either, for that matter," Brendan said.

"I don't think about it much," Lindy said. "Not any more than I can help."

"So how come now you're all excited about a class reunion?"

"You don't mind, do you? I mean that I didn't ask you to come along?"

"Oh, hell no. There's nothing deadlier than going to somebody else's class reunion. It just seemed to come up suddenly, that's all."

"I know. It surprised me, too. I mean, I haven't kept in touch with anybody from high school in all these years."

"So why are you going?"

"I thought it might be, well, kicks."

"You wouldn't kid me, would you, lady?"

She pulled back and looked at him. Brendan had bright, searching eyes that didn't miss anything. The kind of eyes a pilot should have.

"I have to go back, Brendan. If I don't, somebody is going to hurt Nicole. I told you what happened to her face."

"What's her pimple got to do with your high school reunion?"

Lindy sat up suddenly. Her eyes flashed with reflected light from the television. "It was more than a pimple, dammit! It was a warning. Then there was that message on my computer screen. I told you about that."

"All right," he soothed. "Something funny is going on. And I don't blame you for being upset."

Lindy eased back down beside him. "Upset is putting it nicely. I'm scared shitless."

They were silent for a moment, watching without pay-ing attention while Johnny introduced a young female comedian who smiled too much.

Brendan spoke quietly. "Have you considered the possibility that someone screwed around with your computer?"

"Who would do a thing like that? Who would have access to it?"

"Don't get mad now, but what about Nicole?"

"My own daughter?"

"Kids do some pretty strange things."

Lindy touched his hand. "I'm not mad, Brendan, I know you're trying to help. But even granting the possibility that she might have some crazy motive to do such a thing, I doubt Nicole even knows how to turn the machine on. She could no more program a computer than she could build a rocket engine."

"It was just a thought. There's got to be some explanation for what's been happening to you."

"The only explanations I can think of, I don't like." She turned to look at the glowing red numbers of the digital alarm clock. "I hope Nicole's all right."

"She's staying with somebody, isn't she?"

"Yes. She has a friend home from summer school, and her parents were going to take Nicole for the weekend. When she wanted to go over there tonight, I said okay. I didn't want to make a big deal out of being worried about her. Then maybe I was just being selfish in wanting to spend this night with you."

"A little selfish doesn't hurt," he said. "Nicole will be fine."

They were quiet while Johnny Carson brought on a nervous author to close the show.

Brendan said, "I have another suggestion."

"About what?"

"About the peculiar happenings at your house."

"Let's hear it," Lindy said.

"Poltergeist."

"Come *on*, Brendan."

"Maybe it's a little farfetched, but this whole business is something outside everyday reality. Think about it. Poltergeists are mischievous ghosts that toss objects around, break things, make pests of themselves."

"But they're not supposed to hurt anybody, are they?"

"Nicole wasn't really hurt. Just her vanity."

"But messing with my computer?"

"So you've got a high-tech poltergeist. If they can break dishes, who says they can't fool with microchips? Besides, you've got the main ingredient necessary for a poltergeist—an adolescent girl in the house."

Lindy was thoughtful for a moment. "It's an interesting idea, but I just can't buy ghosts. I quit believing a long time ago in anything I couldn't grab hold of. Anyway, I never heard of a poltergeist being so calculating. I mean the invitation, the crazy talk from Nicole, the message on the screen—they were all aimed at getting me back to Wolf River."

"You still haven't told me why you're so reluctant to go back."

Lindy took his hand, kissed the palm, and placed it over her breast. She said, "Darling, are we going to spend the whole night talking?"

He started to protest, but she eased him down on his back. She kissed his mouth and let her hand roam down over his long, firm body. He wasn't ready for her at first, but she stroked him the way she knew he liked and felt his erection grow under her touch.

He kissed her throat and moved his lips down over the swell of her breast. He took the nipple in his mouth and flicked it with the tip of his tongue.

Lindy sighed and gave herself over to the pleasure of being stroked and kissed by her man. When he touched her between her legs she was moist and eager for him.

Almost from the beginning their lovemaking had been creative, sometimes wild. Neither was cramped by inhibitions, and they were attuned to each other's preferences. Tonight, however, Lindy wanted no tricks, no fancy stuff. She just wanted to lie on her back and be taken.

Sensing her mood, Brendan moved over her, gently spread her thighs apart, and entered her. He braced his hands on the mattress and leaned back at the waist, sliding slowly in and out of her. Lindy kept her eyes open, watching him, enjoying the pleasure reflected in his face.

He began to stroke faster. Lindy felt the climax rising in her body. She reached up to take hold of Brendan's shoulders and pull his full weight down on her.

She screamed.

Instead of Brendan's smooth, muscular back, her hands gripped a rough, scaly surface that squirmed under her touch. Where the strong, loving face of her man had been a moment ago, inches away from her own, she now saw the slavering, slime-covered, lizard-tongued face of a demon such as had never walked the earth. Its loathsome touch was all over her body . . . inside her. The stench of it seared her nostrils.

Lindy could not stop screaming.

Then everything snapped back into place. Brendan, on his knees, was gripping her by the shoulders, his face contorted with alarm.

"Lindy! Lindy, for God's sake, what's the matter?"

For a long moment her throat was too dry to speak. She stared up at Brendan, afraid to blink lest he vanish again and the odious monster take his place. Then all of a sudden she let go. Sobs wracked her body. Brendan held her close, gently stroking her hair until the crying fit subsided. It took a long time.

Over cups of hot, strong coffee in Brendan's kitchen she tried to describe the unearthly thing she had seen for that terrible endless moment in bed.

"I don't know what it was," she said. "Hallucination, delusion, vision, premonition. I only know if I had had to look at it for a minute longer I would have gone screaming mad."

Brendan refilled her cup. "Do you think this is somehow related to all the other stuff that's been happening to you?"

"I'm sure it is," she said.

"Then maybe it's time for you to tell me about Wolf River and what happened to you there."

"Yes, darling, I think maybe it is." She drew a deep breath and began. "Twenty years ago I had this little Hummel figure of a shepherdess I kept on my dresser. . . ."

ROMAN

Dinner at the Dixon house in Bellevue was baked Columbia River salmon with lemon caper sauce, creamy scalloped potatoes, fresh baby peas with pearl onions, and sourdough biscuits. There was a shrimp and mushroom salad, and for dessert, German chocolate cake.

Roman leaned back, took a sip of rich dark coffee, and lit a cigarette. If Stephanie could do one thing in the world, she could cook. He was full, and he had the beginning of a headache. He let his belt out a notch and promised himself to start going more regularly to the gym.

The boys left the table early and got out of the house to go wherever it was they went. That suited Roman just fine. The less he saw of the loutish Brian and the skinny, weak-eyed Eric, the better he liked it. The good news was that at seventeen and eighteen they would soon be out of his house for good. God willing.

Roman let the cigarette butt hiss out in a puddle of coffee in his saucer. Might as well break the news to Stephanie that he was leaving for a couple of days, and let her get her bitching out of the way.

Stephanie got up and started clearing the dishes away.

Roman took hold of her wrist. "What's your hurry, Steph?"

"The dishes won't wash themselves."

Damn near, he thought, with the expensive dishwashing equipment he had installed last winter.

He said, "Sit down a while. Let's talk."

"Talk?" She looked at him suspiciously.

"Why not? We don't talk much anymore, the two of us."

"That's for sure." She sat down uneasily in the chair vacated by Eric. "What was it you wanted to talk about."

Something happened to the light in the dining room, as though a momentary shadow had passed over. Roman blinked and looked across at his wife. By God, she didn't look half bad in this queer light.

"Well?" she prompted.

"Nothing earthshaking. Something came up and I've got to go out of town tomorrow for a few days."

"Out of town where?"

Her voice had altered too. The words she said didn't matter; there was a smoky softness to her tone that stirred something in Roman that had long been dormant around his wife.

He realized she was looking at him, waiting for him to speak. "Uh, Chicago," he said, remembering the fiction he had prepared. "Midland Sport Scene is closing two of their outlets there. I've got a chance to pick up most of their stock at a good price."

Roman cocked his head and squinted. Stephanie was growing younger and more desirable before his eyes. She had not been much of a looker even when he married her twelve years ago, but right now she was damn near beautiful.

"This trip came up pretty suddenly, didn't it?"

He couldn't concentrate. "You know something, Steph, you really look great tonight.'

"Are you drunk?"

"Stone sober. One beer before dinner. Are you wearing your hair different or what?"

He got out of his chair and walked over to her. Lord, she even smelled different. All summer and spice. He felt a stirring in his crotch.

"The only thing different about my hair is I haven't had it done in two weeks."

He didn't hear what she was saying. In the strange soft-focus light of the dining room his bony, shapeless, sour-dispositioned wife had somehow turned into this absolutely ravishing woman. Roman wanted her now as he had not wanted any woman since he was a horny adolescent. He took hold of her hands, unbelievably soft and cool, and pulled her gently to her feet.

"You know what we ought to do?" he said.

"What?" The word was a whispered caress.

"We ought to go to bed."

"Now?"

"Hell yes, now. We're alone in the house, no kids to come yelling for Mom. We can get crazy. What do you say, Steph?"

"Are you serious?"

"Jesus, woman, don't I look serious?" He took her hand down and held it against his hard cock. "Doesn't that feel serious?"

She looked up at him, her eyes clear and deep and bright. He wanted to lose himself in those eyes, in that body. God, he wanted her. Roman pulled his wife against him and kissed her openmouthed, the way he had never kissed her even before they were married.

Abruptly the light in the room brightened. A gust of stale fish breath hit Roman's nostrils. His tongue scraped against Stephanie's bridgework.

"You disgusting pig," she said, snatching her hand away from his wilting cock. "What happened, did one of your office whores cut you off so you had to come sniffing around for something at home?"

Roman stumbled backward a step. Jesus, God, how could he have put his tongue into that ugly slash of a mouth? And what crazy trick of the lighting a moment ago made him see this sour husk of a witch as some kind of desirable woman?

He spun away from her and headed for the den.

"Where are you going?" she demanded.

"For a drink."

"I could have guessed that." She followed him to the archway that separated the dining room and living room. "Does Daddy know you're going to Chicago on a buying trip?"

"Fuck Daddy. There are some things I can handle myself."

He made it to the basement door and out of earshot before she could answer. Downstairs at the leather-padded bar he had put in himself, Roman poured bourbon into an old-fashioned glass. He drank thirstily, letting the whiskey burn its way down to his stomach.

For a minute there, just for one brief minute he had relived a sexual excitement greater than anything he had known since . . . since high school. He drank again, and sat down on the bar stool. He let his thoughts drift back to his last year in Wolf River. It had started out as the happiest and ended as the most miserable year of his life.

ALEC

He sat leaning back in the chair with his pants down around his ankles, watching the top of Georgia's blond head bob back and forth between his legs.

Alec concentrated on the dark roots of her straw-colored hair and the tiny flakes of dandruff that clung to the individual hairs. He felt her lips glide expertly along his penis, but there was no arousal.

After a while she pulled back and let his limp member

slide out of her mouth with a wet little *pop*. She held it in one hand like a small sick animal and looked up at him. ''Something the matter, honey?''

The eternal woman's question. *What's the matter?* Hell, everything's the matter, including the humiliating need for a man to stick his joint into a woman to ease the pressure in his testicles.

''I've got a lot on my mind,'' he said.

She kissed the head of his cock and looked at him again. ''Want to keep trying?''

''Let's give it a rest,'' he told her.

Georgia got up off her knees and stood in front of him. She had thrown her imitation fur coat over the back of the sofa and was wearing a soft cotton tank top and leatherette miniskirt.

Alec reached down to pull up his pants, but she stopped him.

''Hey, we're not quitting. Just taking a break.'' She sat down in his lap, arranging his penis so she could rub it against the silky crotch of her panties. He didn't feel anything, but she kept it up.

''Want to talk about it?''

Alec could not help smiling. He might have been in some pop-psych therapy group instead of up in his apartment with a whore who worked out of a phone booth sitting in his naked lap.

''I'm all talked out at the end of the day,'' he said.

''A lot of my clients like to talk,'' she said. ''Matter of fact, that's *all* some of them want to do.'' She gave his member a little squeeze to punctuate her joke. ''Anything special bothering you?''

He leaned back, slipped his hand under the miniskirt to massage Georgia's smooth ass, and closed his eyes. ''Some peculiar things have been happening to me lately,'' he said in a dreamy voice. ''Things I can't explain. All I can think of is that somehow they're connected to my hometown.''

''Where's that, honey?''

"You'll never have heard of it. Wolf River, Wisconsin."

"Funny name."

"Yes, isn't it."

"You weren't happy there?"

Absently he rubbed the back of his head where the tension was.

"Happy? No, no really. But it was bearable. At least until something happened . . . twenty years ago."

Alec opened his eyes and laughed. It was a bitter laugh at his own expense for having no confidante but an Eighth Avenue whore to tell his innermost thoughts to. But by Christ, it was working. He was getting a hard-on.

Georgia stroked him happily. "See, honey? I told you it helps to talk about it. Should we get back to business?"

"Mmmmm." He nodded, keeping his eyes closed.

Georgia returned to her kneeling position and took his cock back into her mouth with little professional sounds of pleasure. She began to work on him.

Alec moved his buttocks rhythmically, enjoying the warm wet mouth sliding expertly up and down the length of his shaft. He began to breath harder. He opened his eyes and bent his head forward. He liked to watch her sucking him off.

Alec's eyes snapped wide. His jaw dropped. The smooth gray hair on the head that was eating him was not Georgia's. The bony thumb and forefinger that circled the root of his cock were not the hands of a whore. He gave a strangled cry.

Startled, the woman looked up at him, his penis still between her lips. The dry, wrinkled skin, the pale eyes behind bifocal glasses were nothing like he remembered, rather they were what she would have looked like had she lived another twenty years.

"Jesus . . . Mother!"

He pushed her away roughly and lurched out of the chair, trying to pull up his pants and get away from the awful apparition at the same time. He banged against the coffee table and fell facedown on the camel brown carpet.

"Honey, what's the matter?"

Her hand was on his shoulder. He tried to jerk away. Frantically he rolled over and looked fearfully up to see . . . Georgia, the friendly whore from the phone booth, with the black roots and the dandruff flakes.

Not a terrible ghost of his long-dead mother.

"You gave me a scare, honey."

Alec scrambled to his feet and quickly buckled up his pants. He pulled a bill from his money clip and gave it to the woman.

"Sure you don't want to try again? We almost made it there."

"Forget it."

She looked at him questioningly for a moment, then, seeing that no explanation would be offered, she tucked the bill away and left the apartment.

When she was gone Alec walked stiff-legged back to his chair, but he didn't want to sit there just now. Instead he went to the kitchenette and poured himself a glass of milk. He sat down at the table and sipped the cold white liquid. It didn't much help his burning stomach.

"God damn you," he said to no one he could see. "God *damn* you!"

CHAPTER 11

Wolf River, October 1966

Frazier Nunley went through the motions of the school day in an agony of anticipation. He had not been thinking with his usual clarity since two nights ago when he watched Lindy Grant unseen through her bedroom window. Today his mind was only fractionally on the words of the teachers and the pages of text. He was way ahead of them anyway.

Frazier's mind was on the bomb in his locker.

Not a real bomb, of course, but it might as well have been. Ever since he had bought it, the Hummel shepherdess from Bonnie's Gift Shop had seemed to Frazier to be alive and ticking.

Never good with his hands, he had spent three hours last night wrapping and unwrapping the figurine in the most expensive gift wrap they had down at the Hallmark shop. The package still looked like it had fallen off a truck, but it was the best Frazier was able to do.

He could have asked his mother, who wrapped things beautifully, to do it for him, but then he would have had to explain to her who it was for and what was the occasion.

He would rather take his chances with his own amateurish wrapping.

Once the shepherdess, well padded with tissue, was wrapped, the next problem to be faced was when and how to deliver it. Frazier's inclination was to leave it on Lindy Grant's doorstep, ring the bell, and run. But that would be cowardly. A nerd he might be, but Frazier Nunley was no coward.

No, he would hand over the shepherdess to Lindy Grant in person. After all, what possible benefit could he gain from leaving the statuette as an anonymous gift? Was not his purpose, at the bottom, to establish some kind of communication with the lovely Lindy?

So why, he demanded of himself, had he let the entire day go by, in which he had contrived to be within a few feet of Lindy several times, without handing over the shepherdess? Easy—he didn't want anyone else around at the crucial moment when she unwrapped the gift, and it was nigh impossible to catch the popular Lindy Grant with no one else around. So the bomb waited, it's gaudy gift wrapping concealed by a brown paper bag, on the top shelf of his locker.

By the end of the day Frazier had nearly despaired of ever getting close to Lindy alone. Depressed and disgusted with himself for not finding the right opportunity, he trudged down the wide concrete steps of the high school. Halfway to the bottom, he came to a sudden stop. Miraculously, there she was, sitting alone on a stone bench along one of the footpaths that wound from the main building toward the new boys' gym. She had a book open in her lap and was reading. A light breeze ruffled her blue-black hair, pushing a lock repeatedly down across her forehead. Frazier found her gesture in brushing the hair back one of such unconscious grace that a lump grew in his throat. He hurried back inside to his locker, retrieved the package, still in its anonymous grocery bag, and came back out.

Lindy was still on the bench. Frazier's heart hammered

as he walked down the path toward her. He carried the wrapped figurine as though it might explode if he jarred it.

In his mind he ran through an opening gambit.

Casual: *Hi, Lindy, I thought you might be able to use this.* No, no, no. Way *too* casual.

Practical: *Say, Lindy, I don't have any place to keep this myself, so* . . Whoa, he'd have to do better than that.

Beseeching: *I hope this will in some way replace your recent loss.* Balls, he might as well crawl up on all fours and lick her hand.

Romantic: *A beautiful piece of work like this should belong to a beautiful girl like you.* Who was he kidding? That was dialogue from the late-late show. Anyway, he could no more get those words out than he could grow a face like Fabian.

The best thing to do was just play it by ear. Let her set the pace. He'd walk up to the bench, maybe sit down next to her. A little preliminary chitchat. Then:

What's in the package, Frazier?

This? Oh, just a little knickknack I thought you might like.

(Did people still say "knickknack"?)

Really? How exciting. May I open it now?

Sure, why not?

(A flurry of unwrapping accompanied by little squeals of excitement.)

Ooh, Frazier, you shouldn't have! (Corny, but he'd love it.) *What a darling you are. I'm going to give you a great big kiss.*

The fantasy popped in his face like a punctured balloon. When he was a dozen or so steps away from her, Lindy Grant was no longer alone. Roman Dixon, grinning and sweaty in his gym shorts, and Alec MacDowell, his faithful hanger-on, had strolled up from the other direction on the path and had Lindy Grant surrounded.

Frazier could not simply turn around now and walk back

the other way. That would be too obvious. His only course was to saunter past them as though he just happened to be passing by on his way to the gym.

The three of them were talking and laughing together now as though it were the most natural thing in the world. How, he wondered did they ever manage it with such ease? Frazier moved to the outside of the path as he passed the trio, shifting the package to his outside arm and concealing it as best he could with his body.

"Hi, Roman," he said, damning the squeak in his voice. "Hi, Alec. Hi, Lin . . ."

But then he was beyond them. None of the three had spoken to him. They hadn't even looked over at him. He might as well be invisible.

Trying to keep his step jaunty and unconcerned, Frazier continued to the new gym, and hung around there just inside the door until Lindy, Roman, and Alec had left and the path was clear for him to go on home.

He managed to get the package into the house and up to his room without his parents seeing him. No way he wanted to answer any questions about what he had in the bag and who it was for.

When the family sat down around the dinner table that night, Frazier's mother knew something was wrong. She kept eyeing Frazier with that gentle yet piercing look she had when she was suspicious about something. His father, of course, saw nothing amiss. He went through dinner relating one of his complicated anecdotes about the adventures of his students at the college, laughing heartily at his own scholarly wit.

As soon as he reasonably could, Frazier excused himself from the table and retreated to his room. He lay on the bed, under which he had stuffed the bagged figurine, and stared at the ceiling where three years before a spider had opened up a mysterious world for him.

His thoughts were not on the spider tonight. Not on escape through his secret window. All he could see was his wimpy failure to give the shepherdess to the girl of his dreams. If he was ever going to assert himself about anything, this had to be it.

With sudden resolve he pulled the package from its hiding place, concealed it as best he could under his coat, and headed for the front door.

His mother looked up from the piano. "Where are you going, dear?"

"Library," he mumbled, finding it hard to get the lie out. He hurried through the door before she could ask any more questions.

He climbed the Elm Street hill, feeling furtive and somehow guilty as he clutched the package to his chest. The night air was crisp and cold and made the insides of his nostrils tingle. When he reached the Grant house he stood for several minutes across the street and stared up at the lighted bedroom window on the second floor. He could see nothing inside from this angle, but sensual memories nipped at his testicles.

Finally, with a huge indrawn breath, he marched across the street, up the front walk, and rang Lindy Grant's doorbell.

He barely had time to think, *Omigod, what am I doing?* when the door was opened by a handsome, graying man with a pipe in one hand. Judge Grant. Lindy's father.

"Yes?"

"I-is Lindy home?" *Of all the goddamn rotten times to stammer.*

"She's upstairs," said Mr. Grant. "Who shall I tell her is calling?"

"I'm F-Frazier Nunley. I'm in her class at school."

Wendell Grant's wise, kindly eyes took in the boy's age, his discomfiture, the ill-wrapped package half-hidden by the too-big coat. He said, "Come on in, Frazier. I'll go up and tell her you're here."

Frazier stood in the warm hallway watching Mr. Grant ascend the stairs, and fighting a sudden need to urinate.

His twanging nerves screamed for him to bolt through the door and run into the night, but his mind told him it was too late for that.

Upstairs Lindy's father delivered the message.

"Frazier Nunley?" Lindy repeated. "What in the world does he want, I wonder?"

"I did not ask the purpose of the young man's call," Wendell Grant said with an amused smile. "I will say it seemed to be of some importance."

He talked that way sometimes when he was having a little fun with Lindy.

"I can't imagine . . . oh well, I might as well see what it's about."

Frazier managed a rictus that passed for a smile as Wendell Grant returned.

"Lindy will be down in a minute," he said. "Would you like to come in and sit down?"

"Oh, no thanks, I don't . . . I won't . . . I can't stay. I'll just s-stand here." *Oh, shit! Stupid stupid stupid!*

"Suit yourself." Mr. Grant gave him a warm smile and vanished into the living room.

Frazier stood fighting his impatient bladder. *Jesus, what if I piss my pants?*

Then She came down the stairs. No film goddess ever descended into a room more gracefully and beautifully than did Lindy Grant to the waiting Frazier.

"Hi," she said, the question clear in her tone.

All the prepared speeches, the clever openings, the ready remarks vanished. Frazier thought for a terrible moment he was going to faint.

"H-hi," he got out at last. "I . . . well, I just thought maybe you'd like this."

He shoved the package toward her, then awkwardly pulled it back to remove the grocery bag. He offered it again. By this time the gift wrapping was bunched and crumpled.

Lindy stared at it.

"It's for you," he said, wishing the floor would open beneath his feet. "Take it."

Lindy accepted the package tentatively from his trembling hands. "What in the world is it? Do you want me to open it?"

"No," he blurted. "I mean open it after I'm gone." Then, an afterthought: "I hope you like it."

And Frazier Nunley turned away from the girl of his dreams and fled into the night. He ran all the way down Elm Street to his own house, the breath wheezing painfully in and out of his lungs when he got there. His big chance—the one he had dreamed and fantasized about for more than a year—and he had screwed it up. At that moment he loathed himself more than ever in his life.

"Your friend leave?" Wendell Grant asked.

"He's not really a friend," Lindy said. She was still standing in the hallway, looking at the clumsily wrapped package in her hands.

"He brought you a present?"

"I don't know why he would." Lindy hesitated a moment longer, then danced up the stairs to her room, leaving her father with a puzzled smile.

Seated on her bed, she tore away the wrapping paper and pulled off the layers of tissue. She gasped as she recognized the little shepherdess, and held it out at arm's length, turning it this way and that.

What a terribly nice and thoughtful thing to do, she thought. She carried the figure over to the chest of drawers and placed it next to the picture of her mother. It was almost a perfect match for the one she had broken. What a strange and really nice thing for Frazier Nunley, of all people, to do. She had badly missed the little shepherdess since the night she—

Wait a minute! How could Frazier have known she'd broken the other one. Lindy had told no one, not even her father. How could Frazier even have known there *was* another one? He'd certainly never been in her bedroom.

She whirled toward the window. The blind was up as always. She hurried over and looked down on a patch of empty sidewalk on the other side of the street.

Why that sneaky, spying little sonofabitch!

She remembered then what she had been doing the night she broke the shepherdess. Trying on the cat costume, dancing around and . . . and . . . *Oh, God!*

Her father tapped on the door and opened it. Lindy blushed as though he had caught her with her hand in her own pants.

Wendell Grant did not appear to notice his daughter's sudden embarrassment. He said, "More company, Lindy. Roman and Alec are downstairs."

The boys were waiting for her in the Grants' basement party room when Lindy came down. Roman was drinking a Pepsi from the bottle while Alec rolled the balls around the pool table.

"Damn," Lindy said by way of greeting.

"Something the matter?" Roman asked.

"I'm just so mad I could spit, that's all."

Alec came over from the pool table. "What's the problem?"

"I don't believe it," Lindy said. "I just flat do not believe it."

"Believe what?" Roman prodded.

"That Frazier Nunley. That kid. The junior brain."

"Frazier?" Roman repeated. "What'd he do?"

"He was out in the street looking through my window the other night. He saw me"—Lindy caught herself—"naked," she finished.

"The hell you say." Alec's eyes were bright.

"Are you sure?" Roman asked.

"Darn right I'm sure." She told them about the broken

shepherdess and how Frazier had brought her a replacement.

"That's pretty nervy," Alec said.

Lindy softened. "I don't know, maybe he meant it as an apology," she said.

"Apology, hell," Roman said. His big hands balled into fists. "I'll pound some apology into that creep."

Roman Dixon was painfully aware that *he* had never seen Lindy naked, and they were supposed to be going steady.

"Should we go get him tonight?" Alec said.

"I don't think you have to beat him up or anything," Lindy put in.

"We can't let him get away with it," Roman said. "You don't want him walking around thinking he can do that anytime he wants to."

"No-o-o," Lindy said doubtfully. "But he's so much smaller than you, it wouldn't be fair."

"Was it fair for him to stand out there and . . . and *look* at you like that?"

"He's really just a kid."

"So what?"

"I don't think you ought to hurt him."

"How about if I just squeeze him a little?"

"Wait a minute," Alec said. "I've got an idea how we can teach the creep a lesson he'll never forget and not hurt a hair on his brainy little head."

The others turned to Alec MacDowell to hear the idea that would change all of their lives.

CHAPTER 12

Frazier managed to stall through the next day by feigning symptoms of the flu. He lay in his bed agonizing over what a jackass he had made of himself with Lindy Grant. Running away, for Christ sake! The worst possible thing he could have done. Sooner or later he was going to have to face her, and staying home in bed today would only prolong the moment.

Besides, he didn't think his mother was fooled. She listened to his complaints of chills and fever, felt his forehead, told him to rest quietly, but her eyes told him she knew there was something much more going on with him than the flu. He almost wished he could talk to her about it, or to his preoccupied father, but he knew he would no sooner do that than he would compare methods of masturbation with them.

The next day he recovered from the make-believe flu and trudged into school like a condemned man. While the rational part of his mind told him to get it over with fast and be done with it, he spent the day darting around corners and slipping into the boys' room to avoid a face-to-face meeting with Lindy.

At the end of the day his nerves were raw. What the hell was he afraid of? What was the worst thing that could happen? How bad could it be, anyway?

She could shove the figurine back into his hands. *I don't accept presents from creepy little shits with acne and fat behinds. So take this piece of junk back and don't ever come around me again.*

Okay, it could be pretty bad.

Frazier felt utterly drained as he slouched down the steps of Wolf River High School after the last class of the day. So deep was he in his personal gloom that he didn't hear the light footsteps hurrying down behind him.

"Frazier? Wait up."

He turned, sick with dread. It was *her*.

"I need to talk to you," she said.

"Oh, y-yes?" God, she was beautiful.

"Not here." She looked around conspiratorially. "Meet me at the Bean House in fifteen minutes." She flashed a smile on and off and walked swiftly away.

Frazier stood looking dumbly after her. He could not believe the sudden turn in his fortunes. Instead of ripping him apart with her scorn, Lindy had actually seemed friendly. She wanted to talk to him. Maybe the gift of the little shepherdess had had the desired effect after all.

The Bean House owed its nickname to some past generation of Wolf River High students for reasons lost in the intervening years. The name on the blue-and-white sign over the service window was Riverview Burgers 'n' Shakes, but nobody ever called it anything but the Bean House.

There was a fast service window and half a dozen Formica tables outside for fair weather. Inside were four small booths and a counter. Frazier arrived five minutes after talking to Lindy and hung around the door trying to look casual and failing miserably.

The familiar candy-apple Chevy pulled up in front and Frazier's heart dropped. Lindy Grant got out, but Roman

Dixon and Alec were with her. He must have been crazy to think Lindy wanted to talk to him alone. Maybe they were going to beat the shit out of him. Right now he didn't even care. At least then it would be over and done with.

"Hi, Frazier," Lindy said, seeming friendly enough, if a little nervous. "Let's go in and get a booth."

Roman nodded at him and grunted some kind of a greeting. Alec have him an oily smile.

The four of them went inside and took one of the small booths and ordered Pepsis. Frazier sat on the inside, painfully aware of the radiating heat of Lindy's body next to him. Across from them sat the broad-shouldered Roman and weasel-face Alec. Frazier could not figure out why everyone was smiling at him. It made him acutely uncomfortable.

"We've been wanting to talk to you since school started," Roman said.

"You have?" It seemed to Frazier there had been ample opportunities.

"That's right," Alec agreed. "We've got sort of an invitation for you."

Frazier searched the boys' faces, looking for some sign of mockery. They seemed sincere enough.

"You've heard of the Wolfpack," Roman said.

"Sure." Who hadn't?

"How'd you like to join?" Roman tossed it off casually enough, but he might as well have asked, *How'd you like to play quarterback for the Packers?*

"M-me?" Frazier stammered.

"Sure," Alec said. "We all figured we could use some brainpower in the Pack, and you've got the best brain in school. We talked it over and . . . everybody wants you."

Frazier thought his ears might be failing him. He looked to Lindy.

She gave him the smile that made his stomach knot. "That's right, Frazier."

"What do you say?" Roman asked.

How much, he wondered, did Lindy have to do with this off-the-wall invitation? He said, "Well, sure, I guess so."

"That's great," Alec said. "We'll shoot you right through the initiation, and you'll be a full-fledged member of the Wolfpack." He flashed his ring with the grinning wolf's head and the two red stones for eyes. "Then you'll be wearing one of these."

"Initiation?" Frazier asked.

"Everybody goes through it," Roman said.

"We just have a little fun," Alec said. "No paddles or anything like that."

"We'll do it Saturday night," Roman said.

"This Saturday? Isn't that the Halloween Ball?"

"Right," Alec said. "This way you get initiated and welcomed into the Pack at the party. How does that sound?"

"Well . . . fine, I guess."

"It'll be kicks," Alec said. "Right, Lindy?"

She touched Frazier on the arm, and he fancied he could feel the flesh under his jacket sleeve turning red. "We'll all be glad to have you, Frazier."

"I don't have a costume or anything."

"Don't worry about it," Alec told him. "We'll pick you up and bring a costume for you and everything. I'll let you know where and what time. Cool?"

"Okay," Frazier said, breaking into a smile. "Cool."

Alec beamed back at him. "Good, good. Glad to have you with us."

He stretched his hand across the table and shook Frazier's. Roman gave him a nod.

Lindy smiled, then looked away. She said, "I've got to get home."

Roman and Alec slid quickly out of the booth to stand with Lindy. She looked as though she would say something more, but turned suddenly and walked out. Roman followed her.

Alec lingered to repeat, "I'll let you know where and when," and he too was gone. The red Chevy roared to life and peeled away from the curb.

For several minutes Frazier sat in the booth staring out the window after them. He could not believe what had just happened to him. The girl he secretly loved had smiled at him and touched him. The star of the football team had asked him to join the most important club at school. From a nothing he had become Somebody. He took off his glasses and wiped them with a paper napkin. Then he picked up what was left of his Pepsi and drained it in a gulp. This was shaping up to be the most important day of his life.

Alec MacDowell laughed, pleased with himself, as the three young people drove away from the Bean House.

"He bought it," Alec said. "Bought it hook, line, and sinker. And he's supposed to be so smart."

Roman at the wheel was grim. "I'd still like to smash in his stupid face."

"This'll be better," Alec said. "You'll see."

Lindy, sitting between them, was thoughtful. "I don't know," she said. "He seems so harmless."

"You ought to know better than that," Roman said. "You're the one he was peeping at."

"And who knows what he might do next," Alec added. "Window peeping today, sneaking into a house tomorrow, the next day . . . who knows?"

"I can't believe he'd hurt anybody," Lindy said.

Roman gripped the wheel. "It's always the quiet ones that go crazy."

"That's right," Alec said. "Lee Harvey Oswald was just a quiet wimp, and you know what he wound up doing."

Roman was scowling at his own thoughts. "Looking at you the way he did, we can't let him get away with it."

Lindy chewed on her lip. "I guess you're right. Just so nobody gets hurt."

"Don't worry," Alec assured her. "I've got everything planned out. It's going to be a kick, that's all."

Lindy sat back and stared through the windshield, saying nothing during the rest of the ride to her house.

CHAPTER 13

At dusk on Saturday, Frazier Nunley stood on the corner of Main and Elm streets with his hands buried in the pockets of his mackinaw, watching his breath make pale puffs of steam. The day had been cloudy and dark, and the streetlights had gone on half an hour ago.

The little kids were already out with their Batman and witch and skeleton costumes, lugging their huge shopping bags to collect trick-or-treat goodies. Halloween officially fell on the following Tuesday, but by common consent the town of Wolf River had agreed to celebrate it tonight.

The *Chronicle* had run the usual editorial about driving safely and watching for tiny ghosts and goblins, and the usual scare stories about the dreadful things evil people sometimes put in fruits and candy in Milwaukee and other large cities. Not that such a thing was likely to happen in Wolf River, but it wouldn't hurt for parents to have a look at the goodies before the kids ate them. Nobody ever paid any attention to the warnings, and the little kids were usually half-sick with stuffing themselves by the time they got home with their loot.

Frazier had never cared about trick-or-treating when he

was a child. He preferred to stay home and read. Dressing up and going door to door for handouts struck him as degrading.

He had been a little concerned tonight about what to tell his parents. Alec had made it very explicit that he was not to tell anyone where he was going. It turned out to be no problem, as his mother was playing for a group of faculty wives and had her mind on her program.

"Going out, dear?" she said, concentrating on gathering her sheet music.

"Uh-huh. Meeting some friends."

"That's nice." If she wondered where her son had acquired friends, she didn't think about it until later.

His father, with characteristic restraint, had looked up from his book long enough to say, "Have a good time, son. Don't stay out too late."

Frazier thought all this secrecy was foolish, but if that's what it took to be with the in-crowd, he would go along with it. He was relieved that he had not been forced to lie to his parents. Frazier was a terrible liar.

Since the other day at the Bean House he hadn't had a chance to talk to Lindy or Roman, and he hadn't heard from Alec. He had begun to wonder if maybe they had forgotten about the invitation. Or maybe it had all been a cruel joke. Then Alec had called last night with instructions to meet them here, and to say nothing to anyone about the initiation.

The idea of secret societies and clubs with passwords and grips and all that meant little to Frazier, but he could not pretend he wasn't excited at the thought of being accepted in the Wolfpack. He would even wear their stupid ring, which he had always thought looked like something you might win at a carnival. You made a lot of concessions to be popular.

"Hey, Frazier."

He started at the sound of his own name. Lost in

thought, he had not seen the candy-apple Chevy drive up Main and roll to a stop a few feet away.

"Get in," called Alec from the window on the passenger's side.

Frazier walked to the car and climbed into the back seat. Roman was driving. He didn't look around. Frazier was disappointed to see that Lindy wasn't there.

The Chevy pulled away from the curb. Alec turned in the front seat and handed a shopping bag stuffed with clothing back to Frazier.

"Put this on."

"Right here?"

"Sure, right here," Alec said.

Roman spoke without turning around. "Don't worry, nobody's going to watch you."

Frazier thought he heard an odd emphasis in Roman's words, and frowned, but he forgot about it as he pulled the clothing from the bag.

"This is a clown suit."

"Right," Alec said. "It's your costume. Put it on."

Had he been allowed to choose his own costume for the party, Frazier would sure as hell not have gone as a clown. Too close to real life. However, since he had no choice, he began awkwardly getting out of his clothes and into the garishly colored suit.

"What should I do with my clothes?" he asked.

"We'll keep 'em for you," Alec said.

Without any more conversation they drove out of town and along one of the little-used county roads that led to Wolf Lake. From the faint aroma of beer in the car Frazier deduced that the party had already begun for his two companions.

When the silent woods closed in around them and still no one had spoken, Frazier finally asked, "Isn't the party at the Hartman cabin? Over on the other side of the lake?"

"We're not going to the party yet," Roman said. "This is your initiation."

Frazier completed the clumsy job of getting into the clown suit. It consisted of baggy green pantaloons, a pull-over polka-dot blouse with a floppy collar, and a pointed hat with a ball at the peak and an elastic chin strap. There were big plastic feet that went over his shoes and a cutout Ping-Pong ball painted red for his nose. He must look utterly ridiculous, Frazier thought, and for the first time a glimmer of doubt crept into his mind as to whether this was such a wonderful experience.

But it was too late for second thoughts. The Chevy crunched to a stop on the gravel next to a dark pier on a little-used part of the lake. Two rowboats, one with an outboard motor, bobbed in the dark water. A line from the outboard was tied to the prow of the second boat for towing.

The boys in front jumped out and stood watching critically as Frazier climbed out in the clown suit.

"Not bad," Alec said.

"It fits him," said Roman, not smiling. He turned to Alec. "Have you got the blindfold?"

"Right here." Alec produced a wide band of dark terry cloth.

"What do you have to do that for?" Frazier said.

"They always blindfold initiates," Alec said. "It's traditional." He reached out and plucked the glasses from Frazier's nose.

"I can't see with out those," he protested.

"There's nothing to see where you're going," Roman said.

"Don't worry," Alec added. "We'll take good care of them."

Reluctantly Frazier turned his back and allowed Alec to tie the cloth behind his head so it blinded his vision. A tickle of panic touched him, but he pushed it away. It was silly, sure, but as Alec said, silliness like this was a part of all initiations.

Then he felt them start to tie his wrists together behind his back and reflexively jerked his hands away.

"Hey, Frazier, it's all right," Alec said. "All part of the ceremony."

"Why do you have to tie my hands?"

"Listen, we don't have to do any of this," Roman said, an ominous note in his voice. "We can just take you back and drop you where we picked you up and forget the whole thing."

"He didn't mean that, Roman," Alec said quickly. "He's just a little nervous. Aren't you, Frazier?"

"I guess."

"Well, anybody would be. But you've got to learn to trust us. Believe me, nobody's going to be hurt."

Frazier hesitated a moment longer, then put his hands behind him, wrists crossed. He had come this far, he might as well go the rest of the way.

"Way to go," Alec said approvingly.

Frazier winced as he felt his wrists bound tightly together with plastic clothesline rope.

They walked him, one on each side, out onto the pier. A chill wind off the lake probed at the floppy collar and reached down inside the clown suit.

Frazier shivered. "Where are we going?"

"For a little boat ride," Alec said. "I'll explain what you have to do on the way."

"I don't swim very well," Frazier said. Hell, he didn't swim at all, if the truth be told.

"Nobody's doing any swimming," Roman told him. "Just stay in the boat."

He was eased down into the rocking rowboat and experienced a pang of dizziness. His foot bumped against the concrete block used for an anchor and he staggered. A grip on his arm pulled him upright and guided him onto the wooden plank that served as a seat. Someone sat next to him. Alec.

He heard Roman's footsteps up on the pier, then a

clump-bump and the wash of wavelets as he stepped into the other boat, the one with the outboard. Alec shifted on the seat beside him.

"Hold on," he said.

There was the grinding sound of a starter cord being yanked in the boat up ahead, and on the third try the outboard motor coughed to life. The plank jerked under Frazier's buttocks as the tow rope pulled taut and his boat began to move forward.

Alec sat close to him. "What we're going to do," he said, talking over the roar of the outboard, "is let you float out here for a bit while the rest of the Pack meets on shore to discuss you as a member and vote on you."

"Vote?" Frazier said.

"Just a formality. You've got Roman Dixon for a sponsor, and that guarantees you get in."

"I have to stay out in the boat alone?"

"Just during the ritual."

"What ritual?"

"From time to time you'll hear our call—like this . . ." Alec loosed a quavering wolf howl into the October night. "When you hear that, you answer back. Let's hear you try it."

"You want me to howl?"

"It's the call of the Wolfpack."

Feeling cold and ridiculous, Frazier gave a halfhearted little howl.

"No, no, you can do better than that," Alec coaxed. "Come on now, let's hear a real Wolfpack howl."

What the hell, Frazier thought. He threw back his head and wailed into the blackness, letting some of his misery come out with the howl.

"That's more like it," Alec said.

Abruptly the pitch of the outboard motor in front of them changed. The boat lost headway, and soon the other bumped alongside.

"Sit tight now," Alec said. "And remember to answer

the call. When we come back to pick you up, you'll be a full-fledged member of the Wolfpack.''

There was a heavy splash. That would be the concrete anchor going over the side.

Frazier gripped the seat behind him with bound hands while the boat pitched as Alec stepped out.

''Remember,'' Alec said, ''listen for the call of the Wolfpack.''

The outboard motor revved then and gradually diminished and died as the other boat pulled away. Frazier was left alone—cold, unhappy, and seriously wondering if he had made one of the more stupid decisions of his life.

Lindy was waiting for them when Roman and Alec docked the outboard at the pier down the bank from the Hartman cabin. Some of the kids had already got there, and the Bee Gees' ''To Love Somebody'' could be heard blasting from the stereo speakers.

The boys looked Lindy over, appraising the sleek cat costume.

''Hey, you look really sexy,'' Roman said.

Alec nodded his agreement.

''Where are your costumes?'' Lindy asked.

''They're up at the cabin,'' Roman told her. ''We brought 'em out this morning.''

Lindy looked out over the lake. ''Did Frazier meet you like he was supposed to?''

''He was there on schedule and came along like a lamb,'' Alec said. ''He's out there now in his clown suit waiting to hear the call of the Wolfpack.''

The boys snickered as the three young people looked toward the shadowy silhouette of the rowboat about a hundred yards offshore. Lindy frowned behind the domino mask.

''I couldn't believe it when you got him to howl,'' Roman said.

''I told you this would work. When he figures out what

an ass we made of him, he'll never show his face again.'' Alec turned to Lindy. ''Want a demonstration?''

''Is he all right out there?'' she said.

''Sure, he's fine. Just listen to this.'' Alec cupped his hands around his mouth and howled out at the dark lake.

After a moment there was a weak answering howl. Alec grinned at the others. Roman bent over to muffle his laughter.

''He's in good voice, huh?'' Alec said.

''How long are you going to keep him there?'' Lindy asked.

''Until he finally figures out he's been had. There's a little paddle in the boat he can use to get himself to shore if he wants to work at it.''

''But if he's blindfolded and his hands are tied . . .''

''I made the knots real easy. A baby could get out of them.''

''But what if he can't?''

Alec shrugged. ''Then we go out and get him when we're good and ready. By that time he'll know better than to go peeking in any more windows.''

''I'm gonna try it,'' Roman said. He cupped his mouth and loosed a full-throated wolf howl toward the lake.

In a moment Frazier's reply drifted back.

The two boys laughed uproariously. Lindy looked out toward the lake. She didn't smile.

''Come on, pussycat,'' Roman said. ''Let's go join the party. Alec and me will get our costumes on, and I can sure use a beer.''

''Me too,'' Alec agreed.

Lindy looked at him in surprise. ''You, Alec? I thought you didn't drink.''

''There's got to be a first time,'' he said, ''and I think this is it.''

The cabin where the Halloween ball was annually held belonged to Amos Hartman, Todd's banker father. It was easily the largest and most expensively furnished of the handful that were scattered along the shores of Wolf Lake.

Actually, it was more of a lodge than a cabin, with a spacious dining hall downstairs that could be cleared for dancing, and four bedrooms on the second floor. Mr. Hartman himself used it for holiday entertaining during the summer, but whenever he wasn't using it he made it available for his son, who was, naturally, a leading member of the Wolfpack.

The Halloween decorations were extensive, if not very imaginative. Black and orange crepe paper streamers draped the beamed ceiling, and the usual black cat, jack-o'-lantern, and witch cutouts were stuck on the walls. Jointed cardboard skeletons jiggled in the doorways.

A bar at the edge of the dancing area had been stocked with soft drinks and, supposedly unknown to the school and Mr. Hartman, a plentiful supply of beer, wine, and vodka.

By nine o'clock the first floor was packed with enthusiastic high schoolers drinking, dancing, laughing, fooling around. Occasionally a couple would slip away and up the stairs for some more intimate fun.

A pair of huge loudspeakers was set up at one end of the dining room with the volume turned to the approved ear-busting level. There were some up-tempo rock songs by the Beatles and the Doors and Little Richard, but more popular were the slow tunes by people like the Association and Frankie Valli and Bobby Vee.

Merilee Lund, in a harem outfit, was having an over-enthusiastic good time dancing with Todd Hartman, who was a slightly pudgy Robin Hood. Merilee didn't seem to notice that her date's eyes followed Lindy Grant all around the floor.

Johnny Mathis crooned "Somewhere My Love," and Lindy clung sensuously to Roman as they swayed together in the center of the floor. Lindy's cat costume was easily the sexiest at the party, and she felt lightheaded and happy after a couple of vodka-Sevens. The salt tang of Roman's sweat and the feel of his bare back under her hand was exciting.

Roman, as usual, had chosen a costume that would display his muscular build. Lindy had to admit that he made a fine-looking Tarzan in his leopard-skin briefs. She could, however, have done without the leering Tarzan-Jane references, which became tiresome with repetition.

Alec, livelier than usual with the unaccustomed beer in him, capered around in a hairy gorilla suit. By eleven o'clock everyone had grown bored with his routine of bowlegged hops, dangling arms, and grunts.

"Why don't you go climb a tree, monkey?" Merilee said, then laughed excessively, as though she'd said something really funny.

"Climb this," Alec muttered behind the gorilla mask, but not loud enough for anyone to hear.

Out on the dance floor Roman pushed his pelvis hard against Lindy. He put his mouth close to her ear and whispered, "Let's go upstairs. I've got a key to one of the bedrooms."

"Are you going to start that again?" Lindy said, but she didn't pull away.

"Come on," he coaxed. "We'll stop whenever you want to. I promise."

He thrust his body even harder against hers, and Lindy could feel his erection under the Tarzan briefs.

"Okay," she said, "but just for a little while."

Roman immediately started to lead her off the dance floor.

"And no sneaky stuff," Lindy added.

"Trust me," he said, holding up his right hand.

As they passed the bar he grabbed a couple of cans of Stevens Point beer from the ice tub and a pint vodka bottle. They started up the stairs just as Alec lurched over in the gorilla suit.

"Leaving us?" he said, his voice muffled behind the ape mask.

"Mind your own business," Lindy told him.

"Yeah, get lost, King Kong," said Roman.

Alec made gobbling monkey sounds and stuck a paw into the ice tub for a beer, nearly losing his balance as he did so.

Roman laughed at him and led Lindy on up the stairs.

When they were together in the darkness of the small bedroom, Roman offered her the vodka bottle.

"Didn't you bring any Seven-Up?"

"Only had two hands. Go ahead and try it straight. You might like it."

Lindy unscrewed the top and took a pull from the bottle. It didn't taste as strong as she thought it would. She tried another while Roman popped a beer can and chug-a-lugged.

Lindy sat down on the edge of the narrow bed and stretched, feeling like the cat she was impersonating. The smell of raw wood mingled with her own sweat and Roman's musky odor in a heady perfume of sensuality.

Roman came over and sat beside her. He found the zipper on the back of her costume and slipped his hand in and around to take hold of her breast. She wasn't wearing a bra. He carried her hand down to his stiff penis. She squeezed it gently.

"Does that cat suit come off in one piece?" he asked hoarsely.

"You think you're going to find out?" she teased.

"Just curious."

He pulled the velvety material down over her shoulder, exposing a breast, pale in the darkness of the room. His mouth found her nipple and took it into his mouth.

It felt good to Lindy. Better than ever before. His cock swelled even larger under her fingers, and she knew then that this was the night she would let Roman do it to her. Still, something made her uneasy.

She pulled back, her nipple making a little *pop* when it slipped out of Roman's mouth.

"What about Frazier?" she said.

"Huh? What about him?"

"You left him out on the lake."

"So what? He can't go anywhere."

"Will you go and get him afterwards?"

"Afterwards?" Roman's grin could be seen clearly in the semidarkness. "Sure. Now let's see how that cat suit comes off."

It had grown colder out on the lake as the night went on. Faint sounds of music and laughter floated across the water from the party cabin. Frazier shivered without letup, feeling more alone and miserable than ever before in his lonely and miserable life.

As the hours passed and he heard no more wolf calls from the shore, the terrible realization came to him that he had been had. He had been an unmitigated jackass. Straight A's in all his classes, scholarships waiting for him at at least three Ivy League schools, and he had been outsmarted by a couple of clods who would be lucky to get into junior college.

Why had they done this to him? He had never offended Roman or Alec or anybody else. And could Lindy possibly be involved in the cruel practical joke?

He tugged at the clothesline that bound his wrists behind him. There was play in the rope, but he didn't have the strength to pull the knots loose. Better work on the blindfold first.

Frazier eased down off the plank seat to the bottom of the boat. The scummy water that had collected there seeped through the seat of his clown pants and chilled his ass. He squirmed around so he could feel along the gunwale with his bound hands. He found the oarlock socket with a screw head that protruded a quarter of an inch. He knelt on the bottom of the boat and bent his head to catch the terry-cloth blindfold on the head of the screw. After several unsuccessful attempts, he managed to pull the blindfold down around his neck.

He struggled back to a kneeling position, vision seriously blurred without his glasses. He just had time to locate the lights of the party cabin on the shore before he lost his balance. He pitched forward, hitting the gunwale with his chest and tipping the boat.

Before Frazier could right himself, and with his hands still bound, he toppled over the side of the boat and into the water. His cry of terror was silenced as the lake filled his mouth.

CHAPTER 14

Wolf Lake, October 1966

How impossibly clumsy; how like Frazier Nunley to fall out of the boat. The picture of the fat clown toppling over the side was so ludicrous that Frazier almost laughed in the split second before he hit the water.

The shock of the icy lake snapped him back to reality. The waters closed over him, and the universal rules of time and space were suspended as he sank.

The seconds he spent underwater seemed to drag into minutes, marked off by his hammering heartbeats. Long minutes of icy darkness with no direction—no up or down, no sense of movement. Just water. Cold lake water in his eyes, his nose, filling his mouth, stopping his lungs. In his ears, a rushing, clanging roar.

Then he broke the surface. Frazier gulped at the precious air, coughed, coughed some more. He struggled to get his arms moving, but they were still bound behind him at the wrists.

Without his glasses he saw the empty rowboat as a blurry oblong shape just six feet away. It bobbed gently, invitingly, offering safety. And life. Short seconds ago that boat had seemed a cruel prison. Now what wouldn't he give to be returned to it.

He began to go down again. He tried to gain some upward momentum by kicking, but the sodden folds of his costume and the awkward clown feet dragged him down in the water. The lake closed over him again.

You're drowning, his mind screamed. *Think, idiot! You've got to do something or you're going to die!*

With an agonizing effort of will Frazier stilled the thrashing of his limbs. He fought to keep from drawing in another lungful of water. He knew the natural buoyancy of his body would eventually take him to the top again. He had to stop fighting.

Tiny lights blinked on and off before his eyes in the depths of the dark water as Frazier fought back panic.

When does my life flash in front of my eyes? God, how boring that would be. I'd rather watch reruns of The Flintstones.

Frazier giggled foolishly, and in doing so pulled more lake water into his aching lungs.

I'm losing it. Getting light-headed. Got to fight to stay lucid. No hope if I get hysterical now.

Once more his head broke through the surface of the lake into the night air. He could make out a smear of light on the shore. That would be the Hartman cabin, where the party was going on. It was no more than the length of a football field away, but it might as well have been on the other side of the world. Frazier opened his mouth to shout, but all that came out was a sputtering, squeaking cough.

And he was under again.

Down for the third time. That was all a drowning person was allowed. Was that fact or was it myth? Was he dying? Frazier's mind could not accept, could not conceive its own nonexistence.

As he slowly sank into the depths Frazier concentrated as he never had before. He cleared his mind of all extraneous thoughts—all images and sensations from the outside world—and focused on a pinprick of blue directly in front of his forehead. Millimeter by agonizing millimeter the spot of blue expanded until it became his secret window. While his body, wrapped in the ludicrous clown suit, rolled slowly in the currents of the lake, Frazier's mind moved out and through the window and rocketed toward the lights onshore.

Up through the dark trees and into the big cabin. On the first floor the Halloween party was a kaleidoscope of sights and sounds. The walls vibrated, the floor thumped with the rhythm of the music. Ghouls and monsters cavorted with warty hags and undead creatures from the grave. Demons and devils laughed and screamed and danced and drank, and the music played louder and louder.

Frazier's disembodied mind bounced from one of the revelers to another like a pinball. With no voice and no power of touch, how could he reach anybody? Tell them he was out there in the lake drowning?

Across the room a staggering figure in a gorilla suit pawed at a female vampire who pushed him away to dance with a laughing ghoul. Frazier had no trouble recognizing the boy under the gorilla disguise. Alec McDowell. Alec was as responsible as anyone for his terrible crisis. Perhaps a bond of some sort might let him get through.

Alec McDowell watched blearily as the vampire gyrated out of his grasp. Nice ass, but not much in the way of tits. Still, he wouldn't mind grappling with her. He tried to follow the girl and her partner but reeled helplessly from one side of the dance floor to the other, bumping into dancers, falling down, getting up, laughing.

He was, he thought dimly, having the best time of his life. How stupid he'd been to be timid about drinking with the other guys. Drinking was fun. He should have tried it a long time ago.

Alec shuffled toward the bar and sat down hard on the

floor. The dancers whirled around the fallen gorilla, ignoring him. Alec looked up at them, grinning behind the mask, and waved. Nobody waved back.

Another beer, that's what he needed. Alec struggled to rise. Something like a wisp of cold air touched the back of his neck under the mask. Where the hell could that have come from? A huge fire crackled in the hearth, and he was, if anything, uncomfortably hot in the heavy gorilla suit.

And yet, for an instant he had felt deathly cold. The cold of the grave. Of the deep, deep waters of Wolf Lake.

Now where the hell did he get a thought like that?

Must be drunk.

Giggling, Alec crawled on hands and knees to a chair, and there pulled himself upright. Something buzzed around his head like a fly caught inside the gorilla mask. Alec flapped a hand against the gorilla ear, trying to shoo it away.

Suddenly he didn't feel so great anymore. His head pounded, his stomach rebelled. Sour vomit rose in his throat. Alec lurched for the door. He covered only three stumbling steps before the beer and chili and chips and onion dip came up and exploded through his mouth, splashing his face and fouling the inside of the gorilla head. He dropped to his knees, tearing at the mask as wave after wave of vile puke pumped up from his stomach and sluiced out his mouth. He pitched forward on his face and lay on the floor in his own slime.

Still retching, he made it to his hands and knees and crawled out through the door into the night air. The sudden chill crimped his stomach again and he collapsed.

Wild with panic, the mind of Frazier Nunley abandoned the hopeless Alec. With instinct born of desperation the floating mind shot up through the ceiling into a bedroom where two naked young bodies were locked together in passion.

* * *

I'm fucking her! Roman kept reminding himself. *I'm actually fucking Lindy Grant!*

She lay beneath him, not taking an overactive part in the connection, but with her legs willingly open, receiving him. A virgin. The first virgin Roman had ever had. They said if you were the first, the woman could never forget you.

He decided screwing a virgin wasn't really that much of a thrill. Kind of sloppy, as a matter of fact. But it would be good in the telling. Roman's thoughts were as much on the way he would tell the story to the other guys as on what he was actually doing.

Something cold tickled the back of his neck. At first Roman thought Lindy had decided to participate, but he opened his eyes to see her hands still at her sides. He shook his head and the cool touch went away.

He felt the climax coming, and tried to hold it until Lindy came too. That would make his story even better.

All Lindy could think of as she lay on her back under the hard-pumping Roman Dixon was *There's got to be more to it than this.*

After the first sharp pain, which was not as bad as she'd been led to believe, it was just a lot of sloppy thrusting and grunting. One of us, she thought, must be doing something wrong.

She wished he would get it over with. To speed things along she raked her nails down Roman's bare back, like the heroines did in the sexy paperback novels she sometimes read. It didn't do anything for her, but it made Roman moan, so she assumed he was enjoying it. With a little more practice she might make a good prostitute, Lindy thought with detached irony.

Suddenly she tensed. A chill that began at the base of her skull enveloped her body, and she shuddered. Roman, mistaking her reaction for passion, renewed his thrusts. A high-pitched keening, like a mosquito, sang in Lindy's ears for a moment, then was gone. At the same time, Roman climaxed inside her, flooding her with his juices. Lindy clung to him with a sick feeling that something was terribly wrong. Gradually the feeling and the chill went away, and she felt nothing at all.

Finally he knew it was not going to work. Frazier could not reach a living soul, not even one of the three who had done this to him. Not the drunken slob that was Alec nor the grunting, rutting pair upstairs in the bed. Frazier had focused all the concentration he could muster on a cry for help directed at these three, tried desperately to somehow enter their consciousness, but he couldn't get through. He was sure there must be a way, if only he knew it. But there was no more time to try. No time at all.

Out of the cabin he flew, back through the dark fringe of evergreens, across the black waters to the empty row-boat bobbing so peacefully at anchor.

The water around the boat was empty and still. The disembodied mind scanned and searched the glistening surface. Nothing. That soft, lumpy, ill-favored body he had so reviled was nowhere to be seen. Oh, how lovely and safe and familiar that body would seem to him now.

Then a ripple showed on the dark water, and then something orange bubbled to the surface. Orange and green. The garish top of the clown suit.

The mind of Frazier Nunley shot toward the floating colors. Home. That poor shapeless body was his home. *Let me in!* he cried silently. *I want to come back!* But he could not enter. There was a barrier that he hadn't encountered before in his astral travels. His mind hovered over the ballooning clown suit as it rolled slowly in the water.

Then the face turned up toward the sky. His face. Poor astigmatic eyes wide and unseeing. No more need, ever, for the clumsy glasses. The mouth, slightly open, leaked water. No more junk food would rot those poor yellow teeth. The pimpled flesh was pale and cold. Acne cured forever.

Dead. Frazier Nunley is dead. I'm dead.

The floating mind was not strong enough to assimilate the terrible fact. The logical, orderly mind of Frazier Nunley exploded into madness. Screaming with no sound, it rocketed off into the night to a terrible, timeless void.

CHAPTER 15

Los Angeles, July 1987

LINDY

The molded plastic seat dug into Lindy's back as she sat stiffly in the boarding area of Terminal 7 at LAX waiting for Flight 541 to Denver and Milwaukee. She didn't shift her position to a more comfortable one, holding on to the small pain to keep ugly thoughts of Wolf River out of her mind.

It had been, however, impossible to think of anything else during the week since Nicole's episode with the horrid pimple. The slightest rash or any tiny bruise on her daughter made Lindy tense with anxiety. Such little hurts could, of course, occur in the normal life of any adolescent girl, but they somehow had a dire message for Lindy.

Then, last night, the dreadful experience in bed with Brendan had almost sent her over the edge. At least it had helped to tell someone the Wolf River story, or most of it. Even though he had listened sympathetically and without comment, Lindy didn't think Brendan had completely bought her theory of a connection between what had happened at the Wolf Lake cabin and her present problems. But at least he hadn't told her she was crazy.

When she left him the next morning, Brendan had walked her out to her car and looked at her carefully. "Are you sure you want to make this trip?"

"I'd rather be doing anything else," she said, "but I've got to go."

"Okay. Call me when you get there. What's the name of the hotel you'll be staying at?"

"Wolf River Inn."

Impulsively she had hugged him and given him a hard, meaningful kiss. "I love you a lot," she told him, and left before he could respond.

Driving away from his condo, Lindy had had a crazy impulse to turn back and say, *Come with me*, but she didn't. This was her problem, and she had to solve it by herself.

The frivolous words from the invitation echoed in her mind like a pronouncement of doom.

Be there or be square.

At last her flight was announced, and Lindy filed through the walkway with rest of the coach passengers and boarded the DC-10. She took her window seat in the smoking section and tried to make herself comfortable. Lindy had quit smoking five years before, but she still felt more comfortable among the smokers, where there would be fewer small children and self-righteous anti-tobacco crusaders.

While the jumbo jet lumbered along in the slow parade to the runway, Lindy flipped through the pocket of the seat back facing her, looking for anything to serve as a distraction. The in-flight magazine was a slick pap of happy-face articles and ads for hotels and car rentals. She shoved it back into the pocket and pulled out the card giving emergency exit locations in case of a forced landing. She had never heard of anyone living through the ''forced landing'' of a commercial jet. She quickly replaced the card and felt around for something more cheerful. All that remained was the barf bag.

Lindy let the pocket snap shut and dug through her bag for the paperback novel she had brought along. It was one of John D. MacDonald's early McGees that she couldn't remember if she'd read or not. When she found herself reading the first paragraph for the third time without comprehension, she clapped the book shut and stared out the window.

It was no use trying not to think about it. The ominous summons to Wolf River and the sinister threat behind it ate at her consciousness like acid. Might as well give up the fight and remember. Remember Wolf River, the terrible Halloween party, and the dreadful year that followed.

Wolf Lake, 1966

The party had finally died as the first streaks of dawn shone over Wolf Lake. There would be a lot of explaining done to a lot of parents, but the Halloween Ball was traditional for Wolf River seniors, and allowances were made. It was the one party of the year when they could stay out all night, as long as they didn't do anything too scandalous.

Most of them didn't. There were the expected hangovers and broken romances the next day, but nothing really horrendous had ever happened to anybody. Not until the fateful party of 1966. It was to be the last Halloween Ball.

Lindy had awakened upstairs in the cabin as the last of the cars was driving off. Beside her in the narrow bed Roman Dixon lay on his back, snoring softly. A trickle of saliva ran from the corner of his mouth back across his cheek to the pillow.

Lindy eased herself out of bed, feeling crusty and rank. She found the rented cat costume and pulled it on, feeling like a ridiculous cartoon in the early daylight. She pulled open the door and slipped out of the room.

Downstairs, she went outside, and, shivering in the early chill, she picked her way down to the lake to clean herself. There she peeled off the costume and stepped into the icy water. With her teeth clenched to keep them from chattering, she lowered her body into the lake. She jumped up at once, cramped with the cold, but forced herself back down. She rubbed her body vigorously, especially between her legs, sluicing away the residue of last night's sex.

Suddenly she straightened. ''Oh, Jesus!'' With a cry of memory returning, she spun in the water and looked out over the lake. The rowboat still bobbed a hundred yards offshore, where the boys had anchored it. No passenger was visible.

Lindy splashed awkwardly out of the lake, stumbling in her bare feet. She gathered up the ludicrous cat costume, wrapped it around her, and ran for the cabin.

Over Milwaukee, July 1987

ALEC

The shuttle flight from Chicago began to lose altitude over Lake Michigan and to bank inland toward Milwaukee. Alec peered out the window at the tiny boats visible below, dragging the white threads of wake behind them on the blue-green water. He finished the last of his Diet Seven-Up and handed the plastic cup to the flight attendant.

They hadn't been happy at Laymon and Koontz about his abrupt departure in the middle of a campaign. He concocted a story about the death of a dear aunt, but even he found it hard to accept. This trip could well damage his career, but there was no way Alec could refuse the summons back to Wolf River. After his session with the gypsy hag he had considered writing the whole thing off as nerves, but when his tongue started to swell on him again twice during the week when he needed to be at his most glib, he had to believe something more than his nervous system was at work here.

He had left the office without elaborating on the dead aunt story. Any damage done there would have to be repaired later.

Ugliest of all had been the horrendous vision with Georgia last night. Alec used all his mental discipline to lock away the picture of his mother with his cock in her mouth. But whenever he started to relax, the sensual memory would return, sending him into a fit of shudders. The worst, most horrifying thing about it was how god-awful good it felt. He shivered with self-revulsion as he thought about it.

Alec knew—he could not have said how—but he knew sure as death that all this had something to do with the hideous Halloween party of 1966. Over the years he had congratulated himself more than once for escaping any serious consequences of that awful night. Now he wondered if he really had escaped.

As the plane dropped toward Mitchell Field he let his mind go back there. Back to the lake. Back to the horror.

Wolf Lake, 1966

The pain had been bearable at first, but the image was not. Some powerful maniac was trying to thumb Alec's eyeballs back into his skull. Then the pain got worse and the image of the maniac faded. Alec tasted dirt. Dirt and pine needles and vomit.

It was dawn. He was lying on the bare ground in the remains of the tacky gorilla suit. Alec was sicker than he had ever been in his life. He groaned. The sound of his own voice expanded the pain in his head. He tried to sit up. His stomach heaved, and he bent forward and retched until the back of his throat was raw, but there was nothing more to come up.

With great effort he slid his ass over until he could sit with his back propped against the trunk of a tree. He smelled himself. He smelled like puke.

''Never again,'' he swore through crusted lips. ''If I ever take another drink, let God kill me. In fact, let God kill me now.''

He sagged against the tree, waiting for the Almighty to accept the invitation. God ignored him.

Footsteps approached. Running footsteps. From the direction of the lake.

''Jesus, what happened to you?''

Alec squinted his eyes open and jerked with the lancing pain of the early daylight. Lindy Grant stood in front of him more or less wearing the black cat costume of the night before. At another time the sight of Lindy near-naked would have grabbed his full attention, but on this agony morning she might as well have been his grandmother wearing a muumuu.

''I'm sick,'' he mumbled.

''You look it.'' Lindy wrinkled her pert little nose. ''And you stink, too. Come on, get up.''

''Can't,'' he managed.

''Well, you'd better. We've got to get Roman.''

''What for?''

''You guys left Frazier out on the lake all night and forgot about him.''

''Oh, shit.'' He did not move.

''Come *on*, Alec. We've got to go out there and get him.''

She reached down, grimacing at the touch of his filthy hand, and pulled him to his feet. He tottered for a moment, then found an uncertain balance.

''Where's Roman?''

''I left him inside,'' Lindy said. ''Let's go.''

She skipped off toward the cabin, her bare ass, wet from the lake, twinkling in the early light. Alec McDowell followed miserably, unable to enjoy it.

Milwaukee, July 1987

The tires of the landing gear squeaked as the plane touched down. Alec jerked out of his disagreeable half dream and braced himself for the landing.

U.S. Highway 41, July 1987

ROMAN

The wide highway out of Milwaukee was as fast as a freeway all the way to Appleton. After that, State 45 had been expanded to a multi-lane limited-access road and routed through Clintonville to bypass Wolf River completely. You had to angle off to the northeast on a two-lane road with cracked concrete and no shoulders.

Roman Dixon kept both hands gripped on the wheel of the rented Monte Carlo as he hummed along at a comfortable seventy miles an hour. Some mindless rock band played on the Milwaukee station he had on the radio. It was indistinguishable from the same kind of station in Seattle, except for the unfamiliar merchants named in the commercials.

It didn't matter to Roman what came over the speaker. All he wanted was noise in the car with him to deaden his worry about what he was going to find when he returned to the town where he was born. For one of the few times in his life Roman would rather have been home with his family than where he was.

He had, in fact, dismissed the idea of coming back after seeing the doctor and getting a clean bill of health. But the message on the prescription blank and a recurrent twinge in his genital area helped him decide to observe the ominous summons.

Stephanie didn't waste much time pretending to believe his story about going to Chicago on a buying tip. Why should she? He had never before shown much interest in the commercial operations of the stores. Then there was that wild hallucination last night, where for a crazy minute Stephanie had appeared to be some fantastically desirable woman. His momentary burst of ardor had convinced her he was up to some kind of hanky-panky. Roman was pretty sure she had called Van Haaglund after that to find out if there really was a store selling its stock in Chicago.

Well, fuck her, he thought. And fuck his father-in-law, too. Let them believe he was off for some wild orgy with a gang of female bikers if they wanted to. Roman had too many other things to worry about to give a damn what they thought.

The names of the towns he passed through, or bypassed on the new highway, awoke memories. Neenah, Menasha, Hortonville, New London, Bear Creek. From what Roman could see from the highway, they hadn't changed a lot. Sidewalks mostly empty, except for a few teenagers hanging out. There were the same drugstores and hardware stores. Same theater marquees with different titles lettered in. Same taverns with names like The Come-On Inn or Harve & Wilma's. The same feed stores and farm machinery dealers with sunburned men out front in jeans and baseball caps. And between the towns lay the same pastureland, with quiet herds of Jerseys or Holsteins, the same clean barns with their phallic silos, the same farmhouses with pickups parked outside. The only differences along the highway were an increase in the number of fast-food places and more billboards.

The first sign he saw with the name on it—WOLF LAKE 11 MILES—took him back with a jolt to that cold, sick morning in the cabin.

Wolf Lake, 1966

Roman had awakened with a start and disoriented feeling of *Where the hell am I?* In a moment the smell of the raw wooden walls and the lingering odor of female and sex reminded him.

He rolled over in the bed and reached out, but she was gone. Too bad, because he had a splendid hard-on and nothing to do with it.

He lay there for a minute or two, reliving as much as he could remember of the night before. He had finally done it, by God; he had finally screwed Lindy Grant.

His only other previous experience had been the two times last summer with the willing wife of one of his fellow construction workers. He had been grateful at the time for the release of his pent-up horniness, but the woman was loose between the legs and had an unpleasant way of snorting in his ear when she came. Lindy, now that had been something else. God, a virgin. Roman wished he had drunk a little less so he could remember if it had really been as good as he thought it was.

The door creaked open. Lindy stood there, her black hair shiny and wet, holding the cat costume in front of her body. Roman thought he had never seen anything quite so beautiful.

Then an apparition loomed beside her. Gray-faced and red-eyed, Alec McDowell stood uneasily in the doorway, yellow-brown puke in a messy trail down the front of his gorilla suit. The head was missing.

Roman sat up in the bed. "What's happening?"

"It's Frazier," Lindy said. "He's still out on the lake. We've got to go get him."

Alec belched, swallowed, and shuddered.

"I forgot all about the little creep," Roman said.

"We all did," Lindy said. "Let's go get him. He'll be half-frozen."

"Serve him right," Roman grunted. He climbed out of

the bed, holding the bloodstained sheet around his middle. "Anything to eat downstairs?"

At the mention of food Alec turned away and leaned heavily against the doorjamb.

"We can worry about that later," Lindy said. "We've got to get Frazier."

"Sure thing, chicken. Just give me a chance to pull my pants on." As he woke up more fully, Roman felt a new sense of power and possession. He had made it with Lindy Grant, and the bloody sheet proved beyond any doubt that he was the first. From here on he would hold the upper hand.

They got the outboard started and headed away from the dock toward the rowboat gently riding at anchor. No head was visible above the gunwale of the boat.

"Guy's probably sacked out in the bottom," Roman said from his position in the stern at the motor.

Neither of the others spoke. Lindy, up in the bow, kept her eyes on the rowboat. Alec had stopped his dry heaves but looked sicker than ever as he slouched in the middle seat.

They drew alongside the rowboat and Roman kicked the motor to idle.

"It's empty," Alec muttered.

"I can see that," Roman snapped. "He must've swam to shore."

"With his hands tied?" Lindy said.

"He told us he couldn't swim," Alec added.

"Shut up," Roman said. "Let me figure this out."

"What's that?" Lindy pointed to a disturbance on the surface some ten yards off the bow of the rowboat.

Roman got the outboard in gear and they approached the floating thing. Orange and green and . . .

"Oh, shit!" Roman said.

Lindy covered her mouth with her hands to stop the scream that wanted to come out.

Alec was leaning over the side trying vainly to puke away his anguish.

Frazier Nunley rolled slowly in the water and looked up at them with dead, empty eyes.

CHAPTER 16

Wolf River, July 1987

LINDY

Twenty years ago the Wolf River Inn had been unquestionably the best place in town. The best hotel, the best restaurant, the best—and only—bar with live entertainment. The Grange and the VFW and the Legion all held their banquets here. Anyone who wanted a "night out" went to the inn.

The exterior was finished in a pseudo Swiss ski resort architectural style. It bothered no one in Wolf River that there wasn't a skiable mountain within several hundred miles. The interior carried out the Alpine theme with white plaster walls and dark beamed ceilings. There was a walk-in-size fireplace in the lobby and another in the Chalet Room.

Any party that exceeded the size of the host's home, and was deemed too classy for the Elks Lodge, was held at the inn. Such sexual fooling around as there was in Wolf River took place mostly at the inn. More than one clandestine tryst was rumored to have been consummated in the cozy rooms on the third and fourth floors, the first two being used primarily for tourists and commercial travelers.

Lindy Grant had things on her mind other than the inn's appearance, but she couldn't help feeling a little sad about the obvious decay. The outside, which used to get a fresh coat of paint every spring, now showed the scars of hard Wisconsin winters. Inside, the lobby carpet was stained in several places. The furniture had a secondhand look, and the smell of long-dead cigars hung in the corners like cobwebs.

The desk clerk was watching a game show on a small television set behind the reservations counter. He was in his early twenties, with a complexion problem and greased-back hair. When Lindy walked in he turned down the volume of the game show and looked her over with the eye of small-town makeout artist.

"I'd like a room," she said.

"We've got 'em." He said. "Fourth floor's the best."

"That's fine."

He slid a registration card over in front of her and leaned across the counter to read upside down as she wrote. "Is that for . . . one?"

Lindy caught the significant pause. She looked up at him with a cold stare until his eyes shifted away. "That's right," she said. "One."

She finished filling out the card and slid it back across the counter. "You do take Visa?"

"Sure. We're totally up to date in Wolf River."

I'll bet you are, Lindy thought dryly. She looked around the lobby. It was empty except for an old man who sat in a sagging plush armchair by the cold fireplace reading a copy of *Playboy.*

"Arc there any activities planned here at the inn for the class reunion?"

The clerk gave her a blank look. "What class reunion?"

"Wolf River High School. Class of '67."

The desk clerk shrugged. "Not that I heard of. Was there supposed to be?"

"I thought so. I guess somebody will contact me."

The clerk shrugged again, anxious to get back to the game show. He selected a room key with a big tab of hard plastic attached.

"Four-fourteen," he said. "Has a nice view of Main Street."

"Can you have someone take my bag up?" she said. "I'd like to walk around town a little."

"Hey, Jed," the clerk called.

The old man looked up from *Playboy*.

"How about taking the lady's suitcase up to four-fourteen."

"You betcha." Jed got to his feet and limped over to the desk. He gave Lindy a smile of tobacco-stained teeth.

She put a dollar bill in his hand along with the key, and he reached for the bag.

"Just leave it in the room," she said.

"You can pick up the key here when you come back," the clerk told her. He eyed her curiously. "Anything special you wanted to look for in the town?"

"Not really."

"You won't find a lot doing in Wolf River."

"I've been here before," she told him, and walked out of the lobby before he could extend the conversation. She could feel eyes on her back.

Her last year of high school was a dim memory for Lindy, deliberately clouded by the internal censor that screens out unpleasant memories. She forced herself now to think about it as she walked the once-familiar streets.

The most painful part of it was the change in her relationship with her father. Wendell Grant had always seemed the ideal parent, the envy of her friends who only wished their fathers could have been so friendly and understanding. Not to mention handsome. Lindy was aware that half the girls she brought home developed a crush on the tall, athletic judge.

After the Halloween thing at the lake, however, it was never the same at home. The conversations with her father, which had flowed so naturally before, became stilted and difficult. Whenever the subject became personal, he eased out of range. The judge began spending more time in the county seat, and when he was home often retired to his study, there to remain until after Lindy had gone to bed.

After she left home with a scholarship to Northwestern, her contact with her father or anyone else in Wolf River dwindled rapidly. After her father's marriage to the young Shawano woman his letters became even less frequent.

All in all, the situation did not disturb Lindy. She had little wish to remember the town, nor did the town seem eager to remember Lindy Grant.

Over the years the judge's letters had described in general terms the steady decline of Wolf River. The people there never fully recovered from the double economic blow in the early 1970s when Moderne Gloves closed up shop due to changing fashions and the Allis Chalmers plant relocated to Sheboygan. Lindy had expected to see some deterioration in the town, yet she was hardly prepared for the pervading atmosphere of rot and depression.

Few of the shops she remembered were still located on Main Street. That might be expected with the passage of twenty years, but there seemed an inordinate number of empty storefronts with FOR RENT signs taped to the windows.

The old Woolworth was now a discount furniture and appliance store. SUMMER CLEARANCE! ALL PRICES SLASHED!

Bonnie's Gift Shop was now an unappealing café.

Where the Dairy Queen had been was an office of Milwaukee Savings and Loan.

The Rialto Theater stood empty and dead—a cobwebby

cave under a broken marquee with a few meaningless black letters still clinging drunkenly to the slots. She could squint her eyes and see *Dr. Zhivago*, *The Sound of Music*, *Alfie*, *Bonnie and Clyde*. All gone now. Dead. Shadows of the past.

Lindy shivered. Abruptly she remembered promising to call Brendan Jordan when she got in. He'd never asked her to do anything like that before, and she was amused and touched by his concern.

She wasn't ready to go to her room at the inn yet, so she stepped into a phone booth—they still had the old-fashioned enclosed kind with a folding door—outside a Shell station. She punched in her credit card code and Brendan's Los Angeles number. After much crackling on the line she got a busy signal.

Lindy was oddly relieved. She would have felt silly saying something like *Hi, I got here safe and sound.* She was not, after all, a twelve-year-old. Still, it was nice to have someone care about you. She would try Brendan again later when she got to the room.

Lindy continued her walk through town. The streets seemed narrower and dirtier. The former might have been an illusion: childhood memories always shrink when revisited as an adult. But there was no overlooking the scraps of wastepaper and other trash that littered the sidewalks and gutters.

Lindy shook herself out of her gloomy mood and walked on. Traffic along Main Street was spotty, consisting mostly of muddy pickup trucks driven by sunburned farmers. There were few pedestrians—washed-out looking women, dispirited men. Almost no young people. If Wolf River was not yet a dead town, it was sure as hell dying.

Without realizing where she was going, Lindy looked up to find herself at the intersection of Main and Elm streets. A montage of old Saturday afternoons flashed through her mind—shiny cars, loud rock music on the 8-tracks, girls dressed as sexily as their parents would allow.

The girls' hair sprayed into flips, boys with D.A.s, curls carefully arranged on their foreheads. Lots of flirting and fooling around. Fun. Plain, simple fun. God, she hadn't really had fun for a long, long time.

There was no conscious decision, but Lindy seemed to be carried along up Elm Street by her memories. Up the Hill. How much less impressive it seemed now than when she had lived there two decades ago. Did all houses grow smaller with the passage of time? Did all hills flatten into insignificant grades?

The houses at the bottom, near Main Street, had not been the most imposing even when she had lived there. They had aged badly. Several were empty now, with taped cracks in the windows and shingles missing from the roofs. In one front yard a rusting automobile sat on blocks, never to run again. A couple of hungry-looking dogs prowled through the weeds of unkempt lawns. Sad. The scene made Lindy want to cry.

And there, of course, was the house where Frazier Nunley had lived. She didn't want to look at it, but it drew her attention, like an accident across the road. It was one of the empty ones, somehow looking even more abandoned and forlorn than the others. The paint was badly weathered. Rusted junk littered the front yard. A faded realtor's sign stood crookedly in the weeds.

A chill made Lindy shiver in the hot July sun. She turned from the old Nunley house and walked quickly on up the Hill.

More quickly than she expected, she reached what she really wanted to see—the Grant house, where she was born, and where she had lived so happily with her father for the first seventeen years of her life.

It was in fairly good repair, thank God, and had a fresh coat of paint. But there had been changes. A second entrance had been added off the front porch, the house split into a duplex. A neatly lettered sign noted that one side was currently for rent.

The house had been repainted a sad shade of blue-gray with white trim and shutters. The combination lacked the warmth and happiness that seemed to radiate from the old brown-and-cream paint her father had freshened every year. Or maybe the color scheme was just fine; it was her depressed mood that made it seem so melancholy.

She closed her eyes for a moment and saw the house as it had been. She imagined the changes over the years as in a speeded-up film. The summer after Lindy's graduation, Ida Krantz suffered a stroke that put her into a convalescent home, the kind where the patients never get better, just become paralyzed and mute. Her father had continued to live alone in the big house, but he seemed to lose interest in keeping it up.

Then, during Lindy's sophomore year at Northwestern, Judge Grant married the woman from Shawano, only a few years older than Lindy, and brought her home to Wolf River. Lindy came home for the wedding, but felt like a stranger. The judge was totally fascinated by his bride, and the young woman did little to hide her hostility to her predecessor in the house. A year later Wendell Grant and his wife moved to Madison, where the judge set up a private practice. That was when Lindy's communication with her father had all but ceased.

Thinking now of her father and the way it used to be drove Lindy even deeper into her funk. She turned away from the house of her happy childhood and walked rapidly back down Elm Street and into the present.

Like the rest of the town, the Chalet Room at the Wolf River Inn was not what it once had been. The high-backed, vaguely Swiss-looking booths of carved oak and rich brown leather had been replaced by red vinyl. The little raised bandstand-stage was still there, but the Baldwin piano was gone and a jumble of amplification equipment was in its place.

The bar was smaller, or maybe like everything else in

Wolf River it just seemed smaller. The only other customer when Lindy entered was a stout gray-haired woman with a deeply seamed face. She sat unmoving except when she raised the stubby on-the-rocks glass to her lips.

Lindy took a stool well away from the silent woman. The tired-looking bartender wandered over and wiped down the bar space in front of Lindy's stool.

"Vodka and tonic, please," she said.

"You got it." He dropped ice cubes into a glass and brought up a vodka bottle from the well. "Staying at the inn?"

Lindy was about to give him a don't-bug-me answer, but stopped herself. Sometimes people just made conversation without being on the make.

"That's right," she said.

He nodded pleasantly, eyeballed a generous shot of vodka into the glass, and added tonic.

"Isn't there supposed to be a high school reunion celebration here?" Lindy asked.

"If there is, nobody told me about it."

She began to wonder if this whole thing was some bizarre practical joke. Get her all the way back to Wolf River for a meaningless hoax. But who would do a thing like that? How could it profit anybody? And how would that explain the eerie messages and what had happened to Nicole's face?

The bartender added a squeeze of lime and set the drink before her. Lindy sipped at it and gave the bartender a brief smile of approval. She was relieved when he went away.

"Miz Grant?"

Lindy started at the sound of her name. She turned on the stool and saw the elderly bellhop named Jed standing there, grinning through his brown teeth, holding an envelope.

"A message come for you. I seen you come in here so I told Jerry at the desk I'd bring it."

She took the envelope from him and scooped up a couple of quarters from her bar change for a tip. "Thank you."

The envelope was cheap drugstore stationery. Her name was written with a black felt-tip pen in an angular hand that was chillingly familiar. With trembling fingers, Lindy tore it open.

The message inside, in the same pointy script, made her throat close up when she read it:

Hello, Cat.
Welcome home.
Remember the clown?

CHAPTER 17

ROMAN

He lay on the brown chenille spread that covered the double bed in Room 416 and tried to concentrate on the cartoon that was playing on television. It was not easy because every minute or so the picture would roll. It was just enough to be annoying, but not enough to make him get up and go turn off the set.

So far the visit to his old hometown had been every bit as deadly as Roman had thought it would be. The streets were empty; the bar downstairs was like a morgue. The geek at the registration desk didn't know anything about any high school reunion, and didn't care. As long as he was here Roman would stay the night, but if somebody didn't tell him what was going on by tomorrow morning he'd haul ass.

Roman poured a healthy shot from the bottle of Jack Daniel's into the water tumbler that had come encased in its little plastic envelope on the glass-topped bureau. He swallowed the whiskey and stared at the animated antics of some insufferably cute little blue creatures called Smurfs.

"Ought to club the little fuckers to death," Roman muttered. "Make a nice blue coat for somebody."

He got up and went over to switch through the channels. News on two of them. He didn't need other people's bad news. Continuing around the dial: *Little House on the Prairie*, *Love Boat*, an old movie with Bette Davis, a Chinese cooking show. He clicked all the way around to one of the news shows from Milwaukee and went back to the bed. At least it was better than Bette Davis.

He drank the neat Tennessee mash whiskey and yawned through the report of some ongoing hearings in Congress. There was a commercial for a tire dealer, then a sleek broad with good knockers came on with the local news. They flashed on a film of a body being pulled from Lake Michigan, and the whiskey turned sour in Roman's throat.

The television screen and the hotel room faded and vanished. Roman was back in the outboard on Wolf Lake in the gray morning after the last Halloween Ball.

He thought he was going to chuck his cookies when the thing in the water rolled slowly over and the dead white face of Frazier Nunley looked up at them. But with Alec already trying dryly to puke over the side, and Lindy just this side of hysteria, he held it in.

"It's Frazier," Lindy said unnecessarily.

Alec got control of his stomach and moved up with the others. "Is he dead?"

"Hell yes, he's dead," Roman snapped. "What do you think?"

"What are we going to do?"

"We've got to get help," Lindy said.

"It's too late to help him," Roman said. "What we've got to do is get out of here."

Lindy turned to face him. "You mean, just . . . leave him like that?"

Roman gave her a narrow-eyed glare. "What do you want to do, take him with us?"

Lindy bit her lip, looked back at the floating corpse, and shook her head.

Roman moved back to the stern. "If we all play dumb they can never connect us with this. As far as anybody knows he just went out in the boat himself for some asshole reason and fell overboard."

"That's crazy," Alec said. "Do you think anybody will believe that?"

"They'll have to unless they can prove something else happened. We'll be okay as long as we keep our stories straight and simple. We went to the party, never saw Frazier, don't know anything about him. That's it."

"What if he told someone where he was going last night?" Lindy said. "And who he was meeting?"

"I made him promise to keep it secret," Alec said. "And he was impressed enough to do it."

"We better hope he was," Roman said. He reached for the clutch lever to engage the outboard motor.

"Wait a minute," Alec said.

Roman and Lindy looked at him, startled by the urgency in his voice.

"His hands are tied."

"Oh, shit," Roman said.

He killed the motor and used one of the oars to move the boat back close to the slowly drifting body. With Alec holding on to him, he leaned over and wrestled the corpse around in the water until the hands, still loosely bound with plastic clothesline, were exposed. He would never forget the cold rubbery feel of the dead boy's flesh. A couple of tugs undid the knots.

Roman unwound the white plastic clothesline and carried it with him back to the stern. He said, "It wasn't even tied good. He should've been able to get out of that."

"Let's make sure we get rid of the rope," Alec said.

"We can't leave anything around to prove it wasn't an accident."

"I don't like this," Lindy said.

"Jesus, who does?" Alec said in a tone he had never before used with either of them.

"Can we please get out of here?" Lindy asked.

"Yeah, right."

There was a chilling minute when the motor died and refused to restart immediately, but finally Roman got it going and steered the boat back toward the deserted dock.

The telephone on the little table next to the bed shrilled in his ear, snapping Roman upright and bringing him abruptly back to the here and now.

"Yes?"

For a long ten seconds the only sound in the earpiece was a crackling hiss. Then a whispery voice spoke to him in a cramped monotone.

"Hello, Tarzan."

Roman's muscles tensed. The telephone felt like some cold, unfamiliar object in his hand.

"Welcome home."

"Who is this?" he got out finally.

"Remember the clown?"

There was a click on the other end and the hollow buzz of a dead line.

After a minute during which he sat frozen on the bed, Roman hung up the phone.

ALEC

The Wolf River library, a wooden frame structure not much bigger than a 7-Eleven store, had no facilities for microfilm. However, they retained, bound in heavy fiberboard covers, copies of the Wolf River *Chronicle* from its start as a single-sheet biweekly in 1889 to its final issue in

1971 when television and regional editions of the Milwaukee *Journal* finally put it out of business for good.

Alec asked for the volume containing issues from the fall of 1966, and waited while the pleasant, middle-aged librarian went into a storage room in the back and brought it out for him.

He leafed through the yellowing pages to the end of October, skipping past the abbreviated wire service accounts of world affairs: Indira Gandhi becomes prime minister of India. Pope Paul IV meets with Gromyko. Albert Speer released from prison in Germany. President Johnson tours the Far East. Israel and Jordan fight a battle over something or other.

The theory held by Alec's father as editor was that national and international news was important to the *Chronicle* only insofar as it affected Wolf River citizens. More extensive coverage was given to the fire that seriously damaged Swanke's Feed and Garden Supply Store, and the local sixth-grader who finished second in the All-Wisconsin spelling bee, and the efforts to unionize the workers at the glove factory.

When he found the headline, it hit Alec like a cold towel slapped across his eyes:

LAKE TRAGEDY
LOCAL BOY DROWNS

The story detailed the discovery by a fisherman from Tigerton of Nunley Frazier's body late in the day, after he had been reported missing by his parents. Local authorities (that meant Police Chief Art Mischock, a bear of a man whose habitual scowl masked a shrewd mind) would not speculate on why the boy had gone boating alone at night. No explanation was offered for his peculiar costume.

The following day the front page carried an interview with Frazier's parents, who denied any possibility that their son might have committed suicide. In their grief, they were also angry. They wanted answers to such questions as: Where were the clothes he left home in? Who provided the boat that was still anchored a hundred yards offshore when Alec's body was found? What had happened to his glasses? Who else was on the lake that night?

An editorial written by Alec's father called for a vigorous investigation by Chief Mischock, including calling in the State Police for help if necessary. Alec remembered the tortured, sleepless night he had spent that night.

Two days later the only mention of Frazier Nunley was an announcement of the funeral. It referred to the boy's death as a "tragic accident."

Alec closed the volume of old newspapers. He sat silently for several minutes at the table, inhaling the varnish and dust smells of the library, thinking about what writing that single paragraph twenty years ago had cost his father.

Alec was in the *Chronicle* office that day working with his mother when Judge Grant came in along with Chief Mischock and Elmer Swanke, head of the local merchants' association. They asked to see Alec's father in private. Trudy McDowell showed the men into her husband's office. There they had stayed for an hour with the door closed. An hour during which Alec suffered as he never had before.

Trudy and Phelan McDowell came out of that meeting pale and shaken. They avoided looking at Alec, and never mentioned to him what went on behind the closed door. Their relationship changed from that day on. His father became silent and withdrawn. His mother cried sometimes alone in the bedroom. They no longer asked Alec to help out at the paper. And after the funeral notice, the *Chronicle* never ran another story about Frazier Nunley.

Gossip and rumors, however, persisted. They ranged from a bizarre theory that Frazier was murdered by dope dealers from Chicago, to a guess that was frighteningly close to the truth: that he had been pushed into the water by partying classmates who subsequently fled.

High school parties were canceled for the rest of the year. The Saturday afternoon cruising ritual was abandoned. Kids who had been best friends looked at each other with suspicion. It was possible to trace the beginning of Wolf River's decline as a town to the October night Frazier Nunley died.

Alec's parents hung on at the *Chronicle* while the paper declined into little more than an announcement sheet for rummage sales and farm auctions. In 1971, a month before the *Chronicle* shut down forever, Phelan McDowell put the barrel of a deer rifle in his mouth and pulled the trigger. Alec came home for the funeral, then returned to the University of Missouri to get his degree in, ironically, journalism.

His mother left Wolf River a few months later and moved to Arizona. There she worked on a tiny desert weekly until she died.

Alec carried the volume of newspapers back to the librarian's desk and left the building to return to the inn.

The desk clerk greeted him. "Looks like you people are going to have a pretty small party."

"What people?" Alec asked.

"You class-of-whatever-it-was reunion types. Only three of you checked in so far."

"Three?" For a moment Alec's field of vision darkened at the edges. He took hold of the edge of the registration counter for support.

"That's it." The clerked turned to the key slots and produced Alec's along with an envelope with his name on it. "You got a message."

Alec walked numbly to the elevator, got into the musty car, and punched *4*. While the car creaked and rattled its way up, he tore open the envelope and read:

Hello, Monkey.
Welcome home.
Remember the clown?

The walls of the elevator car seemed to crush in on him like a coffin, and for a moment Alec could not get his breath. Then it jerked to a stop, the sliding doors clanked open, and he stumbled out into the hallway.

CHAPTER 18

THE FLOATER

Here they were.

At last.

All three of them back where this business had begun.

The Floater drifted about the Wolf River Inn, checking on first one then the other. The temptation to act immediately was strong, but the Floater had waited too long, planned too thoroughly to move this quickly to the climax. No, he would take the time to savor his achievement. Watch them squirm. Make them pay. Make them hurt.

It had not been easy bringing them all back here to taste finally the punishment they had escaped twenty years ago. It had been more difficult than any problem Frazier Nunley had solved when he was alive. More difficult than any problem he could have imagined.

But he had done it. They were all here now—beautiful Lindy Grant, arrogant Roman Dixon, and clever Alec McDowell.

They were here solely at his bidding, and they were under his control. They did not know that yet, though they were beginning to suspect. Their poor earthbound minds did not have the capacity to know what was happening to them. But they would learn soon enough. God, yes, *how* they would learn.

The Floater was at peace now, or as nearly at peace as he would ever be. Over the years he had adjusted to the unnatural state in which he was forced to exist. He had done better than merely adjust, he had strengthened himself. From the first frantic attempts at contacting others to try to save his drowning body, the Floater had perfected his techniques. There had been long torturous periods of failure, frustration, and pain. And there had been some triumphs, too.

The worst part had been right after it happened. Right after he died. The shock of seeing his own dear ugly body dead pale in the water and being unable to reenter had sent the astral essence of Frazier Nunley careering off into an endless void with madness all around him. There was no time, no space, no sensation beyond a terrible indescribable pain.

A mind weaker than Frazier's would surely have snapped, lost its tenuous hold on existence, exploded to astral atoms. And that would have been the end. But Frazier would not let go. The lingering strength of his living mind held together its astral counterpart, and slowly, slowly he began to regain control.

Spatial comprehension returned. The void was a nowhere, but there was a way out. A way back. Frazier put his mind to work; the astral mind, now unencumbered by the need to care for the clumsy body, could stretch its limits. It could return from the Nowhere void to Somewhere. The mind returned, but because of the violent way it had been wrenched from the living body, it would forever be warped.

The Somewhere that Frazier returned to was, naturally enough, Wolf River. That was where he was born, where he had lived the brief fourteen years of his earthly life, where he had died sucking icy lake water into his lungs.

The things Frazier saw as he moved spectrally through the town dismayed him. More accurately, the things he did not see appalled him. Where was the hue and cry over his death, especially the cruel manner of it? Why were the lives of those who had brought him to this state allowed to continue as though nothing had happened? Where was the punishment? Where was justice?

Only in the house of his parents, the house of his birth, did Frazier find any real mark of his violent passing. His mother, the strong, serene Viking goddess of a woman, shattered like a porcelain figurine. After the death of her only child she never again touched her beloved piano. For many months afterward she spent her days sitting at an upstairs window, staring out along the street as though waiting for her boy to come walking home.

Mother! shrieked the astral mind of Frazier Nunley. *Mother, I'm here! I can see you! Please hear me! Know me!*

But Orva Nunley could not hear her son, for he had no tongue. She sat in the window and looked out on the street and waited for her boy to come walking home.

She spoke less and less during those months, and the things she said sometimes made no sense. Ellis Nunley gave up his position at the college to devote himself to his wife. He tried valiantly to cope with his Orva's growing alienation, but it hurt him deeply to see the woman who had been a strong and true partner to him draw steadily away.

Finally, when he could no longer care for her, Ellis drove his wife to the county hospital in Shawano, where they had a psychiatric clinic. Orva was tested for weeks for every known form of physical and mental ailment, but in the end the doctors could not identify her illness. They agreed only that she would need care. More intensive care than her husband could give her at home.

He left her there, standing in the hospital garden with a doctor, not yet comprehending that she was going to stay. When he got home, Ellis Nunley, for one of the very few times in his life, got thoroughly drunk.

He continued to visit her at the hospital regularly for a year. The doctors said Orva might start to get better at any time, but Ellis never saw any improvement. He began to go less frequently. Orva didn't seem to notice. Much of the time she didn't even know when he was there, and the visits always left Ellis drained. Finally, he just stopped going.

During the years that he had tended his wife, both in their home and at the hospital, Ellis grew thinner and aged rapidly. He developed a racking cough and had to give up smoking his pipes.

After a last sad visit to Orva, Ellis Nunley sold the Elm Street house and everything in it. He paid most of the money he had gotten to the hospital to assure Orva's continued care and just wandered away. He was known to have spent time in Appleton, Milwaukee, Chicago, and finally Detroit. There he was knifed to death on the street by a sixteen-year-old boy for the eleven dollars in his wallet.

Orva was eventually released from the county hospital. She found a room in Wolf River, which she paid for from Ellis's insurance money, and was seldom seen on the streets.

As he saw these things happen to the only two people who had ever loved him, the astral mind of Frazier Nunley raged impotently against those who were responsible. Still unable to make his presence felt by the living, he swore to the dark gods that somehow, no matter what he must do or how long it might take, he would have his revenge. And he sank deeper into madness.

But even as the rage sapped his sanity, it gave him strength. The searing hatred of three people kept the essence that remained of Frazier Nunley from flying apart like cobwebs in the wind. He followed the three as they played out the final days of their high school lives. He screamed at them from behind the astral barrier. Called them by the unspeakably foul names they had earned. He rushed around them like a dust devil, plunged through their very bodies like a ghostly sword.

Of course, they could not see him, they could not feel his rage. His screaming curses were silent. Only sometimes . . . sometimes he could sense an uneasiness about one or the other of the three. Just the vaguest sense that something was not quite right. It was not much, but it meant he *could* reach them. That kept Frazier going. One day he would have the power he needed, and on that day these three would suffer as they deserved.

Then the three of them went away from Wolf River, each in his or her own direction, to his or her own destination. The mind of Frazier Nunley writhed in frustration that he could not follow. Not then. He understood that his existence was in Wolf River, the only place he had known in life. Even as he grew in strength and cunning, his power was always here. Only here in the town where they all had their beginnings would he have the strength to control their destinies. Frazier knew then that when he was ready, when he had learned what he must know, he would somehow bring them all back here. And here they would pay.

The days in Wolf River stretched out into years. Frazier worked and strained and concentrated every gram of his essential power into making his presence known to others. That was where he must start. Without the power to communicate, he was helpless.

He hovered about, observing the most intimate activities of the people of Wolf River. He reached out to feel them with nonexistent hands. He shouted at them with no throat. He probed and prodded and poked them with his mind. Except for an occasional unexplained shudder, or a sudden glance back over a shoulder at nothing, there was no response.

In his despair, Frazier floated aimlessly one spring day outside a house not far from his own, where Victor and Nancy Yarrow lived with their year-old baby. The sun was bright, and warmer than usual for that time of year. The child sat on the lawn in a playpen while his mother worked among her flowers. Frazier drew closer to watch.

The delight of the baby in a plastic rattle charmed him. He floated nearer, striving to share the uncomplicated joy of the little child in a silly toy and in its own sense of existence. How blindly people take existence for granted, he thought, whatever their age. How foolishly they spend it.

It was there on the lawn in front of the unpretentious house of the Victor Yarrow family that Frazier Nunley discovered he would no longer have to float aimlessly. He was about to begin learning the extent of his powers.

Nancy Yarrow patted the sod carefully around the base of her ailing rosebush. Her husband had run the lawn-mower carelessly close and bruised the poor stem. However, Nancy was good at nursing living things back to health; she helped out in the summer at St. Martin's Hospital when the nurses took their vacations. She would not have minded working full-time as a nurse, but Victor wouldn't allow it.

She stood up, pulled off the gardener's gloves, and regarded her repair job critically.

"You're going to be okay, baby," she told the rosebush. "And I'll put a little fence around you so no lummox of a husband can push a lawnmover into you again."

Chuckie gurgled over in the playpen. Nancy turned to look. She smiled a soft, mother's smile. After twelve years of trying, she and Vic had almost given up on becoming parents, and then Chuckie had come along. Her smile slipped a notch as she saw Chuckie acting a little more animated than usual. Did his little face look flushed?

She crossed the velvety lawn to the playpen and looked down on her child. Chuckie's plump little face was tight with concentration as he tried to grasp the plastic rattle with tiny fingers that did not yet have the dexterity.

''Hey, Chuckie, what you doin'?''

The child continued to play with the rattle and didn't look up. That was so unlike him that Nancy was immediately alarmed. Always the sound of her voice got his complete attention, with the open happy smile he always had for her. She reached down into the playpen to pick him up. The baby squirmed away from her, giving her a frightening look of almost adult anger.

Nancy flinched away from her baby. Then, recovering from her momentary shock, she reached down and firmly brought Chuckie up out of the playpen into her arms. She felt the child's forehead, detected a light fever.

''What's wrong, little guy? Something hurting you?''

A quick check told Nancy the baby did not need changing, and no errant pin was jabbing him. There was just something in his expression—a look that should not be on the face of an infant. She hurried into the house with him while the baby wriggled in her arms for all the world as though he were trying to get away.

Nancy laid her child down on the bed and felt icy cold inside as she watched the strange workings of the little face. The baby showed no recognition of her as its mother. The eyes darted back and forth as though seeking escape, then gyrated wildly in their sockets.

In a rising panic, Nancy kept one hand on the baby's body to keep him from wriggling off the bed while she pulled the bedside telephone within reach by its cord. She had the telephone in her hand and the first three digits of Dr. Tichman's number dialed when Chuckie began to cry. Nancy's immediate feeling was one of inexpressible relief. The baby's cries were so natural, his distress so babylike, that she sensed that whatever had been wrong a minute ago was all right now.

She put the phone down and held her little son. She stroked him and soothed him and kissed his little head. Gradually the crying subsided to gurgling sobs and finally ceased. The face that looked up at her was tired and red from crying, but it was her child's face. Nancy put him down on the bed, covered him, and almost immediately the baby was asleep.

Nancy completed the call to Dr. Tichman, and the next morning took Chuckie to see him, but nothing was found wrong with the baby. Dr. Tichman suggested an allergy, and told Nancy they would make tests if anything like that ever happened again.

It never did.

It had all transpired so smoothly, so subtly, that Frazier didn't realize at first what a significant breakthrough had taken place. One moment he was watching the baby, concentrating, forgetting for that moment his own terrible loneliness. Then, with no conscious effort on his part, he *was* the baby. No, not exactly. The baby still existed, but Frazier Nunley was in its mind.

He had a body again. Not really his, but for a brief period he was in control. The effort it took was draining. He could feel the unformed mind of the child trying to push back in, and he forced it away. Frazier knew he could not maintain the control for more than a few minutes, but the experience exhilarated him and gave him the energy necessary to hold on for a little longer.

He made the plump little hands reach out and touch the plastic toy. The feel of its smooth, slightly yielding surface brought him intense sensual pleasure. He smelled the fresh-cut grass of the lawn and the talcum on the baby's skin. He gloried in the furry softness of the blanket on which he sat. Frazier put a tiny fist to his mouth and tasted the sweet-salt flavor of flesh.

He could feel the unformed little mind of the child recoiling in confusion, trying to get back into its head. The strength of Frazier's intellect and the powers of concentration he had honed for months allowed him to sustain the thin edge of control.

The mother looked over at him then. Her expression told Frazier she recognized something was wrong with her child. She came toward him and spoke to him. The subordinated infant brain tried to respond.

Get away, damn you! Frazier shouted soundlessly at the mother. *Leave me alone! Let me feel!*

However, as the mother carried him toward the house Frazier could sense the growing panic of the infant mind. He knew as surely as death that if he stayed there fighting for control the mind of the child would be irreparably damaged. It was not that Frazier had any compassion for the fate of the child, but he feared for what might happen to his own astral existence. Oblivion? Madness? Unspeakable pain? He could not give up what he had, especially not now when he had just discovered his road to revenge.

CHAPTER 19

It was with great reluctance that Frazier Nunley withdrew from the mind of little Chuckie Yarrow and returned to his disembodied astral state. He watched from above as the baby's eyes spun crazily for a moment before they settled into frightened focus. Then the little face reddened and puckered and the child began to scream.

The frantic mother dropped the telephone and scooped the child into her arms. Gradually the baby returned to normal, and Frazier drifted out of the house.

He floated without destination for a time, reliving the delicious experience of touching things, smelling, tasting—powers taken for granted by everybody. No one could imagine the devastating loss of having those senses stolen.

But even more than the delight he experienced in returning to the tactile world, Frazier thought about the power he had held for those brief minutes. He was awed by the ease with which he might have crippled or destroyed the tiny mind and body he had so briefly inhabited. Never did the suffering of Chuckie Yarrow concern him. To Frazier, the baby existed only as a vehicle for experiment.

But he was not ready yet for that experiment. He still had much to learn, skills to perfect. But he was at last sure of one thing.

Payback time was coming.

The experience with Chuckie showed Frazier that a child's mind afforded easier entry than the stronger, more resistant mind of an adult. The place he selected to search for his next host body was the Tiny Tots Preschool, run by Alma Zanoff, a kindly spinster, and her sister, Freya. The Zanoff sisters had lived their entire lives in Wolf River and were trusted absolutely by local parents with their children.

Over the months that followed, unseen by the youngsters who played on the swings and in the sandboxes at Tiny Tots, the astral spirit of Frazier Nunley floated just above their heads. He watched patiently . . . waiting, choosing.

No one could say for sure later precisely when or with whom it had started. The behavior of children under five is unpredictable at best, and the early seizures might have been passed off as normal playfulness. Exactly which of the Tiny Tots charges was first to be afflicted was never finally determined.

It might have been little Boone Eisenreich who one afternoon laid open the scalp of Alma Zanoff with the locomotive of a Lionel electric train. Boone had always been one of the more introverted children in the preschool, and after the incident he quickly reverted to his quiet self, showing no memory of having attacked the lady.

Or it could have started with Rosie Schwartz. On an afternoon when several parents were visiting, Rosie slipped into the gingerbread playhouse, took off all her clothes, and emerged dancing nude in a childish parody of lust that she had never learned on *Sesame Street*. She was quickly hustled out of sight by the Zanoff sisters, but for those who were present, it was a memorable sight.

Whoever it started with, it was soon recognized that Wolf River had been hit with some outlandish epidemic among its children that caused them to behave in a bizarre manner. The origin of the strange disease was easily traced to Tiny Tots, and the facility was ordered to close. County health people from Shawano swarmed over the preschool, sampling its food, the air conditioning, the insulation materials, the sand in the sandboxes. No cause for the illness of the children was discovered, but Tiny Tots remained closed. Alma and Freya Zanoff were shunned by the townspeople who had known them since birth, and were eventually forced to sell their property. The last anyone heard they had moved to Milwaukee and opened a flower shop.

Some of the local citizens still considered the Crazy Kids Syndrome to be nothing more than standard childish misbehavior, augmented by mass hysteria on the part of the parents. They were unwilling to accept the possibility that some undetectable virus or whatever was attacking their children. Not until Carol Ann Cernich.

Carol Ann had been pulled out of Tiny Tots by her parents before the official closure by county officials. Her mother, Dolly Cernich, had made up her mind quickly after the episode of Rosie Schwartz and the childish striptease. Dolly was not about to take a chance of something like that happening to her daughter.

When Carol Ann came home she showed no unusual symptoms, and her parents relaxed, thinking she had been spared. Then, one night at dinner, the little girl changed into another person before the horrified eyes of her family. It happened right after Dolly had brought out the dessert. Carol Ann suddenly sat differently in her chair, head cocked to one side, squinting in turn at each of the family members as though she had never seen them before. She grabbed the ice cream from her dish in her bare hands and stuffed it into her mouth, making strangled animal sounds as she devoured it.

She ignored her mother's startled reprimand and proceeded to snatch away the ice cream from her older sister and her baby brother.

"Carol Ann," her father cried, "what on earth are you doing?"

"Fuck you, you sonofabitch," Carol Ann said. Words that were surely never heard in the Cernich home.

When her father jumped from his chair and came around the table toward her, the little girl screamed at him in some wild gibberish and brandished a butter knife.

"Don't come near me, you bastard," she screamed, "or I'll cut your fucking heart out."

Her parents carried Carol Ann to a bedroom, where her father had to hold her down while Dolly called for a doctor. Then suddenly the little girl's screaming stopped, the wild gyrations of her body ceased, and she went limp on the bed, her face dull and expressionless.

She was taken to St. Martin's Hospital that night, and the next day after extensive testing she was found to have massive, irreversible brain damage. The source was never determined, and Carol Ann Cernich lapsed into a coma from which she never recovered. She lived for a year before becoming the first fatality of what was known as CKS.

The death of Carol Ann was of no consequence to Frazier Nunley. Compassion was not a component of the astral being he had become. The girl was important only for what she had taught him about entering the minds of others.

The strange epidemic of crazy kids ended in Wolf River when Frazier concluded that he could learn nothing more from children. He moved on to slightly older minds, being careful now to refrain from behavior so outrageous that it would draw unwanted attention. With high school students this was not difficult, as a certain amount of normal weirdness is expected from that age group.

He was not yet ready to try a healthy adult mind, but

searched until he found a subject he could handle but who would tax his powers more than the children had.

Henry Ulbricht was ninety-one years old and lived with his grandson and granddaughter in a house as old as he was on Flower Street. He had been a logger and a pretty good semi-pro baseball catcher before World War I. The local story was that he had once had a tryout with the Cubs. He served in France in the war, and came home to Wolf River to become a successful Ford dealer until his retirement at seventy-five.

Henry's memories of his baseball years, the war, and the old days in Wolf River were as sharp as photographs. He was sometimes sought out by historians of Wisconsin or the Midwest, and unfailingly provided them with valuable material from his reminiscences. However, his recall of what had happened to him yesterday, or even an hour ago, was fogged. He was nevertheless a cheerful old man whose favorite joke was that the doctor who warned him to cut down his drinking and quit smoking had been dead for twenty years.

Henry was, for a fact, in pretty good shape, except for a bum hip joint that kept him confined to the house, and hands crunched into arthritic claws by years of catching baseballs in the old lightly padded catcher's mitts.

It was Henry Ulbricht that Frazier chose as his next host.

Entering the old man's mind was not so easy. Henry had been tough and smart in his youth, and his grandson said fondly that it was sheer stubborness that had kept him alive for so long. Frazier's initial probings met with hostility. For several days he was unable to get in, but he persevered.

The old man took to complaining to anyone who would listen that "Something's poking at my head." However, so accustomed are the young to patronizing the old that his complaints were disregarded as harmless imaginings. Frazier kept up his efforts, and one rainy afternoon as the old man dozed in his chair by the window, he slipped successfully into Henry Ulbricht's head.

He was very careful not to alarm the old man's grandson and his wife by saying or doing anything to call attention to himself. They noted only that Henry was quieter than usual and seemed tired.

The old man's mind, however, refused to be shunted into darkness. It struggled constantly to push out the intruder. The need to maintain his dominance was a drain on Frazier's energies, and he was angry with the old man for deterring him from the experiments he wanted to try.

Also, he found that the body was not suitable for any real test of his powers of control. The damaged hip made it impossible for him to move far from the chair, and the clawed hands were a constant affront as they lay useless in the old man's lap.

The frustration gave birth to an idea that would open new avenues for Frazier in the use of his powers, and would never be forgotten by those who saw it.

It was Saturday evening, and the family was watching an old Doris Day movie on television. Henry always sat farther away from the set than the younger people because he could see better at a distance. The first indication his grandson had was a sharp popping sound from behind him. He and his wife both turned, and what they saw was to stay with them like scars on the retina.

Henry sat in his chair, staring fixedly down at his lap. There his deformed hands twitched and shuddered. One by one, each of the twisted fingers straightened itself out. The popping sound they heard was the snapping of long-calcified bones and knuckles as the fingers were forced out of their cramped position.

"Grandpa, what are you doing!" cried the young man as a yellow shard of bone ripped through the flesh of a straightened index finger.

Henry Ulbricht looked up at them, his face a mask of unholy glee. There was no sign of pain as he continued to crack the brittle bones of his fingers. Only when he had gone through all ten did the intense, triumphant expression vanish. Then, with his hands a ruined mess of torn flesh and splintered bone, the old man's face crumpled in agony. He began to scream.

The howling of the old man's mind had nearly driven him out, but Frazier had continued to enforce his will until he had broken all ten fingers, proving to himself the capacity he had to hurt.

As he tested his powers and worked to strengthen them, Frazier also learned his limits. He was at his most powerful when he was close to Wolf River—the place of his birth . . . and his death. Although he could travel timelessly wherever he chose, his powers of control diminished as the distance from home increased.

The incursions into the minds of others were not without their costs to Frazier. Depending on the extent of his physical activities, the experiences left him drained of psychic energy. Sometimes, as in the case of Henry Ulbricht, it took many days of retreat back to the void to restore his vigor. Over the months Frazier's endurance increased, but gradually.

One drain on his psychic energy was the problem of repeatedly finding a suitable host for his experiments. To overcome this, Frazier began a search for a body he could use as a semipermanent home for his astral mind. Ideally, it should be a body with considerable physical strength, but equipped with a mind that would not fight back. In searching the streets of Wolf River and the surrounding farms, he soon found what he needed. His name was Roy.

When the people of Wolf River later talked about it, they realized that no one had ever really known much about Roy—not how old he was, or where he came from, or even if he had a last name. He was an Indian, from the looks of his strong nose, copper skin, and straight black hair, but beyond that his origin was a mystery.

He just showed up one day, big and grinning, at Elmer Peterson's farm and said, "Chop your wood for supper?"

It took Elmer a minute to understand that the big Indian did not want to eat his stacked logs, but was offering to turn them into kindling in exchange for a meal. The sheer size of the man was intimidating, but his open face and gap-toothed grin were so disarming that Elmer told him to go to it.

In a little more than an hour Roy had split and chopped the mountain of logs and stacked them into neat piles, a job that would have taken Elmer half a day. The Indian worked with a fierce joy, smiling constantly, and when he was through, devoured the food he was given with the same unfettered enthusiasm.

Peterson did not have enough work on his place to keep Roy on full-time, but he spread the word among Wolf River farmers and merchants, and Roy soon had all the jobs he could handle. The Indian proved to be an eager worker, skilled at any kind of task he could do with his hands, so long as it didn't require thinking. In the powerful man's body was locked the mind of a four-year-old.

Roy became a familiar figure around Wolf River. When he wasn't working for somebody, he could be found by looking for a crowd of children and dogs. They loved him, and followed him about like a fan club. Roy treated them all, dogs and children, as equals.

The town more or less adopted Roy, as a family might take in a dim-witted but lovable relative. They gave him work and fed him and clothed him. They protected him from outside forces like the well-meaning Shawano social worker who wanted to put him in a "home."

There were many beds in town available for Roy. Just about anyone who had a spare room wouldn't have minded letting the Indian use it. He was quiet and clean, and never took anything without returning equal value in work. Nevertheless, Roy preferred to sleep in the open when the weather permitted. When it got cold, he liked the warmth of a barn, where he had the company of animals. People grew accustomed to seeing him around. Roy was always just "there," like the stopped clock in the old courthouse.

Roy was in a barn, sleeping on a bed of straw during an early summer rainstorm, when his life effectively ended. That was the night Frazier Nunley entered his head.

This time Frazier met with little resistance. The pliant, child's mind of the Indian offered no opposition. If somebody else wanted to use his body for a while, that was all right. He'd just go somewhere out of the way and lie down.

Roy's body was a delight to Frazier. He gloried in the Indian's strength and agility, qualities Frazier had never known with his own poor body. He went out into the fields alone to try it out, and was delighted to be able to run faster, jump higher, lift greater weights than he could have imagined.

The interaction with people was more difficult. He was able to arrange the facial features into something like Roy's habitual grin, but the voice was more difficult. Fortunately, Roy never had much to say anyway, so Frazier was able to get by largely on nods, shrugs, and gestures. And although he was unskilled in the kind of work Roy did easily, Frazier found he could relax and let muscle memory take over while Roy's body chopped wood or dug a well or put up a fence.

But to continue the tests of his powers, Frazier would have to make this body perform some act that would have been impossible for Roy. The Indian's love for all forms of life was well known. That gave Frazier his idea.

He would have liked to use a dog. They had always been plentiful wherever Roy went, but something in the animal senses told them that their old friend was different. The dogs that once had followed him leaping and yapping joyfully now shunned the Indian. Frazier would have liked to hurt one of them, do something that would have been impossible for Roy, but he could never get close enough to one.

Some other life form would have to do. After one heavy rain, a stretch of road down by the old millpond provided the answer.

Frogs.

Scores of them hopping about, croaking happily or lustfully, as suited their mood. The frogs had been as much Roy's friends as anything else that lived. He would lie on his side, head propped on his hand, and watch their froggy party as cheerfully as though he were a part of it. The frogs, lacking the brain and instincts of the dogs, did not recognize the change in Roy when Frazier guided his new strong body to their pond.

With the air still wet and the clouds slowly breaking up, Frazier stood quietly watching them. He picked out one of the dozens of frogs, fixed the little animal with his eye, and in two quick steps brought his boot sole down on the creature, squashing it like a ripe plum.

The frog made a satisfying *plop* under his foot. Frazier/Roy grinned happily and looked around for more frogs. *Plop. Plop. Plop.*

A faint tickling sensation was the only indication that Roy's dormant mind objected to the cruel use of his body. Frazier easily put it down. He was enjoying this.

Plop. Plop. Plop.

"Why are you doing that, Roy?"

So intent had he been on killing that he had not heard the approach of the little girl. She was a daughter of one of the nearby farmers. Neither Frazier nor Roy knew her name.

"Why are you hurting the frogs?"

At this crucial moment Frazier could not get the Indian's tongue to form words. All he could manage was a deep growly moan. He waved his hands in a meaningless gesture.

The little girl backed away. "You're not Roy. He wouldn't hurt anything. You're somebody else."

The innocent insight of a child had undone him. The mind of Frazier Nunley, slipping out of its normal logical pattern, made the body of Roy the Indian move forward swiftly and catch hold of the child by her shoulder. When the girl started to cry out he clapped a big copper-colored hand over her face.

Although it must have taken longer, it seemed like only a few seconds until the girl stopped breathing. Frazier, exhausted by the effort and the battle with the aroused mind of the Indian, carried the limp little form to the mill-pond and dropped it in. The girl's body rolled gently in the water so the dead little face looked up at him with milky eyes, evoking memories of another body that had floated years before in Wolf Lake.

Frazier/Roy ran and ran until the powerful body was as exhausted as the astral mind. Exhaustion was part of the reason Frazier didn't take his usual precaution of leaving the host body at a time of peril. Instead he let the body of the Indian instinctively carry him to a stone quarry where Roy had been in the habit of sleeping on fair nights. The sun, out now and hot following the rain, drew steam from the raw, wet granite. Frazier/Roy lay down in the shade of a Caterpillar earth mover.

The anguish in the deposed mind of the Indian over the little girl's death prevented Frazier from fully relaxing to restore his energies. That disturbance also saved him from oblivion.

The operator of the earth mover returned from his lunch break and climbed into the saddle with not the faintest hint that anyone might have entered the quarry and approached his machine while he was away. He started the mighty engine.

The awareness for Frazier began with a heavy vibration of the earth under his head. He was instantly awake, but just in time to feel an explosive, bursting sensation that seemed to come from within him. With a mighty effort he sucked his astral self from the body of the Indian and left the poor stunted brain to be crushed to jelly and ground into the gravel under the tread of the Caterpillar.

The experience taught Frazier two things. He *could* feel pain, or something very much like it, when the host body was in dire jeopardy. And he was *not* invulnerable. He knew, he absolutely knew that had he remained in the Indian's mind a moment longer he would have been squashed out of existence like one of those frogs under a boot. Never again, he vowed, would he be caught off guard like that.

But by now he was ready to get to his real task. He knew the extent and the limits of his power, and he was anxious to take his revenge on the three people who had stolen his life.

Strong-minded people, each of them; Frazier knew it would be too difficult for him to enter and control them in their own surroundings, far from Wolf River. But if he could get them back here, all at the same time, he would deal with them where his power was greatest.

Payback time.

CHAPTER 20

LINDY

The dining room at the Wolf River Inn lay beyond a double doorway leading from the lobby. A menu under a glassed frame was affixed to the wall. From the curled edges of the card, it appeared not to have been changed for many weeks.

Lindy walked over and took a look into the room.

The appearance of the dining room was not encouraging. The lighting was uneven—too dim in the corners and overbright in the center of the room. The white plaster of the beamed ceiling was laced with cracks. Brownish stains were visible in the corners.

A pair of young waitresses, one blond, one a redhead, gossiped near the cash register. Probably high school girls, Lindy thought. Picking up spending money with summer jobs.

The scattering of early diners ate silently, without enthusiasm.

The overall impression of the dining room added to Lindy's gloom. It was not a place to forget her troubles. Still, she had to eat somewhere, and she had seen nothing better on her quick tour of Main Street. She decided one meal in the mausoleum wouldn't kill her.

After the message brought to her at the bar by old Jed of the brown teeth, she had gone to her room, grabbed her bag, and started to leave. She could be back in Milwaukee in three hours and on the first flight back to L.A.

The idea was appealing. She wanted to go, she started to go, but finally she couldn't. The threat to Nicole in the messages that had brought her here was very much alive in her mind. Now there was the nagging sense of being watched, the uneasy feeling of business unfinished.

She turned on the television to whatever channel the last person had left it on, went into the bathroom, and showered with the door open. That way she could fill at least part of her mind with the whoops of game show contestants and the manic patter of the emcee.

She lathered her body as thoroughly as was possible with the tiny hotel soap, stretching the shower time to postpone going downstairs to the gloomy dining room. When the little soap was down to a sliver, she stepped out to dry herself with the rough towel.

She caught sight of her nude body in the bathroom mirror, and some buried memory made her walk out and check to be sure the heavy curtains were drawn over the window that looked out on Main Street.

The room was empty, of course, and the curtains were tightly drawn. Nevertheless, Lindy seemed to feel eyes crawling over her flesh. She dressed quickly and sat down before the mirror to apply her makeup.

Was this, she wondered, where she had been headed during the past twenty tears? All of that just to come back home to Wolf River?

No, not home, she corrected herself. Not anymore. Not since the terrible Halloween Ball. She had no one here anymore. Her father lived in Madison now, presumably comfortable in the work he did for the legislature. The last

Lindy had heard, Judge Grant was sharing a suburban home there with his young wife. Lindy's relationship with the new Mrs. Grant had started out cool, and it had not warmed noticeably in correspondence over the years. It had been a vast relief for Lindy in the fall of 1968 to move out of the house where she no longer felt she belonged.

Lindy's grades and the judge's political connections had got her into Northwestern's prestigious drama school after her graduation. There she showed enough promise in school productions to take seriously an acting teacher's recommendation that she try to make it professionally in New York. The fact that the teacher was sleeping with her at the time didn't seem to Lindy to be a factor in his praise until much later.

Lindy found breaking into the New York theater scene to be a far cry from trying out for college productions. She stuck it out, however, for three years until she finally understood that her talent was not large enough for her to compete in the major acting leagues.

Although her career never got off the ground, two things happened to Lindy in New York that determined the course of the rest of her life.

The first thing was when, with much time on her hands between auditions, she started to write. Little dialogue scenes at first. Then playlets. Character sketches, anecdotes, vignettes, short stories. She eventually sold a little 1,500-worder to *Woman's Day* and knew the thrill of being paid for something created whole from her own mind.

The second thing was that she moved in with a handsome young actor named Barry Paul. Barry had done some Off-Off Broadway and received a good review in the *Village Voice*. Lindy enjoyed his company, but she was not in love with him, nor he with her.

All the same, her Midwest roots made her expect that when she told him about the pregnancy he would "do the right thing." What he actually did was give her fifty dollars to use toward an abortion and move out. The last she heard of Barry, he was sharing a loft with two male dancers from *Grease*.

Lindy thought about getting an abortion, but only briefly. She wrote to her father, who offered to let her come and live with him and his new wife, or to send her money to sustain her in New York until the birth of the child. She could sense his relief when she chose the second alternative.

Nicole was born on a blustery day in March at the Columbia-Presbyterian Medical Center. Lindy had finally made it to Broadway.

As soon as the little girl was able to travel, mother and daughter flew to California, where the climate was gentler and raising a child was less hectic. Over the years Lindy had wondered sometimes what her life might have been like if she had stayed in New York. Or if she had accepted her father's halfhearted invitation and returned to the Middle West to have her child.

But it was useless speculating about the World of If. Lindy had made her choice, and on the whole she was happy with it. . . .

She tried again to call Brendan Jordan in Los Angeles. This time the line was too full of static for her to hear if any connection was made on the other end. Wolf River, she decided, could use an overhaul of its long-distance telephone system.

She snapped off the television set, gave herself a last look in the mirror, and headed for the dining room.

ROMAN

Some sonofabitch was out to get him.

Roman did not know who was after him or why, but he sure as hell knew he was a target. Roman was no coward, but how the hell could he fight something he couldn't see?

Whoever or whatever was after him was for sure no

patsy. Roman well remembered the flaming rash on his private parts for which there was no medical explanation. And the invitation back to Wolf River, the weird behavior of his mother-in-law, the message that didn't belong on the prescription blank, and now the voice on the telephone were not the work of any punk. But whoever it was, Roman vowed he would find the sonofabitch and make him sorry as hell that he'd started fucking around with Roman Dixon.

In the meantime, he was apparently stuck back here in Wolf River for at least another day. The prospect did not make him happy. When he left twenty years before, he thought he had left for good.

After the business at the lake that terrible Halloween, nothing seemed to go right for Roman Dixon. Nobody had actually ever connected him with what happened, not really; but there were whispers. Lots of them. Some of them heard by Roman's father.

Howard Dixon didn't say anything to his son, not about Frazier Nunley and the lake, but from that day on their relationship changed. The old man started drinking more heavily and lapsing into sullen silences from the time he got home to the time the family went to bed. At night Roman could hear low, ugly arguments from his parents' bedroom. Before, they used to yell at each other sometimes but then it was over and they'd be all kissy-face again. Not anymore. The atmosphere at home grew heavy with unspoken anger.

Things were different at school, too. He was still the Star, but the other kids acted like they didn't want to get too close to him. Like he had some kind of disease. Little groups would stop talking as he approached. His friends suddenly had other pressing things to do and even turned down rides in his Chevy. Lindy Grant went totally cold and acted as if they'd never done it that night in the cabin. Alec McDowell still came sucking around, but he was the last one Roman wanted to hang out with after the Frazier business.

About two weeks after the thing happened at the lake, Roman made some little mistake at home like losing one of his father's tools. It was all the old man was waiting for. He started screaming at Roman and pounding him with his fists, and didn't stop until he had beat the shit out of the boy. Howard Dixon had not struck his son since Roman was eleven, and then it was just a regular spanking with his belt. This time the old man, ugly drunk, battered the boy unmercifully as he would have another man.

Roman did not defend himself, even when every instinct cried out for him to hit him back. He knew he could take the old man, but in his heart he knew the punishment was just. He was being beaten not for misplacing some stupid tool, but for killing Frazier Nunley. The irony was that he could hurt his father more by taking his blows than he would have by fighting back.

Finally Howard Dixon stopped hitting him. He stepped back, breathing hard, and looked at his son's bloodied face. Roman could still hear the tortured groan that rumbled deep in his father's chest. There was a moment when Roman thought the old man was going to take him in his arms, but he just turned and walked away. They never again exchanged more than a dozen words at a time.

After that things just got worse. In the Thanksgiving Day game with Pulaski, Roman took one bad step avoiding a tackler and heard something pop in his knee. A second later he felt the pain. A couple of linemen helped him off the field to the cheers of the fans—the last cheers he was ever to hear. The next Friday he tried to play but couldn't accelerate, couldn't cut, couldn't keep up with the slowest of his blockers.

The college scouts vanished overnight. There were no scholarship offers from the big colleges. Not much interest even from the small schools. Roman did get a call from Northern Michigan, but his scholarship there was contingent on his making the team. He couldn't do it, and dropped out to be drafted after a frustrating failure in practice.

In the years since he went into the Army, mustered out at Fort Lewis, and settled in Seattle, Roman had lost contact with his parents. The letters from his mother stopped when she divorced his father three years after Roman left home. She had remarried and moved to Florida. Howard Dixon stayed on in Wolf River. Roman had visited him twice, and that was plenty. The old man's drinking finally cost him his job at Allis Chalmers, and the last Roman heard he was living in some flophouse on the South Side. . . .

Remembering Wolf River and what it had done to him and his parents was depressing. Roman took a last pull on his bottle of Jack Daniel's and headed out of the room to get something to eat.

ALEC

The room they gave him at the Wolf River Inn was faded and depressing. It smelled of pine oil disinfectant. And now his stomach was bothering him. The old ulcer that had been dormant in recent years was making itself felt in a persistent prodding just below his breastbone. Alec belched and made a face at the sour taste.

It was this damn town and what it meant to him that was doing it. The circumstances under which he was here now were hardly reassuring. The message with its reference to "clown" and "monkey" could only refer to that long-ago fiasco on the lake that he had worked for years to put out of his mind. No point in denying it any longer. Somebody had brought him here to account for what had happened to Frazier Nunley.

But could *somebody* speak to him through a gypsy hag

in Manhattan? Make his tongue swell up like an overripe *blutwurst*? Something very bad was going on here.

Alec's instinct, as it had been all his life when real danger threatened, was to flee. Pack up and get the hell out of here. Right now. But what if he did that and his tongue blew up in his mouth and finally choked him? No, this time he would have to stay and see it out to the end.

More immediately, he would have to put something soothing in his burning stomach.

The ulcer had begun sometime in that last year of high school. First there was the terrible fear that he would be caught and punished for his part in what had happened to the Nunley kid. Every time the phone rang or there was a knock at the door Alec's nerves contracted into tiny knots.

His parents became unusually silent around him. His father continued to go to work every day at the *Chronicle*, but the old joy in his job was gone. Alec's lovely mother, with whom he had always had a special close relationship, became cold and distant. He was never asked to help out at the paper anymore.

And at school his life changed drastically. Roman Dixon was having problems of his own and brushed off Alec's attempts to renew their relationship. The other kids, who had pretended to accept him because he was the Friend of the Star, immediately dumped him. Alone and frightened, Alec began to wish ardently for the end of the school year so he could get the hell away from there.

Graduation came at last. There was not much in the way of a celebration for this ill-favored Class of '67, but Alec McDowell found himself even more isolated than most. He walked across the stage and received his diploma to no applause. He walked alone off the stage and out of Wolf River forever. Or so he thought.

His grades were good enough to get him into the University of Missouri, which he chose for their excellent school of journalism. He became editor of the school paper in his senior year, but he discovered his real talent was for campus politics. Not in personally running for office, but steering others to election. He was pleased to see himself as a "power behind the throne," and decided then that that was what he would eventually do with his life.

Ironically, in the same year Alec graduated from Missouri with a B.A. in journalism, the Wolf River *Chronicle* shut down forever. Not long after that, Alec's father went out into their garage, spread a painter's drop cloth over the floor, put the muzzle of a deer rifle into his mouth, and blew his brains all over the ceiling.

Alec went home to Wolf River for the funeral. It was the last time he had been back.

His mother moved away to Arizona less than a year after Phelan's suicide. She got a job there as assistant to the editor-publisher of a desert weekly, and there she stayed for the next ten years.

During those years Alec got Christmas cards and an occasional letter from his mother. The letters were cordial and newsy, but not intimate. There was never an invitation for him to visit. He never suggested it. Then, six years ago, Trudy McDowell died quietly in her sleep.

His mother had expressed a wish to be buried beside her husband. Alec made the arrangements without having to personally return to Wolf River.

With no ties left in the town, Alec never expected to be back here. Certainly not to commemorate the darkest year of his life. Yet here he was, summoned by persons unknown, ulcer hurting, and, let's admit it, scared.

He pushed away thoughts of the past and left his room. He rode down alone in the elevator, crossed the deserted lobby, walked into the dining room, and froze.

CHAPTER 21

When Lindy entered the dining room, the only other customers were a young couple at one of the far tables and a family of four. No one looked up when she came in. The couple was too engrossed in each other, and the family too busy arguing about the menu.

"Just one of you?" the hostess said. She wore a black sheath gown that was at least a size too small. Her hair was frizzed out in an approximation of the style affected by some of the younger movie stars.

"Right," Lindy told her. "One."

The hostess signaled to the blond waitress who was still gossiping with her redheaded friend. With some reluctance she picked up a menu from a stack by the cash register and came over. She had the kind of face that should have been chewing gum, though as far as Lindy could tell she was not. Thank God for small favors, she thought.

The waitress led the way to a table equidistant between the young couple and the fighting family.

"Is this okay?"

"Fine."

Lindy sat down and opened the menu. At least the prices

were reasonable. This unplanned trip would really screw up her budget. A busboy appeared and deposited a glass of ice water and a basket of bread sticks.

The busboy vanished and the waitress took his place. "Would you like something from the bar?"

"I don't think so." She could still feel the drinks she'd had earlier.

The waitress poised a ballpoint pen over her order pad. Lindy waited for her to lick the point, and was vaguely disappointed when she didn't.

"How's the stuffed trout?"

"It's really good," the girl said earnestly. "Fresh every day right out of the lake."

"I'll have that."

"You want soup or salad?"

"Green salad. Oil-and-vinegar dressing."

"Wine?"

"No, thanks. I'll have coffee later."

The girl went away. Lindy took a sip from the glass of ice water. She glanced over at the arguing family. There was a comfortable familiarity about their squabbling that said there was nothing seriously wrong there. On the other side of her the young couple leaned close to each other, laughing softly together. Lindy envied all of them.

A man came in and was greeted by the hostess. He had beefy shoulders and the florid face of a serious drinker. Good hair and even teeth. Probably as a young man he had been—

The glass slipped from Lindy's grasp and bounced on the carpeted floor, splashing ice water over her shoes.

Roman Dixon.

Twenty years older, heavier, and with the mark of defeat on him that he'd not had before. But unquestionably Roman.

He saw her. His mouth dropped open, and he ignored what the hostess was saying. He came toward her, the hostess following uncertainly.

"It's Lindy Grant, isn't it?"

He put out a hand, and she took it. There was a strength in the hand, but it was uncallused. Soft.

"Hello, Roman."

The hostess looked from one to the other.

"You two know each other, then?"

"We're old friends," Roman said. To Lindy: "Okay if I sit with you?"

"Sure, there's plenty of room."

The busboy hustled over with another place setting. Roman ordered Jack Daniel's with a splash, and said give him a few minutes before they talked to him about food.

He leaned back and let his eyes range over Lindy. "So . . . you're looking great."

"You too."

"Where you living now?"

"California."

"No kidding. I'm up in Seattle. Got a chain of sporting goods stores up there."

"Good for you."

The conversation continued in this vein for about five minutes, touching on how they were doing and how long since they'd been back to Wolf River and the old town sure had changed. Lindy was reminded of the old song "The Babbit and the Bromide" as done by Fred Astaire and Gene Kelly in some movie whose title she couldn't remember.

Then the small talk died. They looked at each other with a touch of guilt two decades old.

Roman took a deep pull from his drink. "It doesn't look like this is going to be much of a class reunion."

"It isn't a reunion at all, is it, Roman?"

He took a few seconds before answering. "No, I don't suppose it is." He looked around at the all-but-empty dining room. "But what the hell *is* it?"

"I think we're afraid to guess."

Lindy saw the other man enter the dining room and look

around. He wore an expensive tweed jacket and tailored slacks, but looked frail despite the clothes. When he saw her and Roman he froze. His hair was thinner and his face more pinched, but she knew him. There was no mistaking the pointed, foxy look, or the quick little hand movements.

Alec McDowell.

The hostess brought Alec over and seated him with a cheerful smile. "Well, this table's beginning to look like old home week."

She looked around, but when she got no answering smiles she left quickly.

The men got their food orders out of the way—prime rib rare for Roman, consommé, cottage cheese salad, and dry toast for Alec. Roman ordered another drink.

The waitress left them, and the silence grew heavy.

Alec finally spoke. "I guess we might as well talk about it."

There was silence for a moment. Roman frowned and said, "Talk about what?"

"What we're all wondering," Alec said. "Why we're here. Who brought us."

"All right," Lindy said. "I'll go first. I'm here because I had no choice."

She told them about the messages, the strange voice speaking through Nicole, and the unnatural blemish that had bloomed on her daughter's face, with the threat of worse if she didn't return to Wolf River on the specified day. All she left out was the frightening hallucination in bed the night before.

"I'll be damned," Roman said. "That's the kind of stuff that happened to me, too."

He spoke defiantly, but Lindy could sense the fear underlying his words as he told of the encounter with his mother-in-law. Without being specific, he said some unspecified physical thing that was done to him. Finally there was the doctor's prescription with the ominous message.

"Similar story with me," Alec said. He told them about the voice from the cleaning woman, the strange gypsy, the messages, and the tongue problem. He hesitated for a moment, then said, "Did your messages mention the clown?"

The others nodded.

Roman drained his Jack Daniel's and signaled for another. "There's only one thing it can be," he said huskily. "Somebody knows about Frazier."

"That doesn't make sense," Lindy said.

"What else does a clown mean to the three of us?"

"What if somebody did know?" Alec said. "Why would he wait twenty years to do anything about it?"

"How do I know?" Roman said belligerently. "Maybe he just found out."

Alec wrinkled his nose as the waitress placed another drink in front of Roman. "Maybe you ought to go a little easy on that."

Roman's jaw tightened. "What the hell is that supposed to mean?"

"Just that we've got some serious talking to do here, and we ought to keep our heads clear."

"My head's plenty clear," Roman said. "I don't know about yours."

"Cut it out," Lindy said. "I haven't got time to sit here and listen to you two argue."

"So what's your opinion?" Roman asked, sulking.

"First, I don't think anybody just found out about Frazier, and I don't think anybody waited twenty years to get to us either."

"What else can it be?"

"I don't know," Lindy admitted. "But if you can tell me how somebody could make my daughter's face break out, swell up Alec's tongue, and do whatever it was he did to you, I'll be willing to listen."

No one talked at the table for several minutes. Roman ate some of his dinner and ordered another drink, watching Alec closely. Alec tasted his consommé and salad, drank a little milk, and looked back at Roman.

Lindy reflected that she was sitting with the two men she had spent the most important year of her life with, and she really didn't know them at all.

The quiet couple in the corner got up and left, walking close together. The family of four began arguing about dessert.

Roman shivered. "You'd think they'd put some heat in here."

"Heat?" Alec said. "In July? In Wisconsin?"

Roman looked over his shoulder, then turned back to scowl at Alec. "Must have been a draft for a minute there."

Alec jumped up, yanked his chair out from the table, and stared at the padded back.

"What's wrong?" Lindy asked.

Alec ran his hand over the padded leather of the chair back. "It felt like something in the chair was jabbing my neck."

"It's all that milk you're drinking," Roman said. "When did you get on that stuff anyway?"

"At least I'm not rotting out my liver."

"God, will you two cut it out?" Lindy said. "We've got to get our acts together here and figure out what's going on."

"And what we're going to do about it," Alec said, sitting back down gingerly.

"I'm getting the hell out of here first thing in the morning is what I'm doing about it," Roman said.

Lindy stared at him. "Do you think he'll let you do that? Just walk away after all the elaborate arrangements he made for getting us here?"

"Who do you mean, 'he'?" Roman signaled to the waitress and pointed to his empty glass.

Alec spoke up suddenly. "All right, somebody's got to say it. Are we talking about a ghost?"

Roman waved a hand disgustedly. "Be serious, for Christ sake."

Alec glared at him.

"No, it's worth thinking about," Lindy said. "Things have happened to all of us that there isn't any logical explanation for."

"But *ghosts*? Give me a break."

"The first time it occurred to me I thought it was crazy too," Lindy said. "Ghosts are not my style. But maybe this isn't that kind of ghost. Maybe it's something created in our own minds."

"What are you talking about?" Roman said.

"How does conscience grab you?"

The waitress came over with Roman's drink. Out of habit he gave the girl a wink and patted her on the fanny. The others were silent while he took a thirsty swallow.

He put the glass down. "Are you saying that after twenty years the three of us, in different parts of the country, all of a sudden get conscience-stricken about something that wasn't really our fault to begin with?"

"Not our fault?" Lindy repeated.

Roman backed off. "Well, not really."

"Whose fault was it, then?"

"Nobody's. It was an accident. Hell, you talk like it was something really *bad*."

"Wasn't it?" Alec said, staring at his cottage cheese. "The kid died."

"Look, what did we do, really? It was a prank, that's all. Kids do worse than that every day. It wasn't our fault Frazier fell out of the boat."

"We didn't tell anybody afterwards," Lindy said.

"We got scared, that's all. Hell, they couldn't have done much to us if they'd caught us."

"Maybe they should have caught us," Lindy said. "Maybe we should have turned ourselves in. We could have taken the punishment, whatever it was, and the debt would have been paid."

"I still don't see that we owe any kind of a debt," Roman said. "What happened happened. Anyway, it wasn't my idea. All I wanted to do was shake the kid up a little for peeking in your window."

"Just a minute," Alec cut in. "Are you saying I'm the one to blame for what happened?"

"I'm not saying anything. But it *was* you who thought up the whole dumb idea—dress him up funny and leave him out in the boat to make a fool of himself."

"You sure didn't try to talk me out of it. In fact, who provided the boat? Who brought the rope we used to tie his hands?"

Roman gripped the edge of the table and leaned toward Alec. "You've suddenly got an awful good memory about something that happened twenty years ago."

"You bet I have. And if you tell me you don't remember everything about it, you're a liar."

Roman started to rise. "Goddamn it, I'm not gonna take—"

Lindy hit the table with the flat of her hand. "Stop it!"

The men looked at her in surprise. Roman lowered himself back into the chair.

"Arguing among ourselves isn't going to do any good," she said.

"I don't like being called a liar," Roman grumbled.

"Okay, forget it," Alec said. "I'm upset."

"We're all upset," Lindy said. "Now let's try to calm down and discuss rationally what we're going to do."

"Pretty surely something is going to happen tomorrow," Alec said. "Whoever . . . whatever is behind this business made the date quite definite."

"So what are we going to do, just wait and let it happen?" Roman asked.

"We're ready to hear suggestions, if you've got any," Lindy told him.

They stopped talking at the approach of the waitress. She came across the dining room in a strange stiff-legged walk, carrying something before her in both hands. She reached the table, stopped, and smiled down at them. It was a smile without any warmth. A smile that did not belong on the innocent face of the girl. She held out the covered soup tureen she carried like an offering.

"A classmate of yours sends this over to you," she said. Her voice had an unearthly synthesized quality.

"What classmate?" Roman said, looking around. The other two stared at the unblinking waitress.

"He had to leave. He said you should enjoy the reunion."

She placed the tureen in the center of the table. Lindy, Alec, and Roman looked at each other. Finally Lindy reached out, grasped the handle, and raised the lid.

The waitress screamed.

She staggered back, both hands holding her head. Roman jumped up and caught her as she was about to fall.

"Hey, you all right?"

"I don't know. I had a dizzy spell or something." She blinked several times and rubbed her eyes. "Thanks, I think I'm okay now." She looked down at the contents of the tureen.

"What the heck is it, anyway?"

The tureen was filled with murky water. Floating face-down in the center was a small plastic doll. The doll was dressed in a clown suit.

THE FLOATER

From a cobwebby corner high up on the beamed ceiling he watched the scene below, pleased with the commotion he had caused at the table. He had probed each of their minds, gently, gently, and found the two men would be easy to enter here where his power was greatest. He had given Roman a chill, and Alec a twinge in the back. Just a sample. A very small sample of what was coming to them. The waitress had been easy. A perfect messenger to deliver his "gift."

Lindy was something else. Her mind was stronger in its way then the men. Difficult to enter and control. Difficult, but not impossible. He had managed it deeply enough to give her the hallucination on her last night in California. She would not escape. None of them would. Not now. Not after all the years of waiting and planning.

Lindy looked up from the floating clown at the faces of the others. From their expressions she knew Roman and Alec felt it too. A terrible, inexplicable sense of dread. The feeling that none of them was ever going to leave Wolf River.

CHAPTER 22

The Floater could sense the fear in the three of them as they left the dining room. It surrounded them and clung to them like a cold mist. It followed them across the lobby and to the elevator.

Good. The more afraid they were, the better. Before he was finished with them, they might even know a level of fear that approached the unspeakable terror of sinking under the water, hands bound, unable to do anything, knowing you are going to die.

He rode with them in the elevator up to the fourth floor and floated in the hallway as they said their awkward, nervous good-nights. He watched them enter their rooms and climb anxiously into their separate beds.

Will you dream tonight, Lindy? Dream of your daughter's face and what it might look like when you return?

What's wrong, Roman? No young girl to take to bed with you tonight? The waitress downstairs—she was about the age you like them. She seemed available, too. What's that? You can't get it up? Too bad, lover. Too, too bad.

And you, clever Alec, how will you talk your way out

of this? Whose back will you ride on? There's no one to carry you now.

The Floater let the elements take him then and guide him gently out through the roof of the Wolf River Inn. Up and over the rooftops of the town he flew. Below him the people lived out their unimportant little lives. Sleeping now at the end of one boring day, preparing to wake tomorrow to a day just like it. Miserable, boring little people. How bitterly the Floater envied them.

Only a few cars moved on the streets. Most of the houses were already dark. Faint lights glowed in a few homes where insomniacs watched late-night television. Wolf River was an early-to-bed town. Nothing ever happened here. That's what the young people said. The Floater laughed, a silent, spectral laugh that held no humor. Little did they know.

For twenty years he had planned for this night, and for tomorrow. Practicing, practicing, perfecting his skills. Working constantly to increase his psychic strength, like a bodybuilder with his weights. All this work was about to pay off. The triumphs, the failures, the glorious discoveries, the unavoidable mistakes, had come at last to fruition.

The three people who lay uneasily now in their hotel beds had enjoyed their moment. They had spent their years of normal existence. They had lived their lives.

Now it was his turn.

Now it was payback time.

It was just a month ago that Frazier Nunley, or what was left of him—the part that floated—felt ready at last to exact his revenge. He had the strength now, and the knowledge to do what he had to do.

Locating the three people was the first step, and the easiest. All records and files were open to the Floater. Best of all, he discovered, were computers. In the years since his drowning, the electronic brains had become ubiquitous, not only in business but in homes. With the joy of discovery, Frazier had found how easily his astral mind could blend with the microchips and tiny circuits that powered the machines.

In his short lifetime Frazier's scientific knowledge had far exceeded that of his peers and most of the adults with whom he came in contact. Ever curious, he had mastered the principles of digital and analog computerese while others still struggled with algebra. His knowledge in life made it easier for him in his disembodied state to essentially become one with the machines. It took only a brief sortie into the supposedly sealed files of the giant credit reference companies to find out all he wanted to know.

Having located the three, the next step was getting to them. Timeless travel was one of the early skills he had perfected. Even as he lay on his boyhood bed and projected his other self out and away, he found he could cover limitless distances with no measurable time lapse.

Now he had only to psychically place himself in Los Angeles, and there he was, in the Hollywood Hills, just outside the little house where Lindy Grant lived with her daughter.

It was impossible not to relate the moment to a time long ago in another world when he had floated avidly outside the young Lindy Grant's window and observed her at forbidden acts. There was no emotion now in the spectral presence of Frazier Nunley. No feeling resembling nostalgia. All that remained, all that kept him from raging madness was the terrible gnawing ache for revenge.

It did not take Frazier long to sense the vibrations of the little house where Lindy Grant lived. Nicole, the daughter, was the main focus of Lindy's life. There was a man involved somehow, but he was unimportant. It would be through the daughter that he could touch Lindy most deeply.

Frazier did probe, gently and tentatively, at Lindy's mind, just to test her susceptibility. He was not yet ready to fully enter the minds of his principals. He found Lindy to be tough and resourceful. The Floater was far from home, and his powers at this distance were limited. He moved away from Lindy to concentrate on an easier target—the daughter.

Slipping into the girl's mind was easy. Frazier accomplished it the first time with minimum effort while the girl and Lindy were eating dinner. Nicole's shallow little mind was involved in some meaningless daydream about a teenage movie idol, and Frazier had simply gone in and pushed her aside.

Once inside her head, Frazier found Nicole a thoroughly objectionable child. Self-centered and heedless of the feelings of others, she went her mindless way, accepting the gifts of nature in the beauty of her face and her body as no more than her due. She was, Frazier noted, much the way her mother had been when he had known her. Maybe that was being unfair, but "fair" no longer had meaning for the Floater.

Once inside Nicole, he kept his head down for several minutes, concentrating on the feel of the silverware and the taste of food. It was always a heady experience to enter a living body and enjoy the corporeal senses, but it was also draining on his psychic energies. Frazier knew he must not spend too much time here if he wanted to deliver his message to all three of his people.

He raised Nicole's head and looked across the table at Lindy, studying her closely for the first time. This was the girl, grown-up, who had seemed so desirable and unattainable to him twenty years ago. There was no desire in him now.

Lindy was still attractive. Exceptionally so. But no emotion survived in the Floater, save one. As he regarded the woman who had hurt him so grievously, who had stolen his life from him, she looked up suddenly.

The face of Nicole must have mirrored his thoughts, because Lindy gave a start and spilled wine from the glass she was holding. Not yet ready for a confrontation, Frazier slipped out of the girl's mind as swiftly and easily as he had entered. Lindy continued to look curiously at her daughter, but the girl's normal vacuous expression was back, and the moment was past.

Frazier let a week go by before making his next move. Now that he knew he had the power, he wanted to savor his triumph. To draw it out.

This time the mind of the idiotic child was thoroughly engrossed in what she was doing to a pair of denim pants. Frazier entered her and put her tongue and vocal cords to use.

''Lindy!''

The sound that came out was nothing like the girl's own whining voice, and Lindy had whirled from the sink where she was washing dishes.

''It's payback time.''

That was enough, the Floater decided, for this time. The look on Lindy's face had the beginnings of an anxiety that, before he was through, Frazier would nurse into mind-numbing terror. He left the mind of Lindy's daughter and moved on to the next of the three.

Delivering the message to Roman Dixon had been even easier. The instrument Frazier chose was an old woman whose mind was largely gone anyway. It was not pleasant going into her head—like being in a closed room with something that was decaying. But it would serve his purpose.

''Roman!'' Again the voice came out harsh and gravelly, but the name was clear.

So clear that Roman looked up from the magazine he was reading as though he'd been shot.

''It's payback time.'' Almost a growl. Frazier forced the tired old facial muscles of the aged woman into an

expression Roman could not possibly mistake, then he left. Again, trouble well begun.

The mind of the young Puerto Rican woman he chose as the messenger for Alec McDowell was a much more pleasant place. Her thoughts were simple and sad: she was tired, her boyfriend was fucking her neighbor across the hall, her baby had a persistent cough. None of these mundane problems was of any importance to Frazier; he merely noted them in passing as he pushed the young woman's mind aside and took its place.

"Alec!"

So unaccustomed was he to being spoken to by a member of the maintenance crew that Alec could not believe where the voice had come from. Frazier gave him a minute to peer around the room, looking for some other source, before he continued.

"It's payback time."

"What did you say?" Alec managed, finally understanding that the harsh voice had come from the Puerto Rican.

Frazier spread the woman's lips into a parody of a smile before he left, giving Alec a glimpse of the hatred that had built over twenty years. Then he slipped out of her head, and the young woman's face went slack.

With these initial contacts made, the next task for Frazier was to get the three of them back to Wolf River. Back where the balance of power would shift to him. The idea of a class reunion afforded him grim amusement. The chances that anyone would want to return to celebrate the anniversary of that ill-starred class were remote at best. The likelihood of these three even considering such a thing was nil. Ah, but there were ways to manipulate people in direct opposition to their will. There were ways.

Frazier chose a woman employed at the Wolf River post office to write and mail the invitations. He caught her at the end of the day when she was tired and preoccupied with thoughts of her coming vacation. It took considerable exertion to maneuver the woman's hand through the three short messages, and to address the three envelopes, but Frazier was fired with his mission of bringing the three people closer to him. Here in Wolf River his energies were at their peak, and he was able to complete sending out the invitations in an hour.

Afterwards the woman was troubled by her inability to remember the last hour of her shift. And for some weeks she was plagued by headaches. These things Frazier Nunley neither knew nor cared about. He had but one purpose, and every ounce of his concentration was given over to achieving it.

Revenge.

He knew, of course, that the invitations alone would not bring these people back. They would read them, wonder about them, and probably throw them away. But they would not forget. Lindy, Roman, and Alec would now have one more thing to disturb their sleep.

Frazier was by then approaching the fulfillment of his plans, but still he was in no hurry. Death by drowning took an awfully long time. The Floater would not let his three people get off quickly.

Back to Los Angeles then, and once again into the mind of Lindy's daughter, Nicole. Frazier had learned that once he had entered someone's mind, the next time it was easier. Rather like leaving the door unlocked for reentry. Or—and the astral Frazier Nunley appreciated the analogy—once you had possessed someone sexually, you knew you could do it again. It was an experience Frazier had never had in the flesh, so he had to content himself with the psychic equivalent.

This time he entered when Nicole was sleeping. Easy. The girl stirred slightly, but did not waken.

Frazier didn't need her entire mind, so it was unnecessary to suppress Nicole's intellect. He noted with contempt her silly dreams of clothes and boys and the beach, and he brushed on past. The Floater simply made a small space for himself in the area he wanted, like slipping unseen into a tiny corner of a cluttered room.

He would need to spend only a short time in Nicole. Just long enough to plant the psychological seed. It would be his first practical use of the power he had discovered when he shattered old Henry Ulbricht's arthritic fingers.

He planned nothing so drastic with Nicole; just a little hurt that would get her attention. And Lindy's. There would be time for the real pain later.

Once in the girl's mind, Frazier focused his fierce psychic concentration on one tiny patch of skin on the girl's pert little nose, just where it flared over the nostril.

Pimple, he thought. *Ugly, swollen pimple.*

After a moment he was gratified to feel, through the girl's sleep-dulled senses, a tightening of the flesh over the nose. Nicole mumbled something and reached up in her sleep to rub the spot with one hand.

Now grow. Grow slowly. But grow!

Lindy entered the girl's room then, and Frazier slipped out quickly as Nicole awoke. Only a faint reddening was visible on the side of her nose, but the thought was planted deep in the girl's subconscious, and Frazier well understood the power of the subconscious to affect the physical. By the end of this day it would be a ripe, disfiguring boil. Had he possessed a voice, the spectral Frazier Nunley would have laughed in crazy triumph at this confirmation of his power to hurt and disfigure. But he could not tarry to enjoy the eventual damage. He had other work to do.

With grim humor, Frazier hit the other two where they would feel it most. Roman, the boastful cocksman, he gave a rash in the genital area. The temptation was powerful to rot the bastard's dick off completely, but that would spoil the fun he was planning for later, when he had them all together.

For Alec, the talker, the choice was obvious. His tongue. As the Floater concentrated on the ugly hunk of muscle from the root to the tip, and started making it swell, he reveled in the knowledge of how easy it would be to choke off all the air to Alec's lungs. Let him know how it felt to struggle to the point where the brain bursts for just one more breath of air. That too could wait.

Now that each of the three had experienced a sample, a very small sample, of what he could do to them, it remained only to remind them where the Floater wanted them to be, and when.

Lindy's computer was a perfect device for delivering the message to her. The Floater watched her face as she read the summons that overrode whatever she typed in:

HELLO, LINDY.

WOLF RIVER INN.

SATURDAY, JULY 11.

BE THERE OR THE GIRL REALLY GETS HURT.

Before leaving it, Frazier jammed the computer, making it impossible to erase the glowing green message. Then, from a floating position just over the monitor screen, he enjoyed Lindy's confusion, watching it change slowly to comprehension and, finally, fear.

Good. There would be more to come.

A momentary entry into the mind of Roman's doctor was not difficult to achieve. The man was preoccupied with an impending increase in his malpractice insurance and was giving little attention to the minor complaints of his patient.

He moved the doctor's hand to spell out the message he wanted on the prescription blank. The doctor, without rereading it, handed the page to Roman, and for a moment Frazier thought the ignoramus was going to throw it away. But no, he read it. Frazier was especially pleased with the warning he had put in the last sentence:

I'll make you really *hurt down there.*

Roman almost seemed to *feel* the threatened pain. "Down there" was where he lived. He would show up.

Doing Alec was the one the Floater enjoyed most. It let him get into the old gypsy woman—simple enough with her brain rotting with disease. He had a chance to act, to be, for a few moments, a person again, however common.

The revulsion on Alec's face was Frazier's reward as he breathed the gypsy's foul breath at him and delivered the summons. He had to fight down an impulse to kiss Alec full on the mouth and let his recently afflicted tongue experience the taste of death and decay.

That too could come later.

The plan was in motion. The Floater had done his job well. Perhaps he would pay them each one more short visit just before they were to leave. Until then, he would rest.

CHAPTER 23

LINDY

She slept badly the first night back in Wolf River.

For one thing, the air conditioner had an annoying arhythmic *clunk* that grew louder as the night progressed. She tried turning the thing off, but the hot, airless night pressed down on her like a giant sweaty hand. She decided battling the *clunk* was better than suffocation.

Her dreams, when she did sleep, were not conducive to rest. They were filled with dark memories and floating clowns and a waitress who smiled with somebody else's face. When she awoke, the sheets of her bed were cold and wet, and clung unpleasantly to her body.

When she finally gave up on sleep, the travel alarm she had placed beside the bed read five minutes to seven. Lindy had an impulse to call California to see if Nicole was all right. Or to talk to Brendan. She rejected both ideas immediately. In the first place, it was still the middle of the night out there, and in the second, she really didn't have anything to say. If Nicole was not all right, her friend's parents had the number of the inn and they would get in touch with her. And Brendan would think she was crazy, scared by a plastic doll in a soup tureen.

She showered and dressed quickly, anxious to get out before she had to see Roman and Alec. Being with them made her feel unclean.

She hurried out through the empty lobby to the street. The day was overcast, with a heavy feeling to the air. Lindy walked down Main Street to the drab-looking Kountry Kitchen Kafe, which stood where Bonnie's Gift Shop used to be. A pair of weather-beaten men who looked like farmers were eating breakfast in silence at the counter. They gave Lindy a brief look and returned to their food. She took a stool at the far end and took the menu from the clamp attached to the napkin dispenser.

A waitress brought a glass of water and silverware. She was a fat peroxide blonde with a bitter curve to her mouth. Loose flaps of skin hung on her upper arms.

"Help you?"

"I think I'll just have a sweet roll and coffee. Is the orange juice fresh?"

"Frozen."

"Never mind, then."

Lindy looked up from the menu to see the waitress still looking at her.

"I know you," the woman said.

Lindy searched her memory. Nothing clicked. "I-I'm sorry, I don't think I—"

"Lindy Grant."

"That's right," she admitted.

"Jesus, you look just the same."

Unconsciously Lindy narrowed her eyes. Something about the way the woman tossed her head—a gesture too young for her . . . Good Lord!

"Merilee Lund!"

"That's me. Only it isn't Lund any more. It was Spielman for a while, then Gotschke for too long."

"Well, you look . . . fine."

"That's a crock. I know how I look. But *you.* Jesus, how do you do it?"

"Just metabolism, I guess." Lindy was embarrassed by the physical comparisons. To get off the subject she said, "So you've been married a couple of times?"

"To my everlasting sorrow. A salesman from Milwaukee the first time. Planned to start his own machine tool business. Went through all of his money, then all of mine, then went back to Milwaukee to live with his mother."

"Men can be bad news," Lindy said.

"Hell, Avery Spielman was an angel compared to my last ex. Joe Gotschke. From the Gotschkes out by Split Rock. Maybe you know them."

"I remember the name," Lindy lied.

"I'd like to forget it. Gave me three kids and half a dozen broken teeth. Then he ran off with an Indian squaw, and I never saw a nickel's worth of child support or anything else."

"Rough," Lindy said. She stole a peek at her watch.

Merilee caught the glance. "Oh, hey, I'm not doing my job. That was a donut and coffee?"

"Sweet roll. Cinnamon, if you have it."

"I think so."

She moved up the passageway behind the counter, and Lindy tried not to look at the broad rear end and the varicose veins visible beneath the short uniform skirt. There was no way she could relate this woman to the bouncy, supple-bodied cheerleader she remembered.

Merilee came back with the coffee and cinnamon roll. She placed them on the counter and leaned forward, braced on her fat elbows, obviously expecting more conversation.

"So who'd you marry?" Merilee asked. "Nobody from here, I guess."

"I haven't married anybody," Lindy said.

"Smart."

"I always thought maybe you and Todd Hartman might end up together."

Merilee snorted. "Not likely. You were the one he had the hots for. Last I heard he married some rich bitch from Chicago and went to Washington to be a financial adviser or some damn thing."

"How about that," Lindy said, knowing how witless the comment sounded, but not able to think of anything else to say.

"So what are you doing back here?"

"Just . . . a visit." She took a bite of the roll and burned her mouth on hot coffee to keep from having to say any more.

"Seen your dad yet?"

"My father? He's down in Madison."

"Not anymore. You did know he moved back here, didn't you?"

"Oh . . . yes. I meant to say he *was* in Madison. We haven't kept in real close touch."

Merilee looked at her with a peculiar smile. "I guess nobody does. Well, things change."

"Yes, they do." Lindy took a last swallow of her coffee and left the rest of the cinnamon roll. "Nice seeing you, Merilee." She pulled a bill from her wallet.

"You pay at the cashier," Merilee said.

Lindy smiled at her, walked to the front of the café, and paid. She debated about going back to leave a tip, but Merilee was still standing there watching her, so she decided not to. She was upset enough without hearing any more depressing news from her one-time best friend.

ROMAN

The lobby of the Wolf River Inn was empty when Roman came down at about nine o'clock. That was fine with him. He was in no mood to talk to anybody, least of all his ex-school chums. Christ, that dinner last night had been the pits. First, Lindy Grant acting like he was a piece of dog shit. Just as though he'd never made it with her. Then that little creep Alec McDowell giving him a temperance lecture. To top it off there was that toy clown in the bowl. He didn't try too hard to come up with an explanation for that one. The waitress must have done it.

A sick feeling of dread had followed him up in the elevator last night and got into bed with him between the cold sheets. He forced it back into a closed part of his mind now. All he wanted to think about was getting the hell out of Wolf River without delay.

He found the rental car where he'd left it out in the parking lot behind the inn. He decided to take it now and gas up, then come back here just long enough to throw his stuff in a suitcase and check the hell out. He got into the car and turned the key in the ignition.

Nothing happened.

"What the hell?"

Roman snapped the key angrily back and forth, with no response from the starter.

"Jesus H. Christ, that's all I need."

He tried the lights, the horn, the air conditioner fan. Nothing worked.

Dead battery. You'd think a big outfit like Hertz would make sure they put a good battery in their heaps before they rented them out.

He slammed the door and stomped back into the hotel. The desk clerk was talking to a girl in some kind of white uniform—beautician or manicurist or something. The clerk looked up reluctantly as Roman approached.

"You got a Hertz in this town?"

"Hurts?"

"Read my lips. Hertz. Rent-a-car. They got an office here?"

"If there is, it'll be in the phone book."

Roman spoke with sarcastic precision. "Right. Good thinking. So do you happen to have one? A phone book?"

The clerk pointed across the lobby. "Over there by the pay phones."

"Thanks a *lot*."

With his anger building, Roman flipped through the thin Wolf River telephone directory until he found the local Hertz number.

The phone rang nine times at the other end while Roman's knuckles whitened on the receiver.

"Hello," a woman's voice finally answered.

Roman scowled at the instrument. "Have I got the Hertz office?"

"You would have if it was open, but it's not."

"What do you mean not open?" Roman was shouting now.

"I mean Mr. Jacobs is home with strep throat, and there's nobody else here can run the place, and it won't do any good to yell at me, mister."

Roman swore and hung up. He marched back across the lobby to the registration desk. Struggling to keep his voice level, he said, "Would you know where I can find a mechanic? And don't tell me in the phone book."

"Well, it's Saturday, and it's kind of early."

Roman dug for his money clip and slipped out a five-dollar bill. "This is pretty important to me."

The clerk looked down at the five then back up at Roman. "Jim Dancey two blocks down Main Street at the Shell station does some mechanical work if it's not too big and he's not too busy. You could try him."

"All I need is a jump start. He ought to be able to handle that. Which way on Main Street?"

The clerk gave him directions, pocketed the five dollars, and returned his attention to the girl. Roman walked the two blocks muttering to himself.

At the Shell station he found Jim Dancey, a bald, overweight man in green coveralls. Roman explained the situation, and Dancey sent him back with a kid in a pickup truck.

The kid hooked up the jumper cables and spent ten minutes trying to start the Monte Carlo.

"There's nothin' wrong with your battery, mister," the kid said finally.

"Then why won't it start?"

"Beats me. Jim'll have to look at it. I just do jump starts and tire changes."

"Balls!"

Half an hour later, after having the Monte Carlo towed to Dancey's Shell station, Roman sat in his room at the Wolf River Inn with a glass of whiskey in his hand, staring at the telephone.

There were more calls he could make, but he was oddly reluctant to pick up the receiver. Along with his anger and frustration, Roman had a growing suspicion that he was not going to have an easy time getting out of Wolf River.

Off in the corner of the room, unseen and unheard, the Floater laughed.

ALEC

He heard Lindy's door open and close sometime after seven o'clock as he lay sleepless, staring at the crack of light that showed where the curtains did not quite meet over his window. When he was sure she was not coming back to her room, Alec got up and dressed. He had nothing to say to either her or Roman this morning. And there was something he wanted to do.

He found the place easily on the north edge of town, set away from he neighboring farms by a growth of poplar trees. Even as he walked up the brick steps of the Golden Glade Residential Care Home, Alec wondered if maybe this was a bad idea. He didn't really want to see this man; he was afraid of what he might learn. And yet if he went away from Wolf River, surely forever the next time, he would always wonder.

"I'd like to see Arthur Mischock," he told the pert white-haired lady at the reception desk.

"The chief? He doesn't get many visitors. You a relative?"

"No."

When she saw there would be no further explanation, the lady got businesslike. She ran a pink fingernail down a chart. "Let's see . . . he's had his breakfast, so you can go on up now if you want. He's in Room 214, right off the stairs."

Alec followed her directions, depressed by the old people with vacant stares who shuffled past or were wheeled through the halls by healthy young attendants.

Golden Glade. They always had such tranquil names. The retirement homes and convalescent homes where nobody ever retired and nobody got better. Society's dumpsters. There was only one crime society could not forgive; one illness medicine could not cure. They were both the same—growing old.

Alec climbed the stairs and hesitated for a moment outside Room 214, then knocked softly. There was a muffled reply from inside. He took that as an invitation and entered.

The room was pleasant enough, splashed with morning sunlight through the window that looked out on the poplars. The wallpaper was flowery and bright. The furniture, what there was of it, was in good repair, and it might not be a bad room to live in were it not for the medicinal smell.

The man propped up in the hospital bed bore little resemblance to the bearish chief of police who used to intimidate suspects with his sheer bulk. This man was shrunken and dried. The right half of his grayed-out face hung loose. His right arm was shriveled and folded into his body.

"Hello, Chief," Alec said, trying not to look shocked at the man's appearance.

"H'lo, McDowell." The voice was still strong, although slurred by the paralysis of half the mouth.

"You know me?"

"Sure. I remember you. Not likely to forget. How long ago was it, ten years?"

"More like twenty."

"Whatever. Why'd you come back?"

"I was sent for."

"Who'd do that?"

"I don't know. I thought maybe you could tell me."

"Nope. Wasn't me, I can tell you that much. Had my way I'd never seen you again. Or the other two either. Heard all three of you are back in town."

"You don't miss much."

"Word gets around in a town like this. You oughta know that."

Alec's eyes ranged over the small room that contained the pitiful few relics of a man's life. A police badge mounted on velvet. A framed citation from some civic group. Pictures of Mischock as a young cop standing in smiling groups with other young policemen. A tinted 1930s photograph of a woman.

Standing on the bureau next to a small television set was a bowling trophy with the gold leaf flaking away. A checkerboard was set up and ready to play on a small table. The checkers and the board wore a coating of dust.

"You come to see me for a purpose?" the chief said, jerking Alec's attention back to him.

There was nothing to be gained by being subtle with this blunt old man. Alec said, "As a matter of fact, I wanted to ask about my father. I guess you were on the scene right after he died."

"Blew the top of his head off," said the chief. "Funny way for a man like that to do it. The quiet types are usually pill takers or jumpers."

"What I wondered," Alec continued, "is whether there

was a note or anything. I know nothing was said at the time, but I thought maybe—''

''No note,'' Mischock cut him off. ''Didn't need one. I knew why he done it.''

''Did you?''

''Sure. So do you. It was the Nunley kid.''

''Frazier?''

''I never heard about another one.''

Alec's impulse was to play ignorant, but he knew it would be a waste of time. He said, ''You know about that, too?''

''It wasn't no big trick to figure it out. I traced the clown getup he was wearin' to a costume place in Appleton. Found out the Dixon boy rented it there. Him and you and that Grant girl were all pretty thick at that time. Didn't take any giant brain to put the pieces together.''

''But you never said anything.''

''Nope. Important people involved. Judge Grant didn't want his daughter to get hurt. Elmer Swanke, he said it'd give the town a bad name. Your father, he was for tellin' it the way it happened, but we convinced him otherwise.'' The broken old man stared off at a spot on the ceiling. ''That was a sorry day. Ain't none of us or the town ever been the same since. Your father shot himself; I don't know what become of your mother. Elmer, he's dead five or six years of the liver disease. You can see what kinda shape I'm in. And Judge Grant's got his own problems.''

''It wasn't out fault,'' Alec said. ''Not really.''

He stopped talking suddenly, realizing how absurd he must sound looking for absolution from a crippled old man after all these years.

''Don't matter now,'' the chief said. He closed his eyes suddenly, just like that, and began to drool down the front of his bathrobe. The interview was over.

CHAPTER 24

Brendan Jordan spent a restless Friday night after walking Lindy to her car that morning. She had tried to lighten the mood by making jokes about the size of her hometown and what it would probably be like today, but Brendan could read her very real fear just under the banter.

"Are you sure you don't want me to go along?" he said. "I haven't got anything scheduled this weekend, and I get antsy with nothing to do."

"That's sweet of you, Brendan, but I couldn't put you through that. It's like you said, there's nothing deadlier than going to somebody else's class reunion."

"Call me when you get there," he said.

Lindy had looked long at him then. He was not a man who normally worried about a woman if she was out of his sight.

"I'll call you," she said, and kissed him as he left her in the boarding area.

But she hadn't called. According to his figuring, she would have arrived at Wolf River some time Friday afternoon, but there had been no word. Brendan reminded himself that there were countless reasons why she might not have called, but he didn't like the sound of it. If Lindy promised to do something, she could be counted on to do it.

He got out of bed early for him on a Saturday when he was not scheduled to fly. He turned on the coffee maker, brought in the newspaper, and dropped into a kitchen chair.

He sipped his coffee and tried to read the sports section of the *Times* that he had propped against a napkin container on the kitchen table.

Martina Navratilova was, as usual, playing in the Wimbledon finals against some German girl. The Dodgers were having pitching, fielding, and hitting problems. The Angels were trying to stay at .500. Several more professional athletes had been charged with crimes ranging from drug abuse to manslaughter.

His heart wasn't in the sports page. Lindy had been gone since only yesterday, but he missed her. More than that, he was worried about her. It was a vague, unformed worry that touched on the strange happenings she had described to him. He wished now that he had paid more serious attention when she was telling him about them.

Their last night together before she left had been the worst. For no reason at all, in the middle of their lovemaking Lindy had started to scream. She had pushed him away violently and seemed to be trying to scramble out of bed. It had only lasted a moment, but it took an hour of holding her and saying reassuring things to calm her down.

Afterwards she wouldn't go into detail about what had happened, telling him only that she had had some kind of crazy hallucination. Lindy was not a woman given to hallucinations or to hysterical outbursts. Something was deeply troubling her. Something she didn't want to share with him. Brendan didn't press the subject, but he held her especially close throughout the rest of the night.

The telephone rang.

Brendan tilted back in the chair and uncradled the wall extension phone. The voice on the other end was small and frightened.

"Brendan? This is Nicole."

"Hi, kid. What's happening?"

"It's Mom."

Brendan was instantly alert. "What's wrong?"

"Nothing," Nicole said quickly. "At least I don't think so. I tried to call her this morning, but I couldn't get through."

"What do you mean, couldn't get through?"

The girl's voice began to rise. "Just what I said. I tried to call her at the hotel where she's staying, but I couldn't get through."

Brendan grabbed the notepad from the counter under the telephone. He read from the top page.

"You called her at the Wolf River Inn?"

"Yes."

"Area code 715, 555-0226?"

"I think so. Whatever. But I couldn't get through."

"Okay, sit tight, Nicole. Let me try it."

"I'm scared, Brendan. I don't know why."

"Don't start worrying," he said. "There's a thousand things that can foul up telephone communications. It's been like that ever since they broke up Ma Bell."

"I just have this feeling that something's, I don't know, *wrong*."

"Let me try the number."

"Will you call me back?"

"As soon as I find out anything."

"Thanks, Brendan."

He broke the connection, gave it ten seconds, and dialed the number of the Wolf River Inn.

The receiver buzzed twice in his ear. A male voice spoke. "*The telephone number you have reached is not in service at this time. Please be sure you have checked your directory and are dialing properly. This is a recording.*"

"No shit," Brendan muttered into the phone. He hung up again while he checked his directory, not to be sure of the number he was dialing—he didn't make mistakes like that—but to get the service number of the telephone company.

Ten minutes later, having talked to three different telephone functionaries, the only information Brendan had was that circuits to Wolf River, Wisconsin, were temporarily inoperative, and that all concerned expected the problem to be rectified momentarily.

Brendan sat for a minute scowling into his cooling cup of coffee. Then he made a decision. Lindy might never let him forget it, but it was better to risk looking like a damn fool than to be a whole lot sorry later on.

He grabbed the phone again and dialed the number of the people where Nicole was staying. She came on the line immediately.

"What did you find out?"

"Nothing to worry about," he said in what he hoped was a reassuring voice. "Just some snafu in the telephone lines."

"Did you talk to Mom?"

"No, but they expect to have the problem cleared up anytime now."

"Are you sure?"

"Hey, I just talked to everybody at AT&T except Cliff Robertson."

Nicole was unconvinced. "It's just that . . . things have been so weird."

"Yeah, well, as a matter of fact, I've got a flight out that way this morning. I can check on your mom in person just to ease your mind."

"Oh, Brendan, *would* you?"

"No problem, kid. Talk to you later."

Brendan hung up the phone thoughtfully. The flight to the Midwest was a fabrication. He didn't have another charter assignment until Monday, and that one was a group of corporate executives going to British Columbia. But there was no use letting Nicole know he was as worried about Lindy as she was. Whether it was the girl's fear communicating itself to him or legitimate anxiety on his part, Brendan could not be sure. He had only a powerful hunch that Lindy needed help.

Brendan's charter company, Coastaire, flew out of Santa Monica Municipal Airport, but he kept his personal Cessna 310 at Whiteman Air Park in the San Fernando Valley. There was no tower, no red tape, just a compact little field for private pilots.

The twin-turbo 310 was probably more airplane than he really needed, but Brendan had got a good price on it from Coastaire five years before. He kept the trim little red-and-white plane gassed up and air-ready at all times, so when an impulse hit him to fly to Vegas or Catalina or wherever, he could hop in and go.

He filed his flight plan at Whiteman at nine-thirty Saturday morning. Shortly before ten he settled behind the wheel, scanned the horizon, and took off into a light easterly breeze.

CHAPTER 25

LINDY

The day was darkening with angry clouds rolling in from the north as Lindy walked through the curving streets of 1950s tract homes known as the Meadow. Like the rest of Wolf River, the Meadow was decaying. Although, at thirty years, it was still one of the newest sections of the town, it had fared worse than others.

The two- and three-bedroom houses, put up during the boom of the 1950s, lasted about ten years, then began to fall apart. Neglect and the passage of time had taken a toll, and the cheap materials originally used by the developer speeded the deterioration.

After hearing the news from Merilee Lund that her father was back in Wolf River, Lindy had looked up Wendell Grant in the phone book and found him listed on Lilac Lane, one of the saccharine names given to the streets when they were still paths marked out with colorful flags. She had tried to call, but static on the line kept her from getting through.

Now, as she stood before the house where her father

lived, she was having doubts about coming out here. The look of the house made her groan inwardly.

The paint was flaking from the clapboard walls, the lawn was unmowed and weedy, one shutter was missing on a front window, and another hung awry from a single hinge. Visible in the garage was the dented rear end of a ten-year-old station wagon.

Nothing about this pathetic house reminded Lindy of her father. Not the father she remembered.

She drew a deep breath and walked up the short concrete path to the front door. A three-by-five card tacked over the door was hand-lettered: BELL OUT OF ORDER.

Lindy knocked. She heard movement inside, and the door opened about eight inches. It took her a moment to recognize the pinched, suspicious face that peered out as that of her stepmother. Norma Wirthwein had been a dark, thin girl, pretty and vivacious when Judge Grant married her. Now only the lively brown eyes were unchanged.

"Yes?"

Lindy found her voice. "Norma?"

The woman opened the door wider to look at her. Norma was still thin—painfully so. The cheap print dress hung on her like a badly folded sheet.

"Well, look what we've got here," she said. "It's Lindy, isn't it?"

Lindy nodded.

"You know, we never expected to see you back in Wolf River. Nobody did."

"Well, here I am." When Norma said nothing, she went on. "I didn't know you and my father were back living here."

"We didn't exactly announce it on television. Maybe you didn't hear about the mess in Madison."

"No."

"I guess it wasn't such big news out there in Hollywood, but everybody around here sure heard about it."

Her mouth quirked in a bitter parody of a smile. "I suppose you want to see your father."

Lindy began to get irritated. "That's what I came out here for."

"You might as well come in."

Lindy followed her stepmother into the living room. There was none of the furniture she remembered from the old Elm Street house. The sofa, chairs, and rickety end tables looked like mismatched Sears Roebuck. The sofa had been recovered in a flowered print that didn't match anything else in the room. The carpet had a large dark stain near the doorway to the kitchen. Thc curtains were drawn, leaving the room in gloomy twilight.

"Wendell!" the woman called. "Somebody to see you."

"Who is it?" came a muffled voice from another room.

"A surprise. Come on out."

From out of what Lindy assumed must be the bedroom shuffled a man who superficially resembled her father of twenty years ago. The face was still handsome, though thinner, and he needed a shave. The hair was grayer and poorly cut.

The biggest change was in his bearing. Where Judge Grant used to stride into a room and take possession of it, this man entered tentatively, as though fearful he might be ordered back out. His smile had a guilty quaver. He wore a pair of suit pants that needed pressing, and a gray cardigan sweater over a plaid shirt.

"Lindy? My gosh, it is you, isn't it?"

She wanted to say, *My God, what's happened to you?* but she held it in.

"Hello, Daddy."

He came forward to embrace her, but as his arms went around her Lindy could feel him looking over her shoulder at his wife, as though for permission. He released Lindy and stepped back. "Gosh, you look wonderful. What brings you back home after all this time?"

"Daddy, this isn't my home anymore."

He seemed not to hear. "Why didn't you tell us you were coming?"

"It was a sudden decision. And I didn't even know you were living back in Wolf River."

His eyes shifted away from hers as the old Judge Grant's eyes would never have done.

"I guess we haven't been very good about writing." He came back to her. "You didn't exactly keep in touch either, you know."

"No, I suppose I didn't."

An uncomfortable silence grew in the room.

Norma said, "Maybe I ought to leave you two alone to relive old times."

"No, no, dear," Wendell Grant said quickly. "You don't have to leave."

"I know I don't *have* to," Norma said with peculiar emphasis. "But it will give you a chance to talk about me."

Lindy looked at him curiously, but his attention was on his wife, his eyes pleading.

"I've got some shopping to do anyway," Norma said.

"Have you got enough money?"

"Never enough," Norma said, "but I'll make do."

"Better take an umbrella," said the judge. "Feels like it's going to rain."

Norma shrugged him off. To Lindy she said, "Nice seeing you," and went out.

Wendell Grant clapped his hands together in a charade of heartiness and laughed without feeling. "Well, shall we sit down and have a talk?"

"I can't stay long," Lindy said.

"Too bad." He looked around the cheap living room. "It's not much like the old place, I guess."

"No, not much."

"When we moved to Madison I sold the Elm Street house and the furniture along with it. It was too big, anyway. And Norma said it was too gloomy and old-fashioned.'' Quickly he added, ''She was right, of course.''

''Of course,'' Lindy said dryly. Then she could no longer hold it in. ''Daddy, what's happened to you?''

''Happened?''

''You're so . . . different. Norma said something about a scandal while you were living in Madison.''

Wendell Grant seemed to grow smaller before his daughter's eyes. He walked over to the flowered couch and sat down, patting the cushion beside him for her. His face suddenly showed all of his sixty-seven years.

''There are a couple of things I've done in my life that I'm not proud of,'' he said. ''That was one of them. I was counsel to the legislative highway commission. One of the commissioners got involved in a conflict-of-interest mess. There was a bribery thing involving a construction company, and kickbacks to members of the governor's staff. Very complicated. And very ugly.''

''You were involved in that?''

Slowly he nodded. ''I was. It started out just doing a favor for a friend. Rearranging the names on some corporate documents. I knew it was wrong, but I didn't think anyone would get hurt. Then it kind of got away from me.''

''What happened?''

''There were no indictments or anything. Nobody went to prison. But there were deals made that put some people out of the state government and into retirement. I was one of them. The legal expenses pretty well wiped me out. I was lucky to have Norma. She stood by me through the whole thing.''

''Wasn't she the one who pushed you into getting involved in politics in the first place?''

''I wouldn't say pushed, exactly. She thought there would be opportunities for us in Madison, and there were, until I messed everything up.''

''Oh, Daddy.'' Lindy stared at her father, more shocked

by his feeble acceptance of his fate than she was by the confession.

"But, hey, we're doing all right," he said. "I get a pretty good pension, and Norma does some design work for stores in Milwaukee."

"That's good," Lindy said dully.

"Now tell me, what brings you back to town?"

"Class reunion."

Her father's face darkened. "Your high school class?"

"That's right. What's the matter?"

"It wasn't a very happy class."

"No, it wasn't." She made a decision. "Daddy, there's something I always wanted to tell you about what happened my last year in high school. Something you may already suspect."

He gave her the counterfeit laugh again. "Hey, honey, you were a pretty grown-up girl. Whatever it was, you seem to have gotten over it."

"I'm not sure I did," she said.

"Hey, this sounds serious."

"It is," she said. "And it's important. I want to tell you about Frazier Nunley."

"No." He shook his head. "It's too late to talk about all that old news."

"It's not too late. I think it's because of Frazier I'm here now."

He moved away from her on the couch. "I don't know what you mean."

"Just let me tell you what happened."

Wendell Grant checked his watch. "I wonder what's keeping Norma."

"Daddy, she just left."

"I wouldn't want her to get caught in the storm."

He got up and crossed to the front window. There he pulled the curtain aside to peek out. Lindy waited for him to turn back, but he just kept watching the street.

Finally she said, "You don't want to hear this, do you?"

"Hear what, honey?"

"What I want to tell you about Frazier Nunley. And what happened at that Halloween Ball."

"Hey, I'll talk about anything you want," Judge Grant said. "I was just wondering if maybe I ought to see if Norma's all right."

Lindy sighed heavily, saddened by the slump of her father's shoulders. She said, "Never mind, Daddy. I guess I'd better be going."

Judge Grant turned from the window. His relief was evident. "Do you have to?"

"Yes, I think I do. I'm staying at the inn, if you want to call me or anything."

"The inn," he repeated. "Yes, I've got that. Hey, it was great seeing you, Lindy."

Impulsively she ran into his arms. "You too, Daddy." She hugged him very hard, and for a moment felt the old strength return to his arms as he hugged her back. Then the station wagon pulled into the driveway and his embrace went limp.

"Goodbye, Daddy," Lindy said. She hurried out before she would have to face her stepmother again.

CHAPTER 26

ROMAN

Jim Dancey wiped his hands across the chest of his coveralls, extracted a package of Winstons, and lit one while Roman stood grinding his teeth in an agony of impatience.

"Can't tell you what's wrong with her," Dancey said through a cloud of cigarette smoke.

Thunder rumbled somewhere off in the distance. The sound rolled in through the open lubrication bay of the Shell station with a chill draft.

"What do you mean you can't tell me?" Roman said.

"Just what I said. I don't know what's wrong. Everything checks out okay. She just won't go, that's all."

"I didn't need a freaking mechanic to tell me that."

"You think you can fix her, you go ahead."

"There must be other mechanics in town," Roman said. "Who's a good one?"

"Lots of good ones. Saturday's everybody's busy day. You might have trouble getting her looked at today."

Roman's anger boiled over. "Goddamn it, what kind of

a town is this? First the phones are all screwed up, now you tell me I can't get my car worked on because it's Saturday."

"I got nothing to do with the telephones, mister," Dancey said.

"Well, I can't hang around here and argue with you. Who owns this place? Who's your boss?"

"You're looking at him."

Roman could only groan in his frustration.

Dancey took the cigarette out of his mouth and held it carefully. "Now, mister, I generally try to be patient with people come through here and make fun of our town and the way I do my job, but I got a limit and you just reached it. I think about now you better take your car and get you and it out of my station."

"How am I supposed to get the car out of here if it won't start?"

"That ain't my problem. You plan to pay by cash or credit card?"

"Pay? For what?"

"For the tow from the inn. For my time. For the boy's time. For taking up space in my garage."

With an effort Roman took hold of himself. "All right, look, Jim, I'm upset, and it's not your fault. I'm sorry I yelled at you."

"Accepted," Dancey said.

"If I leave the car here now, and my credit card, will you keep working on it?"

"Prob'ly won't do no good. I checked her over, couldn't find anything wrong."

"Just keep checking, okay?" Roman dug the Shell card out of his wallet.

"No need to leave that," Dancey told him. "You can pay when you come back."

Roman nodded, stuffed the wallet back into his pocket, and left the garage.

* * *

From deep within the complicated electronics that regulated the operation of the Monte Carlo, the Floater watched and laughed his silent laugh.

By the time he got back to the inn, Roman's mood was darker then ever. The angry-looking clouds that boiled overhead and the damp, oppressive heat added to his frustration. The whole world seemed to be in a conspiracy to prevent him from leaving Wolf River.

He strode across the lobby and planted both hands on the registration desk. The clerk eyed him warily.

"Have they fixed the telephones yet?" Roman demanded.

"The problem's not here at the inn," the clerk said. "It's somewhere in the phone company circuits."

"I didn't ask you where the problem was," Roman said. "I asked you if it was fixed."

"I don't know, sir," the clerk said huffily. "Why don't you try the phone in your room?"

"Thanks a lot." Roman spun on his heel and started toward the elevator.

"Oh, Mr. Dixon," the clerk called after him.

"Well?"

"I sent a visitor up to your room."

"You sent what?"

"A visitor."

"You let somebody into my room without an okay from me?" The icy finger of fear prodded his spine.

"He said it would be all right."

"I don't care what he said. You don't do that. You don't send people into somebody else's room just on their say-so. I'm holding you and this hotel responsible for anything that's missing."

"I don't think he wanted to steal anything," the clerk said. "It's your father."

Roman stared at the man for a moment, then turned and continued silently to the elevator.

He rode silently and alone to the fourth floor. He hadn't told anybody he was coming here. Especially not his father. One thing he did not need now was a meeting with the old man.

Periodically Roman had sent checks to Howard Dixon in care of a Wolf River post office box. The checks had been cashed, endorsed with the old man's ragged signature, but there had never been an acknowledgment of any kind. That was fine with Roman. He got a Christmas card yearly from Florida, where his mother lived with her new husband, and that was all the contact he wanted with his parents.

Roman opened the door to his room prepared for anything, but still he recoiled at the appearance of the man who sat in an armchair watching a Cubs game on the television set. Howard Dixon had been a stocky, tough little man, five-feet-eight, but solid, with fierce eyebrows and an uncombable shock of black hair. The man who turned wearily to look at Roman was fat, carelessly fat, the belly spilling out of a T-shirt and over the too-tight khaki trousers. His eyes were watery and apologetic. The few remaining strands of hair lay across a liver-spotted scalp.

Howard Dixon started to get up, changed his mind, and sagged back into the chair. He gestured at the Jack Daniel's bottle and the glass on a table at his elbow.

"Hello, Romey. I helped myself to a drink. Hope you don't mind."

A drink, hell, Roman thought. The old man was shitfaced. He said, "Hello, Pop. How did you find me?"

"Somebody called me."

"Called you?" Roman said quickly. "Who?"

"I don't know. Funny kind of voice. Didn't give a name. Just said your son's in town. Said I ought to come over and say hello."

How come, Roman wondered, the old man's telephone was the only one in town that worked?

Howard Dixon belched. He wiped his mouth, and the whiskers rasped against his callused palm.

"So how you been, Roman?"

"I'm fine." Roman could not stop staring at the ruin of a man who was his father. "Pop . . . you look terrible."

"Well, I've had my share of troubles." The loose mouth turned down in a sneer; the watery eyes narrowed. "Your mother left me and run off with that guy from Chicago. You heard about that."

Roman said nothing. His mother had written to him at the time, telling of the steady abuse she had taken from his father along with the drunken tirades that had finally driven her out of the house. She had met Leonard Simon at her sister's house in Oak Park, and married him a year later. As far as Roman could tell, they were happy now in Fort Lauderdale.

"Then they fired me out at the plant. Fuckin' manager was afraid I'd do my job too good and make him look bad, so he told a bunch of lies about me drinkin', and naturally they believed him instead of me and fired my ass."

"That's too bad, Pop." Roman wished the self-pitying old fart would just go away.

"But listen, I'm okay. Got me an okay room on the South Side. Not too bad. Got my own bathroom. Got a TV, not as good as this one, but it picks up most of the stations." He wiped his lips. "Mind if I have just another little snort?"

"Go ahead," Roman told him.

The fat old man poured whiskey into the glass, carefully leaving a quarter of an inch in the bottom of the bottle. He drank, looked up, and for a moment his eyes held the fierce gaze Roman remembered.

"You let me down, Romey," he said, and his voice was stronger than it had been.

"What do you mean, Pop?"

"You know. I mean what you did to the Nunley kid. You and your friends."

Roman recoiled as though he'd been struck.

"Everybody in town knew," Howard Dixon continued, "even though nobody said anything about it. That Judge Grant and the police chief and the editor of the *Chronicle*, they saw to that. I could never hold my head up in this town again. People were talkin' about me behind my back. Whispering. It's your fault, what happened to me."

"You don't know what you're saying, Pop."

For a moment the old man met his eyes, then something inside him collapsed. He was a fat, defeated old drunk. Nothing more. With difficulty he hoisted himself out of the chair.

"I better go. You most likely got things you want to do."

Roman did not argue.

"Uh, just one thing, I'm runnin' a little short this month, and if you could see your way clear to—"

"Sure, Pop." Roman dug out several bills and passed them to the old man. "I'll send you more when I get back home."

"Thanks, Romey. I-I'll pay you back."

"Don't worry about it."

Roman closed the hotel room door behind his father, and for the first time in many years felt like crying. Instead, he went into the bathroom and brushed his teeth over and over.

ALEC

The cemetery, the old one out at the end of West Road, was not a place Alec McDowell really wanted to be. With the gunmetal clouds pushing down on Wolf River like heavy hands, it had to be one of the least attractive locations in town.

And yet here he was. After the unsettling talk with the old police chief, Alec had wandered around aimlessly, or so he thought, until he found himself at the row of cypress trees that bordered West Memorial Park.

He hesitated a moment, then entered through the tall black iron gates that were never closed. "Why lock 'em?" ran the town joke. "Nobody's going to break out."

He walked among the gravestones—simple carved slabs, most of them, although there were a few more elaborate ones with angels or sorrowing saints. Alec caught himself being careful not to step on the patches of ground directly over the buried bodies. *Ridiculous*, he thought. *What am I going to do, wake somebody up?* But he continued to walk around the sodded rectangles.

The stone seemed to jump up suddenly in front of him. Plain dark marble, no embellishments. Just the engraved legend:

Phelan Alexander McDowell
1912–1971
At Rest

Alec stood at his father's feet, looking down at the simple stone, the unadorned grave. In his head he heard the boom of the long-ago gunshot that had splattered Phelan McDowall's brains over the ceiling of his garage.

"It wasn't my fault," Alec said softly. "I never meant to hurt anyone."

As he stood there, remembering, not wanting to remember, Alec had a growing sense of unease. Someone was watching him. There had been no one else around when he entered the cemetery. He had seen no other person as he crossed through the graves. But now he was as sure as he was of the dead under his feet that he was not alone. Not wanting to turn, he turned.

The woman was tall and broad-shouldered, dressed in

a long gray dress and a gray hood. She stood atop a gentle rise and looked directly, unblinkingly at him.

Alec had a crazy impulse to run. Just turn and run as fast as he could the hell out of that graveyard, through the iron gates, all the way back to town and out of town, never to return.

He fought down the urge and stood his ground as the woman came toward him. He couldn't see her feet beneath the flowing gray dress, and she seemed to float over the graves as she approached. For a moment Alec thought she was going to collide with him, but the woman stopped when their faces were just inches apart.

Her skin seemed unnaturally smooth, the flesh tinted pink, the blue eyes clear and sharp. It was a much younger face than was suggested by the strands of white hair that straggled from beneath the hood.

After what seemed like an agonizingly long silence, the woman spoke. "You're back," she said. Her voice was low-pitched and cultured.

"W-what?"

"You've come back. All three of you."

Jesus God, no, haven't I had enough of this?

The woman put out a hand. Her movement was surprisingly swift; before Alec could get out of the way her fingers had clamped onto his upper arm. The strength of her grip was astonishing.

"Excuse me," Alec said, trying to pry loose the grasping fingers. "I think you've made a mistake."

"I made no mistake." The woman's voice took on an uneven quality. For the first time Alec noticed that the blue eyes were a shade too bright. "My son made the mistake. Twenty years ago. My son trusted you."

Alec could only shake his head dumbly.

"Did you come back to see him now?"

Alec pulled harder at the gripping fingers. He could not dislodge even one.

"I'll show him to you," the woman said, her voice now moving rapidly up and down the scale.

Before he could protest further, the woman was pulling him across the graves, her fingers digging painfully into his biceps. Alec looked around frantically for help, but the two of them were alone in the cemetery. He had no choice but to let himself be pulled along, striving to keep his balance as the woman swept back up the rise toward the spot where she had been standing.

They came to a stop before a pink marble headstone.

"There!" said the woman. She leveled a bony forefinger at the stone, keeping her iron grip on Alec with the other hand.

Squirming around in her grasp, he read:

Frazier David Nunley
1952–1966
Beloved Son
Taken Too Soon

"There he is," the woman continued. "There is my son, where you and your friends put him."

Alec pulled at the hand that was squeezing his arm to numbness. "Mrs. Nunley . . . please . . ."

Abruptly she released him. Alec staggered back a step before he caught himself.

"It's wrong," the woman said, madness now twisting her face. "My son is dead, and you are alive. You should have to pay for that."

She rose to her full height and seemed to Alec to tower over him. He had a terrible moment when he thought she was about to draw a hatchet or something from the folds of her dress and split his skull. The, as suddenly as she had appeared, Orva Nunley turned and drifted away from him over the graves.

Alec rubbed his aching arm and hurried toward the gate. To the north, thunder grumbled.

Suspended over the bordering row of cypress trees, the Floater observed the scene.

Don't worry, Mother. He will pay. They will all pay.

CHAPTER 27

Lindy and Roman watched silently as Alec came into the inn and crossed the lobby to the registration desk. His face was pale, his thoughts unreadable. He didn't see the two of them standing near the elevator.

The clerk took a single sheet of paper from the pigeonhole marked with his room number and handed it to Alec. He read the short message, and for a moment looked as though he were going to be sick. When he saw the clerk looking at him oddly, he righted himself and headed for the elevator. He pulled up short as he saw the others. They started toward him.

"I guess you got the same message in your box that we did," Roman said.

Alec stared at him wordlessly and handed over the folded sheet. It read:

Big Reunion Party Tonight!!
At the Wolfpack Cabin.
For the Hero, the Monkey, the Cat . . . and the Clown.
Don't miss it or you'll be sorry!

"What are we going to do?" Alec said.

"I don't know about you, but I'm sure as hell not hanging around to see what that party is all about," said Roman.

"It seems to me that's what you said last night at dinner," Alec reminded him. "Something about getting out of here first thing this morning."

"Jesus, don't you think I've been trying? Is it my fault the damn car is screwed up and the dumbass mechanic can't fix it?"

"Are you saying that your car is the only way out of this town?" Alec said.

"It might as well be. The only car rental outfit in town is closed, if you can believe it."

"There's got to be a bus out or something."

"I came in from Milwaukee on a bus," Lindy said.

"Great. So why don't we catch one right back out of town?" Alec said.

"Don't you think I thought of that?" Roman said. "I just came from the Greyhound depot. There's exactly two buses a day out of Wolf River. The last one left at five o'clock. Just over an hour ago."

"There has to be something we can do."

Roman scowled at him. "If you've got any bright ideas, let's hear 'em. How did you get here?"

"I hired a driver at the airport in Milwaukee."

"Oh, well, lah-de-dah."

"I don't drive myself. In New York you don't have to."

"Same old Alec," Roman said. "You always did mooch a ride with somebody else. Mostly me."

Alec ignored the dig. He said, "Well, let's call around. There's got to be a way."

"Call?" Roman sneered. "Call on what? Have you tried to use the telephone?"

"There was some problem with the lines earlier. Surely that's been repaired by now."

"Oh, yeah? Why don't you try it?"

"It's true, Alec," Lindy said, "but go ahead and make sure."

Alec looked from one to the other, then walked deliberately across the lobby to the pay telephone. He picked up the receiver, dropped a coin in the slot, and listened. He jiggled the switch hook several times, tried the dial, finally replaced the receiver and walked back, not bothering to retrieve the coin that rattled into the return slot.

"It's dead," he announced.

"No kidding," Roman said dryly.

A peal of thunder reverberated through the lobby.

"I wish that storm would either move in or go away," Roman complained. "It's making me jumpy as hell."

"It's a funny kind of storm," Lindy said. "It just sits there outside of town, like it's waiting."

"Are we going to stand around and talk about the weather?" Alec demanded.

"Like I said before," Roman told him, "if you've got any bright ideas on how to get out of here, lay 'em out."

"I don't think we *are* going to get out of here," Lindy said quietly. "Not before . . . whoever or whatever is doing this is through with us."

"Now what does that mean?" Alec said. "Are we talking ghosts again? The supernatural? Some mystical power holding us in town?"

"*Something* is holding us here," Lindy said. "The telephones, Roman's car, that odd storm hanging over us. And you'll have to admit some pretty strange things have happened to us. Things that can't be explained away easily."

"I suppose so," Alec said grudgingly. "But we can worry about explanations later. There must be something we can do now."

"One thing we can do is buy a gun," Roman said. "Either of you see a gun shop or a sporting goods store open anywhere?"

"I didn't see much of anything open," Alec said. "If there was ever a dying town, this is it."

Lindy was staring at Roman. "A gun? What in the world are you going to shoot? Your car? The telephone? A plastic toy clown? A storm that won't move in or away? Come on, Roman, use your head."

"I'd still feel better if I was armed," he grumbled.

"I think the important thing now is for us to stay together and not panic," Lindy said.

"Nobody's going to panic," Roman said. "At least I know I'm not."

"And what good does it do to stay together?" Alec said. "We were all together at dinner last night, and somebody still pulled off that trick with the floating clown."

"That was the waitress's idea of a joke," Roman said. "It had to be."

Alec snapped at him. "You know better than that."

"The important thing," Lindy said, "is that nobody was hurt. There may be strength in the three of us."

"Do we have to stand around here in the lobby?" Roman said. "Why don't we go into the bar?"

"That will help a lot," Alec said, "for you to get smashed again."

"Listen—" Roman began darkly, but he broke off, and they all turned as the street door to the lobby pushed open and a gust of cold air washed over them.

Jim Dancey entered. He started for the desk, then saw the three of them standing by the elevator and changed his direction. "Your car's ready," he told Roman.

"You mean it's fixed?"

"I mean it starts and it runs. Nothing I did, it just decided it was ready to go."

"Are you sure?"

"I just drove it over here, I'm that sure. It's out front now if you want it."

"Hell yes, I want it. How much do I owe you?"

"I figure forty dollars will cover it. If you're gonna use the credit card we'll have to go back to the station."

"No, here, I'll give you the cash," Roman said quickly. "I don't want any more delays."

Dancey accepted the money and looked at each of them. "You'll be leaving town? All of you?"

"That's the plan," Roman told him.

"Good." Dancey turned, walked back across the lobby, and out. The street beyond the glass-paneled doors was dark and forbidding.

"What did he mean by that?" Alec wondered.

"Who cares?" Roman said. "Me, I'm outta here. Anybody coming with me?"

After a moment's hesitation Alec said, "All right, I'll come."

Lindy said, "I'm not sure it's a good idea."

"Why the hell not?" Roman wanted to know.

"It's too convenient, that's all, having the car suddenly get well like that."

"Stay if you want to," Roman said, "but me, I'm not spending one minute more than I have to in this miserable town."

Lindy pursed her lips. "No," she said finally, "I'll come along because I still think we should stick together. But we might be making a big mistake."

"I'll be packed and ready to go in ten minutes," Roman said. "We can meet back down here."

Fifteen minutes later Lindy was standing at the registration desk while the clerk processed her credit card to settle the bill.

He said, "Sorry you couldn't stay with us a little longer. Wolf River is really a nice little town."

"I know," Lindy said. "Like the sign says, 'A nice place to live.' "

"There's those who think so."

She could see Roman jittering impatiently by the door

while Alec stood by, waiting for her. *Just like the old days*, she thought. *Only much, much different.*

She signed the credit slip, took the cardholder copy, and stuffed it into her handbag.

"Glad I don't have to go out tonight," the clerk said. "I don't like the looks of the weather."

"Neither do I," Lindy agreed, "but sometimes you don't have a choice."

She picked up her bag and carried it with her toward the two men.

"Come on, come on," Roman urged. "It's getting darker than hell out there."

So it was, Lindy saw. It was barely seven o'clock, which should be reasonably light at this time of year in northern Wisconsin, but the gloom that had hung in the town all day had darkened to restless night. The streetlights had been turned on, but they seemed unable to penetrate the unnatural dark.

When they went outside, a cold, wet wind eddied around the three people as though probing for a point of entry. Lindy pulled her sweater closer around her while Roman keyed open the trunk.

Their three bags fit easily into the trunk of the Monte Carlo. Roman and Lindy got into the front, while Alec took the back seat. Unwanted memories returned of the same riders in other times and another car on these same streets.

Roman fired the engine, which roared to life immediately. He looked around to the others with a smirk of triumph as though he personally had fixed whatever was wrong.

"Are we going to leave or are you going to sit here revving the engine?" Alec said.

"Keep your pants on," Roman told him. "I'll have us back in Milwaukee before you know it."

He started away from the curb.

"Aren't you going to turn on the lights?" Lindy said.

"They're on," he told her.

"What's the matter with them? I can barely see in front of the car."

"I don't know, but we're not stopping for that. As long as this baby runs, I'm heading out of here and away."

As they drove down a deserted Main Street no other cars were moving in either direction. It was as though they were all alone on a ghostly highway.

Roman snapped on the radio. Nothing but crackling static greeted them.

"Damn storm," he said. "It's fouling up everything. That's probably what jimmied the telephones, too."

"Maybe," Lindy said.

"What else?"

Alec leaned forward from the back seat. "Could we stop talking about it now and just concentrate on getting us out of here?"

Roman turned so his face was close to Alec's. "Look, pal, only one of us can drive this car at a time, and that one is me. So give it a rest, okay?"

Alec subsided, muttering to himself.

Lindy sat straining forward, trying to see into the blackness ahead of them. A mist began to coat the windshield, cutting visibility even more.

Roman turned on the wipers, but they only smeared a greasy double crescent across the outside of the glass, making things still worse.

"Try the washer," Alec said.

Roman's head snapped around. "Dammit, I'm not going to tell you again—"

"Will you two cut it out?" Lindy broke in. "All of us have frayed nerves. Let's at least try to get along while we have to be in close quarters."

Roman poked at the button bearing the symbol for the windshield washer. Nothing happened. Repeated jabs brought no result. He swore under his breath and drove on.

Neither of the men said anything for the next several minutes. Roman drove fiercely, rubbing at the windshield with the meaty part of one hand while he gripped the wheel with the other. Since the greasy mist was on the outside of the glass, his efforts had no effect.

"What the hell are you doing?" Alec said suddenly.

"What do you think I'm doing? I'm trying to drive us the hell out of here."

"Look over there."

Lindy and Roman turned in the direction Alcc was pointing. There, through the misty gloom, was the familiar entrance with the gilt lettering on the door: WOLF RIVER INN.

"You drove us in a damn circle," Alec complained.

"Like hell. I never turned once."

"Then there must be another Wolf River Inn," Alec said with heavy sarcasm.

"Maybe if you'd shut up and let me drive we'd get somewhere," Roman growled.

Alec let a breath escape through his teeth and moved over to a corner of the back seat.

Lindy said nothing. She suddenly felt terribly cold.

After five more minutes of strained driving, a pale glow appeared up ahead on their right. Roman slowed the car. Lindy rolled down her window, the better to see where they were.

The pallid glow behind the glassed doors was chillingly familiar.

"Oh . . . shit," Roman said.

Alec groaned softly.

The gilt lettering, faint but legible, spelled out WOLF RIVER INN.

CHAPTER 28

"You're driving in circles!" Alec shouted.

"Like hell I am," Roman yelled back. "You think you can do a better job, fine, get your ass up here."

He yanked the wheel over to steer the car to the curb. Abruptly it was jerked out of his hands and the car lurched back toward the center of the street.

"What the hell!"

"Now what are you doing?" Alec demanded.

"I'm not doing a damn thing. The fucking car's doing it all by itself."

"Are you drunk?"

Lindy spoke up. "Shut up, Alec. Can't you see the car's out of control?"

"What do you mean, out of control?"

As though in answer to Alec's question, the accelerator pedal sank to the floor without assistance from any human agency, and the car roared wildly into the misty night. Roman continued to struggle with the steering wheel and the other controls, but his efforts had no effect.

"Shut off the engine." Alec cried.

"I'm trying, goddamn it!"

Roman's knuckles whitened as he tried to twist the ignition key, but it was frozen as though mounted in stone.

Alec fought with the handle of the back door. "It's locked," he said. "I can't even get out."

Lindy tried her own door. It too refused to budge.

"We're trapped in here!" Alec cried.

Roman said, "Jump out at this speed and you're a dead man anyway."

"What are we going to do?" Alec said. "We can't just let a runaway car take us to . . . God knows where."

"I doesn't look like we've got any choice," Lindy said, as levelly as she could manage.

Alec's voice took on an edge of hysteria. "It's going to kill us. This crazy car is going to kill us."

Roman turned in the seat and slapped him hard on the side of the head.

Alec rubbed his jaw. "You didn't have to do that."

"Somebody had to," Roman said. "You were losing it." He turned back and clamped his hands on the steering wheel, though he no longer fought to control it, and stared stoically ahead.

Lindy wrapped her arms around herself and tried to relax as the car careered on through the darkness.

The lights of the town, dimly seen through the mist, were soon left behind. Dark shapes of trees and bushes alongside the road swayed and danced as a wind picked up. The growl of thunder could be heard even above the roar of the engine.

A few miles beyond the last lights of the town the steering wheel spun suddenly and violently to the right, tearing itself from Roman's reflexive grasp. With a screech of rubber the Monte Carlo went into a long sideways slide and seemed in immediate danger of rolling.

Lindy was thrown hard against Roman, who was forced against the door on the driver's side. Alec fell all the way across the back seat.

At the moment when it seemed the car had to tip, it

was righted and plunged straight ahead into what looked like impenetrable brush at the roadside. The three people inside braced themselves for the impending crash.

But there was no crash.

The car burst through the barrier of brush and plunged ahead on a faint, weed-grown double-rutted trail that was barely discernible under the headlights.

"Where are we?" Alec said in a choked voice.

"Don't you recognize it?" Roman said.

"How can I recognize anything at night in the woods?"

"I know what it is," Lindy said. "It's the old road to the Wolfpack cabin."

The three of them held on to anything they could as the car bumped and jounced along the old rutted road. Roots and boulders banged off the underside of the Monte Carlo. Red warning lights on the dash blinked on as the oil pressure dropped and the temperature rose dangerously. Steam spurted back from under the hood, making the visibility even worse as it obscured the windshield. Trees loomed in their path and jumped out of the way as the car jerked from side to side, steered by an unseen hand. Brush slashed against the sides of the car. Tree branches banged on the roof.

After an endless nightmare ride, the Monte Carlo jolted to a stop. In the sudden silence, steam hissed from the ruptured radiator and a steady leak of some fluid splashed on the ground under the car.

Lindy was the first to try her door handle. It worked. The door swung open with a protest of tortured metal.

She stepped out unsteadily onto the spongy ground. Roman followed, then Alec. They could feel the damp chill of the nearby lake. In the glow of the headlights they could see the broken, listing shell of what had been the Wolfpack party cabin dead ahead.

"We can't stay here," Alec said.

"We can't do anything else," Lindy told him. "Even if

we were able to control the car, look at it. It's not going anywhere now.''

The Monte Carlo settled slowly as a front tire went flat. Steam spilled from under the sprung hood and beneath the car. The headlights dimmed perceptibly.

Lindy looked toward the sky. No stars were visible under the heavy cloud cover. A momentary flash of lightning off to the north lit the trees with a ghostly silver glow. A moment later came the thunder.

''We're going to need some kind of light,'' she said.

''I've got a flashlight in my suitcase,'' Roman said.

They opened the trunk and retrieved their bags. Roman found the heavy-duty flashlight in his and led the way toward the cabin.

The ragged ends of wires hanging down from terminals under the eaves told them immediately that the electricity that had once come from power lines to the road was no more.

Heavy brush had overgrown the path leading from the cabin to the lake. An untidy pile of wood leaned against one wall, with the blade of a rusty ax still biting into the end of a log.

The glass from the cabin windows was gone, the door was unhinged, roof shingles littered the ground. Roman kicked debris—cans, papers, soiled clothing—out of the way as they entered.

''Looks like bums and teenagers have been using this place for a dumping ground.''

They pushed their way inside, and Roman aimed the flashlight around the big downstairs party room. Trash littered the floor. Cobwebs hung thick on the beamed ceiling. Gray-green fungus crept down the walls.

Small unseen animals skittered away from the light.

''What a mess,'' Alec said.

''Looks like nobody's used it in the last twenty years,'' Roman said. ''Except for the transients and kids.''

"That figures," Lindy said. "Didn't Mr. Hartman close it up right after . . . after the last Halloween Ball?"

"Offered it for sale, if I remember," Roman said. "Never could find a buyer."

"At least the fireplace still looks operative," Alec said. "If that wood outside is dry enough, we can build a fire and get warm."

"What for?" Roman said. "You don't think we're staying here?"

"I think we have to," Lindy said. "At least until daylight."

"Not me," Roman said.

Lindy faced him. "I wouldn't want to try to find my way back to the road through the woods. Not on a night like this."

"There's enough of a trail to follow," Roman said. "I can't see just sitting here waiting for . . . for whatever he's planned for us."

"Whatever *who*'s planned for us?" Alec said.

Roman whirled on him. "Why don't we cut out the bullshit. Frazier Nunley, that's who. He's the only one who could be behind all this."

"Frazier Nunley is dead."

"You think you're telling me something? I was there with you right out on that lake the morning we found him. While you were puking over the side I was looking him right in the face. Hell yes, he's dead. But he's doing this. Don't ask me how, but he's doing it."

"That's crazy. I'm not saying this isn't connected with what happed to Frazier, but he's *dead*." Alec put an icy emphasis on the word. "It could be somebody acting in his place. A relative or something. Leaving messages for us, sending over that toy clown."

Lindy said, "Alec, no earthly power took control of that car and brought us out here."

"If that's so, I don't want to think about what it might be," Alec said.

"Then if we're all agreed, let's get out of here," Roman said.

"We haven't agreed to anything," Lindy said. "I think Alec's right about building a fire, and I think we ought to look around and see if there's some way we can get some light. Didn't there used to be kerosene lamps kept in the closet under the stairs for emergencies?"

"That was twenty years ago," Roman protested.

"So? It can't hurt to look."

With Roman shining the flashlight beam ahead of her, Lindy crossed the trash-strewn floor to the door that led into the triangular storage space under the stairs. The rusty hasp gave with a protesting shriek, and Lindy pulled open the stubborn door. She brushed aside a thick spiderweb and stepped inside.

Roman came up behind her and played the light around the filthy interior. No lamps were in sight, but Lindy found a crumbling cardboard box that contained a dozen candles.

"Let there be light," she said, holding the package up triumphantly.

"All right, all right, come on out of there," Roman said.

A blaze of lightning outside made the many cracks and chinks in the wooden walls stand out in stark blue-white. Thunder boomed seconds later.

"Looks like that sonofabitching storm is going to finally break," Roman said. "I wish it would hit us and get it over with."

With Alec and Lindy doing most of the work, a roaring fire was built in the fireplace, and candles were placed around the room to push back the encroaching darkness. Roman sat on a sagging cot and watched them glumly.

Wood smoke rolled out of the fireplace and filled the room, exiting through the broken windows.

Roman coughed. "Can't you do something about that smoke?"

"The flue's clogged," Alec told him.

"Maybe if you'd help us we could ream it out or something," Lindy said.

"The hell with it," Roman said. "I'm not staying here. That's what he wants us to do. You can stay if you want, but I'm getting out."

He started for the door.

"Don't do it, Roman," Lindy said. "If we split up we're easier prey."

"Ah, let him go," Alec said. "He's no good to us here."

Roman reversed his direction and came back to stand nose to nose with Alec. "You're a pretty big talker now, aren't you? Hot-shot New Yorker. Well, listen, buddy, to me you're still a worthless little ass-kisser who couldn't do a damn thing on his own. You got anything you want to settle with me, let's do it here and now."

Alec held up his hands. "Look, I didn't mean anything. I'm upset. We're all upset. I don't want any trouble with you."

"Now, that sounds like the Alec I remember. Lots of big talk, but pure chickenshit if anybody called him on it." Roman turned to Lindy. "Sure you don't want to come with me? This chickenshit little creep isn't going to be much help if you need it."

"I'm staying," Lindy said. "I wish you would too."

"No way," said Roman. "See you sometime. Maybe." He pushed the broken door aside and went out.

Roman paused in the weakened glow of the Monte Carlo's headlights and looked back toward the cabin. A capricious wind snatched the wood smoke that spilled from the windows and whirled it up and away. The flickering candles inside grew ghostly shadows on the walls. He felt terribly alone.

"You had your chance," he said softly to the cabin and the people inside, then he turned toward the woods.

The wind played tricks with the brush and the trees ahead of him, turning them into ogres waiting for him to enter their world. Roman hesitated. He walked back to the house and grabbed the handle of the rusty ax. He levered the blade from the log where it was sunk and hefted the ax. It felt good. With the flashlight in one hand and the ax in the other, he started down the weeded ruts that had once been the cabin road.

The lightning flashes came closer together as Roman made his way along the faded path. Thunder crashed in his ears, branches clutched at him like bony fingers.

Keeping the pool of light steady on the path before him, and the ax held comfortably by the throat, he plodded on. He could not judge the distance they had come into the woods, so wild had been the ride. He tried to remember his high-school days, the laughing, happy trips he had made to the cabin. It hadn't seemed far from the main road back then. But all distances are shorter when you're young.

The figure appeared so suddenly in front of him that Roman stumbled and almost fell. He dropped the flashlight and had to scramble in the weeds alongside the road to retrieve it. When he had it back he righted himself and took a step backward, brandishing the ax and steadying the flashlight on the figure standing in his path.

It was a woman. A woman he recognized. It took him a moment to place her. She smiled at him, holding out her hands innocently.

The blond waitress from the Wolf River Inn. The one who had brought the floating clown.

"What are you doing out here?"

"I know what's being done to you," she said. "I know who's behind it."

"What are you talking about?"

"I can help you. I can get you out of here safely."

He looked back toward the cabin.

"Just you," she said, reading his thoughts. "I can't help the others."

"What's going on, anyway?" he said. "How can you help?"

The woman came closer, moving lightly over the rutted path. "There isn't time to explain everything now. We have to hurry. Will you come with me?"

"Come where?"

She was standing immediately in front of him now. Inexplicably, Roman felt himself getting a hard-on.

The waitress reached out and touched him. "Trust me," she said.

Lightning blasted the scene, and he looked down into her soft, pleading smile.

"Let's go," he said.

CHAPTER 29

The weather was clear all the way from Los Angeles. With favorable tail winds Brendan made excellent time. The fuel load he carried gave him a range of 1,790 miles, which might have been just enough to get him to his destination, but rather than chance going dry somewhere over Wisconsin, he stopped once to refuel at Omaha.

He got airborne again in less than thirty minutes, and brought the Cessna 310 in for a landing at Nut Tree Field in New London, Wisconsin, at just after eight o'clock Saturday evening. The small, privately operated strip was the closest field he could find to Wolf River.

There was still enough daylight when he came down so that the field's lack of landing lights was no problem. The sky was beginning to darken in the east, but to the west the sun still rode dark red on the horizon.

As Brendan taxied to a stop, a stringbean of a man in overalls strolled toward him from the small hanger. Brendan was out of the plane standing on the tarmac when he got there.

"Howdy. Your name Jordan?"

"That's right. I filed my flight plan in Los Angeles."

"I got it. My name's Wally Mathes. I'm pretty much the whole show here—manager, mechanic, you name it."

"Can you service the bird for me? I may be leaving in a hurry."

"I'll gas you up and give it a once-over."

"Good. You got a telephone here, Wally?"

"Inside on the desk. Help yourself."

Brendan trotted off toward the small hangar while Mathes walked slowly around the Cessna. He had tried to call Lindy at the inn from Omaha, but he got the same recorded message about problems in the circuits, delivered by a different voice, that had answered him in Los Angeles. He hoped for better luck here, where Wolf River was practically a local call.

Inside the hangar were a clean-looking Piper and a beautifully restored Stearman. Normally Brendan would have enjoyed having a look at the planes, but he had other urgent matters on his mind.

The "office" turned out to be a cubicle in one corner of the hangar with a rolltop desk, a creaky swivel chair, and a telephone with greasy finger stains on the handset and dial. Brendan picked up the phone and dialed the number of the inn. He listened for a moment to the loud crackling in his ear, then swore and banged the handset back into the cradle.

He went back out onto the field, where Wally Mathes was already wiping down the Cessna.

"Why didn't you tell me your phone wasn't working?" he asked testily.

"Phone's workin' fine. Least it was ten minutes ago when I talked to the wife. What's the problem?"

"I tried to call Wolf River and all I got was static."

"Oh, well, why didn't you say so? Line to Wolf River's been on the fritz all day. I expect it's got something to do with the storm."

"What storm? I had clear weather all the way from the Coast."

"Maybe so." Mathes pointed off to the north. "But I call that a storm."

Brendan shaded his eyes and peered in the direction the man was pointing. A heavy gray-black smudge lay on the horizon.

"Could be smoke?"

"Could be, but it ain't. Fire that size, I'd hear about it. Nope, it's storm clouds all right. Been just sitting right there all day."

"Weird kind of storm," Brendan said.

"It's that, all right. How long you plan to be staying?"

"Not long. What kind of transportation is there to Wolf River?"

"Bus."

"That's it?"

" 'Fraid so. Not much call for that kind of travel around here. Next one leaves, lemme see, noon tomorrow."

"I mean I want to leave *now*," Brendan said. "Where can I get a car around here?"

"Hard to say, this time of night."

"What do you mean 'night'? It's hardly dark yet."

"Night comes early in these parts. Not like your Los Angeles."

Brendan summoned up as much patience as he could manage. "Look, Wally . . . I do not mean to insult your town or your life-style or anything else. It's just damned important to me that I get to Wolf River as fast as possible. Now, do you have any suggestions?"

"Well, I got a Jeep Comanche I might let you use. For a price, I mean."

"You got a deal," Brendan said.

He agreed to the airport man's price, climbed into the compact pickup, and leaned out to ask, "What's the fastest way to Wolf River?"

"Only one way. Take 45—that's it you see just beyond the end of the runway—head north past Sugar Junction to the Wolf River cutoff. Town's about seven miles farther on. There's a map in the truck if you need it."

"How will I know the cutoff road?" Brendan asked. "The one to Wolf River?"

"It's just the other side of Indian Head Rock. You can't miss it. That's the big rock looks like an Indian."

"No kidding. Will you be needing the truck back before morning?"

"Nope. Wife'll pick me up here when I close down. You can drop her off anytime after six tomorrow."

"Thanks."

Brendan shoved the Comanche into gear and drove out onto the highway, where he gunned it in the direction Mathes had indicated. If there was a posted speed limit, he never noticed.

Can't miss it, my ass, he thought twenty minutes later. As he drove north it grew rapidly darker. The strange storm clouds seemed to roll toward him, swallowing the setting sun as they came. He had passed the sign for Sugar Junction, driven by a couple of granite outcroppings that might have looked like Indians, but had seen no intersecting road for Wolf River. Now he was coming into Clintonville, and he knew from the map that he had gone too far.

He turned the Comanche around and headed back the way he had come on Highway 45. He drove more slowly this time, stopping to shine the spotlight on signs he couldn't quite read. It was almost completely dark when he found a narrow, unmarked road angling off to the northeast just before a big more or less Indianlike rock. A curtain of mist almost obscured the turnoff.

"Why the hell don't you put up road signs?" he asked the countryside, and steered the Comanche down the poorly paved cutoff.

Wolf River was on him before he knew it. Only a few lights shone in the houses. Nothing seemed to be open for business. No one walked the streets. Overhead no stars broke through the clouds. The storm felt imminent.

The Wolf River Inn wasn't hard to find. It was the largest single building on its block, and a light shone behind the glass doors, making the lettering of the name legible even through the mist.

Brendan parked in front of the inn and entered. He crossed the deserted lobby to where a young desk clerk was in agitated conversation with an older man wearing a suit. They looked up reluctantly as he approached the desk.

When Brendan asked for Lindy Grant, the clerk and the other man exchanged a look.

"Checked out. All three of them," said the clerk.

"Three of them?"

"That's right. Miss Grant along with the other two." He checked a register file. "Mr. Dixon and Mr. McDowell. I guess they gave up on the so-called class reunion."

"So-called? You're saying there wasn't any reunion?"

"Not that I heard about. Couldn't have been much of a party with just the three of them. Is there anything else I can do for you? We've got kind of a problem here."

Brendan leaned across the desk and showed the clerk his teeth. "You listen to me, pal. I don't know what your problem is, but mine is that Miss Grant might be in some kind of serious trouble. Now suppose you tell me what you know that might help me with my problem, and I'll leave you to solve yours."

The clerk looked worriedly at the man in the suit, who spoke to Brendan.

"My name's Kinderman. I'm the owner here, Mr. . . ."

"Jordan," Brendan supplied.

"Mr. Jordan. Please excuse our preoccupation, but we had a waitress walk out on us earlier tonight without any kind of notice, and Saturday is our one big night of the week in the restaurant. Not that we're getting much trade tonight, but that's the fault of the weather. Now, about your Miss Grant—Charlie, is there anything you can tell Mr. Jordan?"

"All's I know is they left in Mr. Dixon's car. All three of them. Goin' like the devil was after them."

"Which way were they headed?"

The clerk reached down behind the desk and retrieved a slip of paper. "Maybe this'll help. They all got one today. I think they all read the same."

Brendan took the folded sheet from the clerk and read the short message:

Big Reunion Party Tonight!!
At the Wolfpack Cabin.
For the Hero, the Monkey, the Cat . . . and the Clown.
Don't miss it or you'll be sorry!

"What's this Wolfpack Cabin?"

"It's a place out by the lake the kids used to use for parties. Been closed up for years."

Lindy's story of the last Halloween Ball in her senior year returned to Brendan. He said, "How do I get there?"

The clerk shrugged and looked at Mr. Kinderman.

"Head north out of town about three miles. There used to be a dirt road there off to the right that led in through the trees to the cabin and the lake. I don't think it's been used in a long time."

"Thanks." Brendan stuffed the wadded message into a pocket and strode out of the lobby. Kinderman and the desk clerk watched him go.

Lightning now crackled every minute or so, washing the woods on both sides of the road with a ghostly gray-green light. Brendan drove rapidly, but kept his eyes steadily on the thick brush along the right side.

The entrance to the old road wasn't hard to find. The brush was torn and flattened in a gap the size of an automobile. Without hesitation, Brendan turned the Comanche in and bounced along the matted tracks where he could see another vehicle had traveled earlier.

About two minutes into the forest he jammed on the brakes. The little pickup slewed sideways and stopped just short of a body that lay prone in the roadway. Leaving the engine on idle, Brendan leaped out and ran to the unmoving figure.

A woman. Blond, young, in a uniform that might have been a waitress's. He turned her over. She moaned softly. Her face was smudged with dirt from the roadway, but there were no visible signs of injury.

Brendan carried her to the truck and propped her in the seat next to him. "Are you hurt?" he said. "Can you hear me?"

The girl moaned again. Her eyes snapped open. For a moment she didn't focus, then she jerked away from him fearfully.

"It's all right," he said gently. "You're all right now. What happened out here?"

The girl only whimpered and shrank back against the door on her side.

"I'm not going to hurt you," Brendan said. "Do you know where the cabin is? The one they call the Wolfpack Cabin?"

"He got into my head," the girl muttered.

"What? What's that?"

"He got into my head. He pushed me way back into the dark and he used my body. I couldn't do anything."

The girl, he decided, was on the edge of delirium. Apparently she'd been raped and dumped out here. He had no choice but to take her along.

He took her hand and pressed it. "Look, you try to relax. I'll get you to a doctor as soon as I can, but there's something I have to do first."

The girl started to cry then. Deep, steady sobs. Brendan took that as a hopeful sign. God only knew what had been done to her. Crying now might help wash some of it out of her memory.

He jammed the Comanche into gear and drove on deeper into the forest.

CHAPTER 30

The flashes of lightning outside the cabin followed so swiftly now, one upon the other, that the pale splotches of light provided by the candles were hardly necessary. The boom of thunder was unrelenting. Outside a wet wind lashed the brush and tree branches into a fury.

In the fireplace the last of the ashes glowed dark red. Lindy sat with her back to the brick hearth, her knees drawn up and her arms wrapped around them.

Alec paced back and forth across the bare wooden floor, dirt gritting under his feet with each step.

"Why doesn't the rain come?" he demanded.

"It would almost be a relief," Lindy agreed.

"This crazy weather just makes the whole thing seem worse than it is."

"Mmm." Lindy did not say so, but she wondered if Alec was aware of the depth of their trouble, weather or no weather.

"Do you think Roman made it back to town?"

"I wouldn't want to guess."

"Would he send help for us, even if he did make it?"

"What kind of help would you expect?"

"I don't know. People. Men with lights and weapons and some way to get us out of here."

"Don't hold your breath," Lindy said.

"We shouldn't have let him go. Not and take the flashlight and the ax with him."

"I didn't see you trying to stop him."

"Did you ever try to stop Roman when he wanted to do something?" Alec said.

Lindy smiled grimly in the darkness, remembering. "Plenty of times," she said.

Alec stopped his pacing for a moment and looked at her. Then he resumed. "He's not coming back for us, even if he finds his way to town. All he cares about is Roman Dixon. That's all he's ever cared about. All I can say is that he deserves anything that happens to him out there."

"Maybe we all do."

"What do you mean by that?"

"It's payback time, Alec. Don't you remember the message? I got it through my daughter. Roman heard it through his mother-in-law. It was a gypsy woman with you, wasn't it? But it wasn't really any of those people who sent the message."

"That's crazy. It doesn't mean anything to me."

"Quit it, Alec. There's no use in pretending we don't know why we're here."

He spun away from her. "Don't!"

"No, you've got to listen to this now. We have to face it. We were brought back here to Wolf River, you, me, and Roman, because of what we did to Frazier Nunley."

"But that was twenty years ago!"

"I know when it was," Lindy said quietly.

Alec turned back to face her, silhouetted against a lightning flash outside the empty window frame. "But it's not right. We didn't really *do* anything to him."

"For God's sake, knock it off. We tied the kid up, put him in a boat, set him adrift on the lake, and forgot about him. Maybe you didn't personally buy the rope, and maybe I didn't push him overboard, but we were all a part of it."

"It was a kid's prank, that's all. What happened wasn't our fault."

Lindy continued as though he had not spoken. "He went over the side into the lake and he drowned. He was tied up so he couldn't help himself, and he was blindfolded so he couldn't even see. Yes, it's our fault—yours and Roman's and mine, just as surely as though the three of us had held his head under the water."

For a moment Alec seemed about to say more, then he sagged and turned away. "The fire's going out," he said.

"Let it."

He ignored her. "We should keep the fire going," he said in a toneless voice. "I'll go out and see if there are any logs small enough to burn well. Roman took the ax, so I can't chop any more."

Lindy leaned forward, trying to see his face in the guttering candlelight. "We don't need a fire, Alec."

"Well, I need some air." He rolled his head and rubbed at the base of his skull. "The smoke in here or something is giving me a headache."

Lindy hugged her knees tighter and let him go.

The air outside the cabin didn't help. The wind seemed to suck away his breath, and the grinding pain in the back of his head worsened.

All his life Alec had hated the outdoors. Once or twice his father had made the gesture of taking him fishing. Both of them hated it, and both were grateful when the fishing trips ended.

That was one reason he chose to live in New York City. Even when you were outside there, you had good solid concrete under your feet, and solid, reassuring buildings on all sides of you. Central Park, with its two-legged forms of wildlife, was an example to Alec of the threatening outdoors brought to the city. He looked around now at the trees thrashing in the wild night wind and swore never again to leave Manhattan.

Resolutely he bent down to poke through the remnants of wood at the base of the pile, looking for something burnable. He really didn't care if they had a fire going or not; he just needed to get away from Lindy and her chilling accusations.

He straightened suddenly. The pressure in his head increased, and for a moment he was overcome with dizziness.

"Alec."

The voice was gentle and breathy, so much so that he thought at first it must be the wind.

"Alec."

This time he heard it clearly and looked toward the voice. Lightning blazed and revealed a pale figure standing some ten yards away from him on the weed-choked path that led to the lake.

"Come along, Alec."

The tone of the voice, the expression, the stance of the figure he had seen in the lightning—all were achingly familiar. But they couldn't be true.

His head throbbed.

"Come along, Alec. It's time."

He didn't want to, but Alec found himself taking several halting steps toward the voice.

Lightning slashed the sky again. Thunder blasted his ears. She stood a little farther on down the path to the lake now, her long white dress strangely unaffected by the violent wind. She beckoned to him, turned, and walked on down the slope toward the dark lake.

"Wait!" Alec cried into the wind. "Mother . . . wait!"

He followed her, stumbling along the uneven ground, while his mind shrieked at him that this could not be happening.

She turned once to look back at him. It was his mother's face, without a doubt, as she had looked twenty years ago.

More beautiful, if anything. Her hair was loose around her shoulders, and the white dress now seemed more like a negligee that clung sensually to her swelling breasts and gently rounded hips.

"Come, Alec," she said, and turned to continue down the path. She seemed to float, her feet never quite touching the ground. And strangely, even in the darkness between the jagged streaks of lightning, Alec could see her clearly, as though she were followed by some spectral spotlight. He watched her swaying, provocative ass, hating himself for doing it.

She came to the lip of the shore, with the vast blackness of Wolf Lake beyond her, and turned. She smiled at Alec, a smile of terrible seductiveness.

You're not my mother, he tried to say, but no sound came from his throat.

"Come to me, Alec," she said in that breathy, throaty voice that was his mother's, and yet not quite his mother's.

She opened her arms and he moved toward her, drawn by a terrible force far stronger than he was. Her arms went around him, soft and insubstantial, like arms made of gauze. She pulled him close.

Her lips pressed against his. They were warm and moist. He resisted for a moment, then gave himself to the kiss. The soft sensual mouth opened on his. His mouth answered to receive . . .

Worms!

Dozens . . . hundreds or squirming, wriggling worms spewed from the other mouth into Alec's, bulging his cheeks, sliding back down his throat.

Frantically Alec fought to pull away, but the gauzy arms held him like bands of steel. The obscene wormy kiss went on and on. The pressure increased on the spot at the base of his skull until he screamed in pain and horror. Then abruptly it stopped.

The figure of his mother shrank back away from him and collapsed into dusty nothingness as he watched. He gagged and spat, but his mouth was dry. There were no worms. No woman.

Alec tried to turn back toward the cottage, but he couldn't move. He no longer commanded his body. The *other* was inside his head now.

I've got you.

Alec tried to retreat to merciful darkness, but the *other* would not let him.

Oh, no, Alec. I want you here, sharing your body with me. I want you to know everything I am going to do to you. I want you to see it. I want you to feel it. It's payback time.

A prisoner in his own mind, Alec felt his body jerked one way and another. Before his bulging eyes his right hand was raised in front of his face. He watched in helpless revulsion as the little finger stiffened, then started to bend back toward the wrist. He screamed, silently, as the tendons strained and tore. He tried to will himself unconscious as the bone popped loose at the knuckle, but something held him awake.

One by one the other fingers bent backward to be dislocated with a nasty *pop*, each bringing a fresh burst of pain.

Do you think that hurts, Alec? That's nothing compared to what I still have for you. Watch. Feel.

Alec obeyed. He watched his uninjured left hand clumsily unzip his jacket, then open the buttons of the shirt underneath. The hand that he no longer controlled grasped the neck of his T-shirt, and with more strength than Alec could have summoned, ripped it open down the front, baring his narrow chest and the small pale bulge of his stomach.

Now . . . watch . . . closely.

It began just below his breastbone. A pressure. Something poking him. From inside.

He saw it then, a lump growing on the flesh at the bottom of his chest. As he watched, it protruded, as though a finger were jabbing outward from inside his body. The pain increased as the skin stretched and stretched. No pain Alec had ever experienced was quite like that when the skin finally split and a gout of blood spurted out and down the front of his pants.

Before he could fully grasp the horror of what had happened to him, something crunched inside his chest cavity. Above the burst bit of flesh, and off to one side, the jagged pink end of a rib stabbed outward through the skin.

Alec's mind, clamped in a state of agonized helplessness, recoiled but could not retreat from the reality that he was being killed, bit by bit, from the inside.

Then the thing that was in him started to work on an eyeball.

Lightning ripped across the tops of the trees, revealing for a moment the black boiling lake. Thunder exploded.

And at last the rain came.

CHAPTER 31

When the rain finally came it hit the rickety cabin with the force of a freight train. Water sprayed in from a hundred chinks and cracks in the walls and the roof, instantly dousing half the candles.

Startled, Lindy jumped to her feet and ran to the doorway. She had heard nothing for several minutes from Alec; not since he went outside, where she could hear him talking to himself.

She pushed the broken door open and looked out into the downpour. No living thing was in sight, just the sagging wreck of the rental car.

"Alec!" she called. "Alec, are you out there?"

No answer, except the rain.

Maybe he had wondered off in search of firewood, she thought, and took shelter somewhere from the rain.

You don't believe that for a minute, Lindy told herself. *Something has happened to Alec. Something bad.*

There was no use going out to look for him. She couldn't see more than a few feet in the rain, and in her heart maybe she didn't really want to know.

Lindy backed into the cabin and with difficulty pulled

the broken door shut. She looked around, trying to find a fairly dry spot to sit. She was alone now. More alone than she had ever been in her life. All her pleading that the three of them stay together had been wasted breath.

She picked out a corner of the cabin where the floorboards were reasonably dry. A wadded-up blanket lay over against one wall. Lindy picked up the blanket and shook it out, wrinkling her nose at the rank odor. She pulled it around her shoulders like a shawl and sat down huddled in the corner while the rain lashed the cabin and the three remaining candles guttered in the gloom.

She waited.

Other nights spent alone flickered in and out of her memory. The empty time after her mother died when for one reason or another Daddy could not be there. The icy darkness when she was pregnant with Nicole and fearful that the labor pains would start early and no one would be with her. The many later nights spent at her typewriter, and later her word processor, trying to force out the stories that lived within her. Lonely nights all, but nothing like this.

The storm crashed and boomed outside like a war. A tree fell past one of the cabin windows, making Lindy cringe back against the wall.

As she sat wrapped in the foul blanket, listening to the chaos all around her, she gradually became aware of another sensation. One even more unpleasant than the cold and the wet and the loneliness.

Something was in there with her.

Watching her.

The feeling of being watched grew stronger. Lindy's eyes burned into the darkness that was scarcely relieved by the pitiful candle flames. She knew . . . *knew* something was there, but there was nothing to be seen, nothing but shadows.

The probing began then in the back of her head, just at

the little indention where the skull joined the neck. A subtle, insinuating *poke . . . poke . . . poke.*

The pressure increased. It began to hurt. Lindy remembered Alec before he had gone out into the storm, rubbing the back of his head. *Something . . . is giving me a headache.*

"*No!*" she cried. She jumped to her feet, letting the blanket fall. "Get away from me!"

The pain grew more intense. Lindy held her head with both hands as though to keep it from bursting.

"Get away! Get out of my head!"

She reeled around the room clutching at her head, crying with the pain. She swore, she sobbed.

She fought back.

I will not let you in! Never!

And at last the pressure eased. Blessed relief from the terrible pain washed over her like a warm bath. She looked down at her hands. She felt herself. She closed her eyes and thought about things—about home and her work and her daughter and her man.

She was all right. Lindy laughed aloud with relief. Her mind still belonged to her. She had won this round.

Then quickly she sobered.

It had not taken her mind, but it was not gone. The battle was not over.

Shivering now, Lindy picked up the fallen blanket and wrapped it around herself. She sat back down in the corner and thought of games to keep her mind functioning and alert. To keep out whatever was trying to get in.

Run through the alphabet with movie names. *American Graffiti*, *Bridge on the River Kwai*, *Charlie Chan at the Circus*, *Dog Day Afternoon . . .*

It went quickly until she got to *X*. When she couldn't come up with one, Lindy let herself get by with *Madame X*. Why not? She was making the rules. With *Yankee Doodle Dandy* and *Zorba the Greek*, the game was quickly over. Lindy was still dissatisfied with *Madame X*, and she promised herself she would look it up when she got home.

When? Better make that *If*.

Lindy shuddered and returned to her surroundings. The rain had let up a little. Or else she was getting used to the steady pounding outside and the dripping inside.

At least she had repelled whatever was trying to get into her head, Lindy reminded herself. But she knew the battle was not over.

A footstep outside on the wooden porch startled her like a gunshot. Pulling the blanket more tightly around her, Lindy tried to disappear into the wall.

The crooked cabin door pushed open. Lindy peered up from the folds of her blanket at the figure standing in the doorway.

"Hey, anybody here?"

A flashlight beam hit her in the eyes.

Roman had returned.

Lindy stumbled to her feet, casting off the blanket.

"What are you doing back here? Never mind. I don't know when I've ever been so glad to see a human being."

"If I'd known I was going to get a welcome like this, I'd have come back a lot sooner."

He set the flashlight on a table so the beam was directed upward, giving an overall muted light to the cabin's interior.

"Alec's gone," Lindy said.

"Where?"

"I don't know, but I think he's in trouble."

"Let's not worry about him," Roman said. "Alec always knew how to take care of himself."

She looked at him oddly for a moment. A dark, troubling thought nibbled at her mind. She shook it away. "Seriously, what happened? Why did you come back?"

"Trying to walk out by myself in the storm was a bad idea. You were right. We should have stayed together. Anyway, there's still the two of us." He brandished the ax. "And I've got this to discourage anybody or anything that tries to get in."

"Do your really think an ax is any good to us now?" Lindy said.

"Maybe not, but I'd a whole lot rather have it than not have it."

The rain had definitely slackened now to a gentle patter. The wind had died, and the night was almost peaceful. For a little while Lindy allowed herself to think that maybe, just maybe, they were going to come out of this all right.

Roman leaned the ax against a wall and came toward her. For the first time she noticed something strange about the way he walked.

"Did you hurt yourself?"

"I fell down a couple of times. It's tough going through the woods at night."

His voice seemed odd too. Different. Strained.

"Are you sure you're all right?" she said.

"Fine. Don't worry about me."

Lindy was standing with her back against the wall, and Roman kept coming until their bodies were almost touching. The flashlight was on the table behind him, leaving his face in deep shadow.

"Roman, you're crowding me," she said.

"Is that nice? I come all the way back here to see you, and you tell me I'm getting too close?" In a sudden movement his hands shot out and grasped both of her wrists.

"What are you doing?"

"As long as we're stuck here together, just you and I, we might as well have some fun."

The voice lost all resemblance to Roman's. It became a harsh growl, chillingly like the voice that had come from Nicole back in Los Angeles a month ago when all this started.

Lindy tried to pull free. "You're hurting me," she said.

He threw back his head and laughed. An inhuman, unearthly laugh that was more like the bark of an animal.

"You think that hurts? You have a lot to learn about pain. An awful lot to learn."

He was strong. Inhumanly strong. Lindy was no weakling; she worked out regularly at the North Hollywood Health Club and prided herself on keeping in shape, but she could no more free herself from the hands that held her than she could have burst a set of chains.

"No, you can't get away," said the voice that no longer pretended to be Roman's. "Not now. You were strong enough to keep me out of your mind this time, but there are other ways to hurt you."

"This time?" Lindy said.

"Oh, yes, I've been in your head. Why do you think you saw what you did your last night in Los Angeles? When you were naked in bed with your boyfriend?" He spat out the last sentence with the venom of a hellfire evangelist.

Lindy fought against the panic she felt rising within her.

"I know who you are," she said.

"Aha, you know that I am not the fabled Roman Dixon. The high school football hero who became a drunken, womanizing storekeeper. Well, you're right. And it's a relief not having to pretend. I'm just using his body for a little while. Roman is still in here, but way, way in the back. If he were alert now, he would thank me for keeping him senseless."

"What do you mean?"

He let go of one of her wrists, but seized it immediately with his other hand, holding as immobile as before.

"Your friend Roman lost something a while back," he said. "Something that was very dear to him. Maybe you will recognize it."

He plunged his hand into a pocket of the jacket he wore and brought it out again, clenched into a fist. He held the fist up in front of Lindy's face and slowly opened the fingers.

In his palm lay what looked like a limp, pale sausage, raggedly torn on one end. He rolled it back and forth, and Lindy gasped, recognizing the lump of flesh for what it was. Roman's hand and the thing it held blurred and swam before her. She drew in a deep breath and did not faint.

Without wanting to, she looked down at Roman's lower body. Mixed with the water and mud and dirt from the forest floor, a wide, dark stain fouled the front of his pants.

"That's right," said the voice that came from Roman's mouth. "He lost what was most dear to him. You should have heard him scream. At first it was simple shock and pain. Then came the realization of what had been done to him. I let him appreciate that for a while before I deadened his pain sense. When I'm through with his body, I'll let him hurt some more before he dies."

"Why are you doing this to us?" Lindy's voice was little more than a whisper.

"You know."

"You're . . . Frazier?"

"I am what is left of Frazier Nunley. A phantom, a will-o'-the-wisp, an energy field . . . a floater. Whatever you call it, I am not much. Nothing I could ever do to any of you would equal the years, no, decades, of agony that you gave me."

"We . . . we never meant to hurt you."

The laugh came then. Rasping and unrestrained it tore at Roman's vocal cords. The laughter went on and on, and Lindy knew whatever she was trapped with in this crumbling cabin, it was utterly and irretrievably mad.

As suddenly as it had started, the laughter stopped. Roman's features twisted into the mask of hatred Lindy had seen so fleetingly on her own daughter.

"You . . . never . . . meant . . . to!" the voice mocked, spacing the words viciously. "Do you think that means anything to me now? Do you think that makes everything all right and now I will let you walk away free and unhurt? Think again."

"Alec?" she said, not wanting to hear the answer.

"Oh, yes, Alec had been dealt with. Alec the clever, cowardly hanger-on. I don't think you would recognize him now."

With a wicked sidearm pitch he flung Roman Dixon's penis across the cabin. It splatted against the far wall and thumped to the floor like a small dead animal.

"Now, Lindy, it's your turn. Your mind is tougher than your friends'. Oh, I could get in there all right in time, but I want to finish this tonight. Since our friend Roman has been kind enough to lend me his body, or most of it, I will make use of it."

Lindy tried to pull away, but could not dislodge the grip of steel.

"Do you remember how you tied me up that October night before leaving me to drift alone on the lake?"

"I wasn't there," Lindy protested. "I didn't know."

"Ah, but you were a part of it. In fact, you were the reason for all of it. Your guilt is no less than the others. I'm going to give you a sample now of how it feels to be tied hand and foot, and helpless. It doesn't feel good, Lindy Grant, as you shall see."

Moving with powerful efficiency, he tightly bound her wrists and ankles with what looked like electrical wires ripped from the rented car outside. Lindy watched the mad gray eyes that no longer reflected anything of Roman Dixon. She did not scream, she did not struggle. It would have been useless and would cost her energy she might still need.

Lindy fought to construct in her mind some sort of barrier against the horrors to come. She tried to recall the class she had once taken in transcendental meditation. No good. She hadn't been able to do it then; she would never manage it now.

He slid both arms under her body and picked her up as

though she weighed nothing. He carried her over to the table where he had left the flashlight and stretched her out there on her back.

''Now let's have a look at you. A real look.''

Working swiftly and with purpose, he tore away her cardigan sweater, then the plaid shirt she wore underneath. He lingered there for a moment, searching her eyes for a reaction. Lindy forced herself to meet the mad gaze.

With a swipe of his hand he ripped away her brassiere, feeling her breasts. They rose and fell rapidly with her breathing, the nipples shrunken and small.

He said, ''This is how everything started, you know. A boy looking at a girl. An accidental look, at that. An innocent young boy looking through a window at a pretty naked girl playing with herself. Isn't it ironic how many lives had to be destroyed over such a small thing.''

Lindy rolled her head from side to side, but said nothing. There was nothing to say.

He grasped the waistband of her jeans with both hands and easily ripped them down the front.

''You still like blue underwear, I see. Oh, yes, I remember. I remember every tiny detail about that day. Just as I remember everything about the day I died. Or the day my body died. You cannot know how often I have wished that my mind had stayed in that poor body when it went under for the last time and the lungs filled with water and burst. But the mind did not go down. The mind floated, buoyed for all these years by one thought. Revenge.''

Rip! The blue bikini panties vanished as he snatched them away with one hand.

''So here we are again, Lindy. You and I. You naked again, I the onlooker. Full cycle. Except this time is different. This time I am not ashamed. And this time looking is not enough.''

He spread a hand over Roman's bloody groin. ''But what shall we do? Roman is no longer equipped for what he did to you here that night. The night Frazier Nunley was sucking in water, unable even to call for help."

Lindy tensed, putting all her strength against the wires that were twisted around her wrists and ankles. No use. She could not achieve even the slightest play.

"I know," he said, the voice harsher and more charged with violence than ever.

The nerves jumped all over Lindy's body as he planted a hand on each of her knees and forced her legs apart. She felt cold and exposed and terribly, terribly helpless.

"I think I'll eat you." He waited. "Maybe it isn't what you're thinking. What I'm going to do is eat you bite by bite. And chew you up and swallow you."

He laughed again, the hoarse maniac's laugh. Then the mouth that had been Roman's opened until the jaw creaked. The strong white teeth came toward her.

CHAPTER 32

Lindy turned her head away and squeezed her eyes shut as the gaping face that had been Roman Dixon's descended on her. She felt the heat of his breath and braced for the pain to come.

The gentle patter of the rain was nullified suddenly by the roar of an engine outside the cabin. Lindy opened her eyes and turned toward the door.

Roman, the thing that was Roman, raised his head, a terrible scowl distorting the features.

Outside a car door slammed. Running footsteps slapped across the mud and thumped on the wooden porch. Something heavy hit the crooked door, and it split from the single hinge and slammed to the floor of the cabin.

"Brendan!" Lindy cried.

Brendan Jordan came to a stop in the doorway and looked around at the scene, garishly lighted by the upturned flashlight.

"What the hell is this?"

Roman moved back a step from the table where Lindy lay bound. Using the Roman voice again, he said, "I just found her like this. I think she's hysterical."

"Who are you?"

"My name's Roman Dixon. I'm a schoolmate of Lindy's."

"Don't listen to him," Lindy cried. "He's not what he seems."

Brendan looked from one of them to the other. "What the hell is going on here?"

"She needs medical attention," Roman said. "If you have a car we can get her to a hospital. Mine is outside, but it's not running."

"She's tied up," said Brendan.

"Yes, I know. I was about to set her free. She hasn't been able to tell me what happened."

"Brendan, don't believe him! He's lying. He did this to me."

"She doesn't know what she's saying," Roman said, his voice beginning to crack.

"You just back off, mister," Brendan said. "I'll take care of her."

"Sure, pal. Anything you say."

Roman moved back away from the table where Lindy lay. Brendan eyed him carefully, then stepped forward and began working on the wire that bound her wrists.

A shadow fell across her eyes. "Look out, Brendan!"

He half turned, moving just enough to deflect the full force of the blow that was aimed for the back of his head. He stumbled across the room, finally righting himself and turning to face Roman.

"It's your bad luck that you found us," Roman said. The voice was again the rasping growl of the Floater. "I have nothing personal against you, but now there is no choice. You are going to have to die."

Brendan set himself and, as Roman charged in, slammed a fist into the middle of his face. Roman's nose broke with a loud pop and blood spilled down over his lips.

Roman laughed, spraying blood and spittle. "You can't hurt me. Nothing you do to this body can hurt me." The laughter died, and Roman's eyes burned with anger. "But I can hurt you. Watch."

He began windmilling blows at Brendan without any attempt at science or defense. Most of the punches missed, many were taken on the arms, but some got through and smacked against Brendan's face.

From her helpless position, bound on the table, Lindy watched as the men fought.

Brendan was easily the harder hitter and the more accurate puncher of the two. With Roman putting up no defense, he smashed blow after blow into his unprotected face and body. Although the skin swelled and split under the attack, and blood from Roman's face spattered both men, nothing slowed him down. The mind of Frazier Nunley, ignorant of the skills of physical combat and impervious to injury, kept flailing away, careless of the damage to Roman's body.

Lindy could see that Brendan was weakening—growing tired from the sheer effort of hitting the other man. Roman's wild punches were getting through more often, and were beginning to take a toll.

Seeing his adversary slowing down, Roman lowered his head for an all-out charge. As he thundered in, Brendan sidestepped and wrapped both hands around Roman's chest. With a groaning effort he lifted the other man off his feet, spun halfway around, and threw him against the wall.

Something crunched as Roman bounced off and the point of his shoulder hit the floor. He dragged himself erect and stood unsteadily with his left arm dangling. He grasped the wrist with his right hand, lifted it, and dropped it. The arm fell lifeless against his body.

"You seem to have broken something in there," he said. "But that doesn't matter. I still have one arm, and that should be enough. You see, you can't stop me, no matter what you do to this body."

Brendan stared. He looked over at Lindy, still bound on the table. "What *is* it?"

She could only shake her head as the tears ran down her cheeks.

Roman stumbled across the room, and with his good right hand snatched up the rusty ax from where it leaned against the wall. He smiled through bloody lips as he raised the ax and started forward.

Brendan ducked low, and the ax whistled just over his head in a deadly arc. The handle slipped from Roman's bloody grip and pinwheeled across the room, banging on the frame of one of the broken windows before falling outside the cabin.

While Brendan's eyes followed the flying ax, Roman stumbled to the table and seized the flashlight. With the beam making crazy dancing patterns of light and shadow, he rushed at the pilot.

Brendan heard him coming. He turned and started to raise an arm to ward off the blow. He was a fraction too late. The metal flashlight case banged hard against his temple. He dropped heavily to his knees, seemed about to speak, then pitched forward and lay still.

Roman stumbled back and replaced the still-glowing flashlight on the table next to Lindy. Standing in the light, he looked down at himself. He nudged the useless arm. He wiped his still-functioning hand across his bloody mouth, probing at the broken teeth in front.

"I'm afraid Roman's body is no longer equipped for what I intend to do to you," he said. "Fortunately, we have another body I can use. One that appears to be in fairly good shape."

"No!" Lindy cried. "Don't hurt Brendan any more. He wasn't any part of what happened to you twenty years ago."

"Then it's too bad he intruded here tonight. While he is unconscious like this, it will be easy for me to move out of Roman's poor battered head and into his. You might prepare yourself for some screaming when I let Roman feel the pain of all that's been done to him. He won't be able to move around much, but he will hurt. Oh, yes, he will hurt."

"Don't do this," Lindy said. "It's wrong."

"Wrong?" he repeated, drawing the word out into an ugly growl. "Do you think I share your concept of right and wrong? Frazier Nunley might have done so once. When he was a boy. When he had a body. Now I make my own right and wrong."

Lindy realized then how hopelessly mad was the creature in Roman's body. She understood that there was no way to reach him on a human level. No way out.

"That's right, Lindy," he said. "There is no way out. Not for you. But before I am through, you and I still have things to settle. Things to do to you. It may make it easier for you if I use the body of your friend here. Now if you will excuse me for a few moments while I make the transfer . . ."

He limped over in Roman's ruined body to stand above Brendan. As he looked down, an apparition appeared in the doorway.

Lindy screamed.

Roman turned slowly to face the thing that stood there in the muted glow of the flashlight.

It stood upright on two legs, it had a kind of head and two arms, but was barely recognizable as human. Tatters of clothing hung from ragged flesh that had been torn, gashed, slashed, and otherwise violated over every visible inch of the body. The face was a quivering mass of bloody bone and muscle. One misshapen eyeball hung like a congealed egg low on the torn cheek.

Lindy's throat tightened in horror as something in the way the bloody figure stood brought recognition.

"Alec!"

The grisly head turned slowly toward her. The remaining eye fixed on her for a moment. Slowly he raised a hand in a ghastly greeting—a terribly mangled hand with the fingers twisted and smashed. She saw then that the other hand gripped the ax.

The voice from Roman's body said, "You surprise me, Alec. In the condition I left you, I never expected you would find the strength or the courage to—"

With startling suddenness Alec swung the ax up over his head and brought the blade down with splitting force in the center of Roman's skull.

Roman fell, the split-open head smacking the floor in a splatter of brains and blood.

The ax thumped down beside him, and on top of it the ragged remains of Alec McDowell. Alec quivered for just a moment, then was still.

From where she lay Lindy sensed another presence in the cabin at the moment Roman's skull was cleaved by the ax. Something ephemeral and lost. It floated for an instant as though looking for an exit, then exploded forever into nothingness.

Someone groaned.

Slowly Brendan Jordan pulled himself up. He stood for a moment staring around him at the carnage in the room. Then he stepped over the mangled bodies on the floor and came to Lindy.

Gently he began to unwind the wires from her wrists.

CHAPTER 33

The drone of the Cessna's engines and the warm sun coming through the cockpit windows relaxed Lindy to a point just this side of falling asleep. She reached over and touched Brendan's arm. He smiled back at her, the sun glinting off his tinted glasses.

"What's our E.T.A., Captain?" she said.

"We should touch down in another three hours."

"God, it will be good to get home. It's hard to believe it's only been four days. I don't think I'm ever going to leave again."

"We might have to go back to Wolf River for the inquest, you know."

Lindy frowned. "Do you think so?"

"No, not really. The local police seemed willing enough to write the cabin scene off as two drunken tourists killing each other."

"Nobody really believes that," Lindy said.

"Maybe not. But nobody wants to think about the alternative, either."

Lindy suppressed a shudder. "I don't blame them."

After a moment she said, "I don't know if I ever properly thanked you for coming to my rescue."

"Some rescue," he said. "I was flat on my back unconscious at the finale."

"All the same, you were magnificent."

He grinned at her. "I guess I was, wasn't I?"

They flew on in comfortable silence for twenty minutes, then Brendan, looking straight ahead said, "So, now that your twentieth reunion is out of the way, I suppose you'll be making plans for the twenty-fifth."

Lindy allowed a full minute to pass before she answered. "Flyboy, the only reason I am still sitting here next to you is that you didn't give me a parachute."

He reached over and pulled her close. They sat like that the rest of the way to Los Angeles.

About the Author

Gary Brandner was born in Sault Sainte Marie, Michigan. He went to nine schools in eight states from New Hampshire to Oregon before receiving his B.A. in journalism at the University of Washington, Seattle. He is the author of the successful Fawcett novels THE HOWLING, THE HOWLING II, THE HOWLING III, WALKERS, HELLBORN, CAT PEOPLE, QUINTANA ROO, THE BRAIN EATERS, CARRION, and CAMERON'S CLOSET. Gary Brandner lives in Northridge, California.